Winning Texas

Nancy Stancill

To Roz –
My friend and
africa companion!
all the best,
Nancy Stancill
2/10/17

BLACK ROSE
writing™

ISBN: 978-1-61296-683-0
PUBLISHED BY BLACK ROSE WRITING
www.blackrosewriting.com

Printed in the United States of America
Suggested retail price $16.95

Winning Texas is printed in Adobe Caslon Pro

For Len Norman

My husband, my best friend and partner in all things.

Winning Texas

CHAPTER 1

The female body slipped into the oily waters of the Houston Ship Channel one night and surfaced early the next morning, floating by the Valero petroleum refinery where it spooked a middle-aged cleaning woman savoring a cigarette.

Annie Price heard about it on news-talk radio as she drank coffee and scanned two newspapers at her kitchen counter. She jumped off the bar stool, scaring Marbles, her cat, who was lurking underneath. She hurried to her bedroom, pulled on a pair of black jeans and a red blouse and twisted her hair into a low bun. Five minutes later, she backed out of her narrow driveway in the Heights neighborhood in her old white Camry, heading east to the ship channel.

She'd half-hoped for a light day filling in for Travis Dunbar, a reporter for the *Houston Times,* who normally covered daytime police. Travis had gone to the Rio Grande Valley to a court hearing for Phil Cantoro, a drug kingpin. As his editor, she made sure police was covered – day and night. Today, she was the only person available in the thinly staffed newsroom to work the early shift.

As she maneuvered through the early-morning traffic east of downtown, she tried to remember when she'd last worked police at the *Times.* Probably in her early thirties, not long after the paper hired her. She'd become an assistant metro editor three years ago, when her prized job of investigative reporter was eliminated. At forty, she might be the oldest reporter at the scene. Would any of her old sources be there to help her out? She wished she'd had time to wash and blow-dry her thick black hair, which she considered her best feature. Not that it would look good for long in this humidity.

A familiar mixture of excitement and anxiety welled up in her chest. She'd never outgrown a reporter's stage fright, even now as a fairly experienced editor. She was spending too much time at her desk editing other people's stories. Would she still be able to coax enough details out of the police? Could she frame her story fast enough to be competitive? Would she get all the details right? Timing was everything on the police beat, especially now that Houston's radio, TV and newspapers all had fiercely competitive websites. She was definitely rusty and she'd always performed better on longer stories with more expansive deadlines. But she knew that once she got to the scene, she'd stop worrying and her skills would take over.

She opened the car window to gauge the heat of the morning and was assailed by the very particular odor of Houston's eastside. It was acrid and earthy at the same time, the corky burnt smell of the refineries in nearby Pasadena and the funk of heat and humidity with the faint aroma of overripe bananas. She wrinkled her nose, but didn't mind it as much as outsiders did. The August weather drove hordes of Texans to Colorado or other, cooler mountain retreats, but Annie prided herself on having developed the stoicism of a native. If you outlasted the blast-furnace heat of Houston's August, you'd be rewarded with balmy temperatures in February.

She pitied whoever had been unlucky enough to meet her fate in the opaque waters of the ship channel. Annie had gone on a Port of Houston tour one time, expecting eye-popping waterway views and insights into the city's massive shipping industry. But the big tour boat had lumbered along for what seemed like hours, passing rusty hulls of workhorse vessels slung along the sides of the channel like old beached whales. At the tour's end, she still felt mystified by the workings and the appeal of what resembled an oversized ditch.

Up ahead she spotted a swarm of activity at an industrial marina with a shabby wooden building. She saw the knot of police cars and a few media trucks, so she eased the Toyota into a spot and got out quickly, carrying her old-fashioned leather notebook and straw purse. She scanned the group of uniformed police and rescue workers loading a body bag onto an ambulance. She was happy to see a familiar face, Detective Matt Sharpe. He'd been one of her best sources ten years earlier and apparently was the lead detective at today's scene.

He stood at the water's edge, talking and gesturing to the clump of workers. She'd always marveled at the easy manner and unforced leadership with which he commanded everyone's attention. A few uniformed men took notes and others listened intently, drinking coffee from paper cups they'd gotten at the marina. She walked up and nodded to Sharpe, but stayed about eight feet from the group, knowing he wouldn't want to be interrupted.

He grinned at her and walked over immediately when he finished, giving her a hug.

"Annie Price! Girl, what are you doing here? Aren't you the big dog editor who stays in the office?" Sharpe drawled in his small-town Texas accent. He was a middle-aged, barrel-chested cop who always looked rumpled, especially after being summoned to a scene at 5 a.m. He moved more slowly than usual, his brown eyes swollen and red around the edges, but he seemed to be in a decent mood.

"Sometimes they let me out on good behavior," Annie said. "So glad to see you, Matt. I'm subbing for Travis Dunbar. He's working on a story in the valley."

"Coffee? There's a joint a few blocks from here," Sharpe said.

"You always know the best joints," she said. "That Greek place? Meet you there in ten."

She gathered a few details from the public information officer handling reporters, called the *Times'* website editor to bolster the bare-bones story he'd already posted and said she'd be back with him in a while.

Minutes later, she joined Sharpe in a battered orange booth at the ancient café and both ordered the $5.99 breakfast special – eggs, sausage, grits, biscuits and coffee. Soon they were sipping from steaming brown mugs. Annie stretched her long legs under the table, feeling human again. She badly needed coffee to make up for the half-full cup she'd left on her kitchen counter.

How she'd missed this, she thought, taking in the sight of Sharpe in his navy chinos, short-sleeved shirt and bifocals. He'd been one of her favorite police officials during her reporting years and they'd occasionally enjoyed coffee, diner lunches and dissecting the roiling mysteries that cropped up daily in the big city.

Annie thought about the times she'd sat in similar cafes with news sources. She'd always considered cultivating sources her greatest reporting strength. She'd been born shy, but she enjoyed people and relished getting them to talk and share secrets that she'd parlay into stories – while protecting her sources' confidentiality. She loved flushing out things that the top brass wanted to keep hidden. And while most of her sources were male – men mostly still held the power on the major urban beats – she was friendly without being flirtatious. She thought that her tallness – nearly six feet in her favorite ballet flats – and her looks, more girl-next-door than vamp, helped her in some ways. Her height, a bugaboo as she was growing up, now worked to her advantage. Questioning stubborn men at eye level, standing tall and refusing to go away without answers, was surprisingly effective.

"So what's your best guess on the body?" she said, pushing a few strands of hair back into her twisty up-do. She leaned forward, eager to hear whatever the detective had to say. From past experience, she knew that Sharpe could deduce more from a scene than most of his bosses.

"Female in her twenties, and she's not from around here."

"How do you know?"

"The body markings and the tattoos make me think she's from Eastern Europe," Sharpe said, stirring his grits into the runny yellow of his fried eggs. "One of her tattoos apparently is in a Slavic language. That's not for publication until the medical examiner weighs in."

"Accident, homicide or suicide?"

"Best guess, homicide. Maybe someone smuggled her into the port on a cargo ship. Something went wrong and she ended up being disposed of."

"Seen anything like that before?"

"About three years ago. A biker gang was paying the Russian Mafia to bring girls in, but three suffocated in the hold before the ship landed."

"Nasty. I remember seeing those stories. Can't recall the name, but wasn't it some big homegrown Texas gang?"

"The Brazos Boys. They were bringing girls from Eastern Europe and sending them to biker bars in Houston, Dallas and San Antonio." Sharpe held up his hand and the waitress came over and refilled their cups.

She sipped the café's inky brew, enjoying his companionship and gauging how much time she could spend catching up before heading to the office and filing a new top to the story. He seemed to be in a reflective mood, so she decided to go with it. It was intoxicating to be out of the office, talking to a human being about something besides deadlines and personnel problems.

"The Boys still around?"

"Not to speak of. The judge charged the head honchos with racketeering and murder and sent them away for life. The gang as we know it is kaput."

"So who do you reckon is responsible here?"

"Don't know. Could be another prostitution ring, or something entirely different. Could be just a stowaway. I imagine we'll get more clues from the autopsy."

They sat for a few more minutes while she picked his brain about human trafficking in Texas. One of the dubious distinctions of Houston, he said, was its notoriety as a hub of trafficking in men and women for the sex trade, and for agricultural work in near-slavery conditions.

"You got the port, the interstates that connect through Houston and the direct access to the border," he said. "Dream territory for smugglers."

Annie listened and took more notes until her cell phone rang. She saw that it was Hugh Heller, the website's editor. She excused herself and walked outside to talk. The parking lot of the popular diner was filled with pickups and beat-up compacts, but work loomed and more were leaving than arriving. She saw Sharpe's fading blue Crown Vic parked not far from her Camry.

"Hey, Hugh. Got more details about the body. I'm coming in to file."

"You better feed me what you've got and I'll top what we already have." Hugh was a legendary rewrite man, a pint-sized, wizened reporter in his sixties who always wore a starched white shirt and skinny dark tie. He could put a story together faster than anyone in the newsroom. He prided himself on usually being first with breaking news on the region's websites.

"Sure, let me tell my source goodbye. Call you back in a minute."

As she hung up, Sharpe shambled out the diner's front door, looking wide-awake at last.

"Think you inhaled enough battery acid?" She joked. His ability to drink mug after mug of bad coffee had always amazed her.

"Nope, just getting started," Sharpe said. "Annie, don't be a stranger. Call if you need anything."

"Thanks, Matt. You know I will."

CHAPTER 2

Travis Dunbar woke to the sound of less-than-ladylike snoring next to him on the blow-up mattress. He'd never bothered to get a real bed because he kept moving from one small, barely-respectable apartment on the north side of Houston to the next. During the three years he'd been at the *Houston Times*, his financial circumstances hadn't improved.

The stentorian sounds emanated from Lila Jo Lemmons, his occasional lover and fellow card-playing enthusiast, who'd stayed over after a long night of Texas Hold'em in an upscale neighborhood about five miles from his apartment. High-stakes poker was illegal in Texas, but underground games flourished in Houston, mostly in private homes away from police scrutiny. It hadn't taken Travis long to find games and Lila Jo was much more connected than he was.

Neither had found any luck last night. He'd blown a few hundred dollars, a serious dent in his meager bank account, while she was out nearly a thousand. Lila Jo, who worked sporadically in real estate and occasionally burnished her finances by selling a multi-million dollar mini-mansion in the Houston suburbs, could absorb her losses a lot easier than he could. He reminded himself that he hadn't gotten a decent raise in the years he'd worked as a police reporter for the newspaper – and they'd hired him cheap to begin with.

He looked at Lila Jo, whose snoring was amplified by too many glasses of cut-rate bourbon at last night's games. Her tousled curly hair was dyed a red not seen in nature and she carried an extra twenty pounds around her waist and hips. But he liked her easy laughter and fun-loving approach to life. She was what his parents would probably call a good old Texas gal, though they'd be horrified if they knew he was sharing a mattress on the floor with a woman at least fifteen years his senior. But what could they expect? He wasn't much of a prize for sophisticated Houston women his own age, he reflected, looking at the love handles slopping over his plaid boxer shorts and white T-shirt. He was short, round and his sandy blond hairline was receding faster than his bank account.

His passions were just two – journalism and Texas Hold'em, but they warred against each other for control of his life. He'd started playing the popular poker game while he was a student at UT Arlington and had gotten hooked. But he'd settled down and managed to get his journalism degree, and even gave up the game for his first few years as a reporter in the boondocks. Then he'd gotten a big-city job in Houston and stumbled into the city's incredible feast of underground poker. He'd always heard that Houston was the poker-playing capital of Texas, but he hadn't counted on the number of opportunities that existed for playing every night, if he wanted. Once you earned the trust of regulars, the illegal network flung its doors wide open.

He'd resisted regular play until he met Lila Jo at a game three months ago. She helped organize games for a deep-pockets investor and had introduced him to a flamboyant new crowd, where the quality of the play was more comparable to Vegas and the stakes were higher. Now he played with her a couple of nights a week, which he couldn't afford, but it was hard to stay away.

"Hi, Trav," she said suddenly, yawning and stretching. She wore a large pair of pink panties and nothing else, and gave him a beguiling smile. Travis returned it, but ignored the implied invitation to take up where they'd left off a few hours ago.

"I'll put some coffee on," he said. "Got to grab a quick shower and get out of here. But stick around and have a cup or two if you want."

"Thanks, babe," she said. "I've got an open house to check out, so I'll be gone soon."

"How about tonight?" she added. "There's a game up in The Woodlands."

"Better pass," he said. "I'm broke until I get paid next week."

"You know I'll spot you," she said, rubbing his thigh.

He better go before he succumbed to the pleasures of the flesh, and to the gambling table.

"Thanks. May have to work late," he said, patting her shoulder and getting out of bed.

She was a temptation, in many ways, he thought. Lila Jo had been separated for a few years from her husband, a busy construction supervisor, but she didn't seem in any hurry to divorce since he still paid her health insurance. Like Travis, she was a serial mover and had resided at several different addresses in the last year. He admired her entrepreneurial spirit and acceptance of a fair amount of chaos in her living arrangements. When she saw an especially good deal on a condo or suburban ranch, she'd buy it and live there until the time was right to repaint it, stage it and sell it. She'd offered to cut him in on a deal or two, but he couldn't afford it. As it was, he owed her a few thousand dollars, but she assured him it was no problem. He felt uneasy about it, though. He liked Lila Jo a lot and enjoyed the easy sex, but now he worried about the strings attached to their relationship.

Thirty minutes later, his mood elevated by two cups of coffee, he drove his ten-year-old Honda Accord into downtown Houston, parked in a cheap garage and walked two blocks to the *Times* building. He took his time. He still had a half-hour before he had to be at Annie Price's team meeting.

Because he'd grown up in a desolate stretch of rural Texas west of Fort Worth, Travis was still enthralled by Houston. As he looked down the long streets of sleek high-rises, squat midrange buildings and dusty parking garages, he felt a thrill. He imagined the jostling diversity of humanity inside the buildings, from the starched-shirted bankers to the Gucci-loafered oil barons to the jump suited federal prisoners. He thought about the workers hurrying below him through the city's network of tunnels, designed to shield them from the punishing heat. He knew they'd be lining up for their coffee and egg-and-cheese bagels in the subterranean cafes. Houston was a crackling city of strivers, stragglers and strays, and sometimes he had trouble figuring out where he fit in. He scanned the people on the street once more, but didn't see any signs of anyone committing news. So he walked into the marble-fronted newspaper building and rode the elevator up to the fifth floor.

The newsroom looked like an insurance office, one that was struggling and hadn't been updated in ten years. As a teenager, Travis had loved the movie, "All the President's Men," with its color-coded, accurate representation of the *Washington Post* newsroom. He'd expected the *Times* newsroom to look more like that, vibrant and buzzing with important breaking news. But the *Times* office consisted of a sea of gray carpet with off-white desks and low dividers. Even the conversation of reporters and editors seemed muted and mundane. Small glass offices belonging to editors ringed one wall and the access to sunlight was limited to another wall of windows. Since the *Times* building abutted a taller hotel that had been converted to expensive downtown condominiums, there wasn't much of a view.

He crept in with trepidation. He should've stopped by the office to brief Annie the day before when he got back from the Rio Grande Valley mid-afternoon. But he and Lila Jo already had planned to go to a poker game, so he'd blown it off. He knew his editor had been forced to hustle on the story about the floater found in the ship channel.

In a conference room off the elevator, he saw her preparing for the meeting. He admired her slender figure in a sleeveless black dress. Annie always wore classy clothes that were feminine without being overtly sexy. He liked her brown-flecked green eyes and the black hair with a few silver strands she hadn't bothered to color. He recalled the recent sheet cake celebration in the newsroom in honor of her 40th birthday. Annie had responded to it good-naturedly, as usual, but Travis could tell she wasn't in a celebratory mood.

He knew about her storied history in the newsroom. Formerly an investigative reporter, she'd helped uncover a statewide scandal four years ago that involved two murders and a drug conspiracy to further a secessionist candidate's run for governor. The fallout had been huge – indictments, prison, disgrace and a suicide. His friends in the newsroom teased him about having a mad crush on Annie, but it wasn't really that. He considered her his role model and mentor. He just hoped he could get back on track before Annie found out how messy his life had become.

CHAPTER 3

Annie stood in the newsroom's small conference room, nicknamed the rubber hose room, getting ready for her team's weekly meeting. The dinky conference room got its moniker from its sheltered, out-of-the-way location off a hall from the fifth-floor elevator to the newsroom. With blinds lowered on the window facing the hall and a door that locked, Annie could see why reporters joked about it as a covert torture chamber where recalcitrant suspects could be beaten with a hose.

Before long, she thought, the rubber hose room will disappear into history. Like other struggling urban papers, the *Times* spent considerable energy looking for ways to shore up precarious finances. The latest trend was to sell downtown buildings for their high-value land and relocate the shrunken staffs of papers to cheaper digs in the suburbs. She knew it would happen in Houston before too long, because the McKnight chain had already announced its intentions. The proceeds from the sale, when it happened, would go to the corporation's woefully underfunded pension fund. Annie believed strongly that newspapers should be located in a city's downtown for visibility. On the other hand, maybe she'd need the healthier pension fund if she outlasted the continuing string of departures.

She put planning sheets for each reporter on the table and looked up expectantly as Travis walked in. He wore fresh khakis and a clean polo shirt, but something about his glance told her he'd had a bad night. She sensed that things were amiss with him lately, but couldn't figure out what it was. She suspected that he drank too much, not unlike her and other stressed-out denizens of the newsroom. She also knew that he worried about money, though he'd never shown an inclination for hungering after an affluent lifestyle.

"Hey, Trav," she said. "How was your trip back from the Valley?"

"You know that route, slow trucks and fast cars. Thought I'd never get back."

"But the cuisine is so great," she joked. "Did you find any barbacoa?" She knew he enjoyed the spicy Mexican meat made from the heads of cows or goats. It made her gag to think about it, but it was his favorite Tex-Mex treat.

"Nope. Strictly fast-food burgers the whole time," he said.

"Great job on the court hearing. We managed to wrestle it to Tuesday's page one. You see it down there?"

He rewarded her with a smile. He so badly wanted his stories on the front page that he came close to sulking when a good story didn't make it. He worked hard, too, but her bosses often resisted her efforts to elevate the best crime and courts writing to page one.

"Thanks. Seems like I can't find the *Times* in convenience stores in Brownsville any more. What gives?"

"Circulation has cut back on supplying the truck routes again. They don't pay for themselves, as the brass keep telling us."

"And this place calls itself a major newspaper," he complained under his breath before lapsing into silence and sliding into a seat. She didn't have time to worry about his moodiness.

Her three other reporters, Nate Hardin, Maggie Mahaffey and Brandon McGill had filtered in and found places at the table. She let them settle in while she went to get the refreshments she'd left on her desk. When Annie had become an editor, she'd had no training in leadership, so she'd started out overcompensating with food. Her philosophy stressed eating together and pulling together as a team. She regularly set up team lunches, coffees and happy hours. But recently one of the top editors, in a rare lecture on management, had said assigning editors shouldn't try to act as substitute parents for the younger reporters. Annie worried that perhaps her behavior could be construed as mothering. So she had to remind herself often not to meddle, worry, or try to solve her reporters' problems. God knows she had plenty of issues of her own, and what did she know about mothering anyway? However, she wasn't going to cut out the food and drink just yet.

"Hey, guys," she said, setting a plate of kolaches on the table. The fruit-filled, doughy pastries were a Czech specialty she couldn't resist from a downtown bakery. "Let's get started. We need to keep it short. Who wants to go first?"

Maggie, a petite blonde who usually wore bright shades of pink, scads of jewelry and stiletto heels, put her hand up. Annie thought she did a decent job covering state politics, but couldn't figure out how to motivate her to probe deeply into more complicated stories. She suspected that Maggie used her feminine wiles as a shortcut for working harder.

"I'm starting to look at something new I'm hearing about – the German-Texas movement," Maggie said.

"What's that all about?" Annie asked, making notes on the legal pad she carried in a leather folder.

"Those folks apparently are lobbying to get most of the Hill Country formally designated as German Texas, emphasizing German culture, language and traditions," she said. "Kind of like the push for all things Gaelic in Ireland."

"Who's behind it?"

"The leaders are business people and history buffs from New Braunfels and Fredericksburg. As soon as I'm sprung from covering the legislature, I'm going up to the Hill Country and nose around."

"That's a few weeks away," Annie said. "Can it wait that long?"

"I think so. I'm going to interview state Senator Satterfield about it next week."

A strange look passed over Annie's face as she heard the name of her former fiancé, now one of the most powerful state government leaders. But she quickly composed her face into a pleasant mask again and turned to Nate Hardin. Just a few years out of college, his curly dark hair and lanky figure reminded her of an overgrown teenager. He was still fairly new to Houston, a hard-working reporter and openly gay. Annie wanted to nurture his talent and couldn't help worrying whether he'd be distracted by the attractions of the city's numerous gay bars.

"Nate, what have you got for me?"

"Actually, boss, I might have something for Maggie on this German Texas thing."

"You do? Spill it." Maggie gave him the high-megawatt smile she usually reserved for influential lawmakers.

"Does the name Kyle Krause mean anything to you?"

"Never heard of him."

"Isn't he one of the topless club owners you're looking at?" Annie leaned in to hear more.

"Yeah," Nate said. "Krause runs the seven Texas Girls clubs in the Houston area. He's one of the biggest strip club owners in town and definitely the most interesting."

"In what sense?" Annie said.

"There are plenty of older, entrenched owners. He's different – young, enterprising and a political animal."

He turned to Maggie, who was taking notes. "What you said about the German-Texas movement rang a bell. Krause grew up in the heart of the Hill Country, supports politicians from there and recently wrote a big check to some German-Texas group in Fredericksburg."

"Did you look at his campaign contributions?" Maggie asked.

Nate nodded, flipping through pages in a reporter's notebook filled with neat, cramped writing. He found what he was seeking.

"I thought so," he said. "Last month, he sent a $25,000 check to the German Texas Political Caucus. There may be more out there."

"The German-Texas caucus is the group doing the lobbying," Maggie said. "Isn't Krause kind of a German name? Strange if there's a connection."

"Isn't everything in Texas connected?" Travis asked. "Have you heard the term six degrees of separation? In Texas, it's only two."

"Good tip, Nate," Maggie said, ignoring Travis's attempt at humor. "I'll ask my sources about the strip-club king."

"And I'll keep you and Annie abreast of things," Nate winked.

Maggie groaned and Travis kicked Nate under the table, saluting his pun. Annie hid a smile.

"Kyle Krause sounds like a good profile," she said. "Give me a memo summarizing what you've found and we can decide where to go from there. Travis?"

He offered a recap of the kingpin's trial in the Valley.

"What about the floater in the ship channel, Annie?" he said. "By the way, thanks for going out there yesterday."

"Could be nothing more than an unfortunate accident," Annie said. "But who was she and how did she get there? Obviously, you should follow up on the autopsy. The human trafficking angle sounds intriguing. Why don't you look for sources outside the police department, maybe folks in the shipping industry?"

"Will do, boss."

"Your turn, Brandon," she said. "What's the latest on the West Texas secessionists?"

At fifty, Brandon McGill was the team's senior reporter. Since the gutting of the investigative team, he was the nearest thing to a projects reporter. His title was general assignment reporter, but Annie tried to keep him out of the general-assignment rotation that often led to stupid stories ordered by clueless higher-ups.

"They've been laying low for a while," Brandon said. "But I talked to a source today who told me there's trouble brewing in the Nation of Texas ranks."

"There's always trouble in the secessionists' ranks. What's new?" Annie asked.

"Only that Dan Riggins and Alicia Perez have been spotted in West Texas."

"Are you kidding?" Annie said, turning over her coffee cup. She mopped up the mess, but her hands wouldn't lay still. "Can we confirm this?"

"Probably not," Brandon said. "They were hanging around some of the border towns and then they disappeared, according to my source. But I'll try."

"Okay, Brandon," she said. "Can you find me after lunch to map out a plan? We need to get cracking on this."

"Did you know those two personally, Annie?" Travis couldn't help asking. "You reported that whole secessionist scandal, but you never talk about it."

"You guys have probably read the clips," she said. "It was four years ago, really old news."

"You never talk about it," Nate said. "Tell us what really happened."

"Well, here's a capsule summary," Annie said. "Dan Riggins was the leader of the Nation of Texas secessionists. He also ran the gubernatorial campaign of Tom Marr, his college buddy, and secretly used drug money to pay for it. Riggins's girlfriend, Alicia Perez, was an assassin who murdered two people, including my friend Maddy Daniels, a *Times'* investigative reporter. Perez tried to stab me and kill Mark Ingram, a Texas Ranger, when we got close to the truth. She was captured, but Riggins and the secessionist goons freed her in a terrible shootout. Perez and Riggins escaped and the Texas Rangers think they're hiding in South America."

"That was a crazy good series of stories you did. Those were the glory days of this paper," Brandon said.

"Thanks. It was an exciting, but scary time," Annie said. "Riggins and Perez have been fugitives for a long time, so we need to find out what's going on. I can't believe they're brazen enough to cross the border."

"What about Tom Marr, the secessionist candidate for governor?" Travis asked. "Did he go to prison?"

"No, he paid a fine, gave up politics and went back to his ranch in West Texas," Annie said. "He believed in the secessionist cause, but didn't know about the murders, drug smuggling and other stuff Riggins orchestrated behind his back. I think he was a decent man, just misguided."

She checked the time. Five minutes remained before she should leave for the editors' news meeting. She needed to wrap it up with a message that might inspire them. But she still felt rattled.

"Guys, I'm proud of what you're doing on your projects." She looked around the table at each of them. "I know that it's hard keeping up with your beats. But we all know that just feeding the daily beast isn't satisfying. You need to feed your soul with a great story."

"You sound awfully serious," Brandon said. "Know something you're not telling us?"

She hesitated before speaking, but decided nothing would be gained by pussyfooting. She always tried to be honest with them.

"The usual. The paper's had another awful quarter. There may be more budget cutting ahead. I hope our jobs are safe – for now."

"Doesn't sound very promising," Maggie said, buffing a fingernail with an emery board she'd pulled from her designer purse.

"I can't lie to you, Maggie. You guys shouldn't count on raises when we may get furloughs before the year ends."

She stood up, picked up the platter with leftover kolaches. She searched for some reassuring words.

"Don't feel like our glory days are behind us. Try to carve out time each day to work on your own great story. Don't worry about the state of the newsroom. Just focus on your best work."

CHAPTER 4

A few days later, Annie shook hands with State Senator Sam Wurzbach in front of Treebeards, her favorite downtown restaurant. Wurzbach, a Fredericksburg legislator who spent much of his time in Austin, had called the day before saying he'd be in Houston and wanted to take her to lunch. He said he was interested in her experiences reporting on the secessionist movement. She'd quickly said yes.

She liked his lopsided, friendly smile. He was thin and wiry with close-cropped dark hair and a ski-jump nose. She guessed he was about 40.

"Great to meet you, Senator Wurzbach," she said, appreciating his direct gaze and firm, but not bone-crushing, handshake.

"Annie, please call me Sam," he smiled. "I've been researching the Nation of Texas group and it sounds like you're the go-to expert."

"That's flattering, but probably not true," she said. "My experience with the secessionists was four years ago, but I'm happy to talk about it. Shall we get in line first?"

She'd only had to walk a few blocks from her office to Treebeards. The Houston café, located beside a leafy square, served generous plates of spicy Cajun food to downtown workers at lunchtime. It was too far north of the main commercial area to attract casual visitors or tourists, but it thronged with lawyers and government workers from the courthouse complex a few blocks east.

She and Wurzbach joined the cafeteria-style line that snaked from the outside entrance all the way to the back of the cavernous restaurant. It was a bit dark inside, but nicely appointed, with dark-green walls and rows of wooden tables and chairs.

She rarely took time for a real lunch because it was so much easier to duck into the tunnel under the newspaper building and grab a salad or sandwich at one of the outlets underground. She could eat while she edited stories, updated budgets and dispatched paperwork that sucked time from an editor's day. It was a treat to be out, even in the blazing sun, and spend an hour with someone new.

"Did you say you have business in town?" Annie said. "What brought you to Houston?"

"I'm meeting with an old friend this afternoon," he said. "It's kind of a long day trip, but I'm driving back tonight."

Annie was curious. "Who's your friend in Houston? Anybody I might know?"

He laughed and evaded her question.

"Annie, I can see why everyone says you're a great reporter. But I'm not willing to give up all of my secrets yet. Let's get to know each other first."

"You can't blame a reporter for trying," she smiled. "I understand you own a chain of German bakeries?"

"Yeah, we started Wurzbach Bakery in Fredericksburg and we've expanded to ten locations around the Hill Country," he said. "Hopefully, we'll cover the whole state before too long. You haven't tasted our apple strudel?"

"No, but I've heard it's delicious. Next time I'm in the area, I'll look for it."

As they moved to the head of the line, Annie ordered a salad, a dish of collard greens, jalapeno cornbread and iced tea.

"That cornbread looks amazing," he said, looking at the thick slab with a big glob of butter. He asked for it too, along with red beans and rice topped with a sausage.

They unloaded their trays at a table for two and began to talk above the din of a few dozen animated conversations.

"My best friend in the legislature is Jake Satterfield," he said. "You two were engaged a few years ago, right?"

"Yep. I'm surprised you know about Jake and me," Annie said. "We broke up, he remarried his ex-wife and had another child. End of the line for us."

"You probably haven't heard that he and Jeannie separated recently. Second time wasn't exactly the charm for them," he said, pausing for her reaction.

"Really," Annie said as coolly as she could manage after hastily swallowing a lump of cornbread. "Should I care?"

"Maybe you don't, after all this time," Wurzbach said. "Just thought I'd mention it because he speaks so warmly of you. He was the one who told me I should talk to you."

"Nice of Jake. Tell him hello."

Despite her attempt to play it down, Annie felt excitement deep inside her body. Just thinking of Jake affected her powerfully and that didn't end when she broke up with him three years ago. She tended to find other men pallid in comparison. He'd been a wildly electric lover, with a knowing confidence about her needs and wants that she'd found in no one else. She still dreamed about having sex with him, reveling in his imagined closeness and waking up desolate.

"Sorry, didn't mean to dwell on a sore subject," Wurzbach said. "Jake's told me more than once he should have married you instead of reconciling with Jeannie."

"He made his choice," Annie said. "But that's another story. Let's not waste your time. Tell me why you're interested in the Nation of Texas."

"Can you keep this information confidential for the time being?" He leaned forward and looked at her intently. "When I'm ready to go public, your newspaper can have it first."

She nodded, noting that his smile had vanished. He looked around quickly before lowering his voice, though no one was looking their way.

"I'm a proud German Texan whose ancestors came to the Hill Country in the 1840s," he said. "Growing up in Fredericksburg, my family's heritage was really important to us, as it is to most people in the area with German ancestors.

"About three months ago, I started meeting with business and civic groups about trying to get the state to designate ten counties as German Texas," he said. "A bunch of us have talked about the idea for years, but it was the first time we'd gone public with it to the local media."

"What exactly would that mean?" Annie asked.

"We'd get the legislature to do certain things, like requiring signs in German and English and emphasizing German language and cultural education in schools. We'd ask for money to help make those things happen."

"Nothing wrong with that, I guess," she said.

"We'd also revive a lot of traditional clubs with German dancing, shooting and games," he said. "The state's biggest outlay would be for a

German Texas museum and cultural center in Fredericksburg."

"That all sounds like a quaint throwback in today's world," Annie said. "Do you think many folks in the Hill Country really care about its German heritage?"

"Absolutely. We've done private polling and the idea is a hit. So many people have German ancestry and strong ties to their roots. But even those who don't are excited about the economic possibilities."

"Like what?"

"Tourism, Annie," he said. "German Texas could attract more visitors and industry to our small towns. We could use our new status to bring in businesses like German-style craft breweries and maybe German industries like Mercedes-Benz."

"Sounds intriguing. So what's the problem?"

Wurzbach slumped in his chair and lowered his voice again.

"We believe the Nation of Texas is doing everything it can to sabotage us."

"Do you have any evidence?" Annie asked. "The secessionists are operating underground since the scandal. Have any members contacted you?"

"Indirectly, yes. I've gotten hate mail from people who claim proud membership in the Nation of Texas. Most is unsigned, but it all contains the same thread of bigotry."

"Can you give me examples?"

"Most emails talk about fulfilling the state's destiny, vowing that nothing will stop the Nation of Texas from making Texas an independent republic, like it was after the Texas Revolution."

"They've been saying that for years," she said.

"But they go much further, saying the new country of Texas won't tolerate German Texans, who are just Nazis in disguise. One message even threatened death to any German Texan who dares to interfere in the Nation of Texas's goal of winning Texas."

"Winning Texas? That's an interesting way to put it," Annie said. "The Nation of Texas hasn't come close to winning Texas – and probably never will."

"They've left no doubt where the group stands."

"Sounds ugly," she said. "Have you gotten the local police involved?"

"Not at first," he said. "But then bad things started happening, mostly to me since I'm the person out front. Several of my bakeries have been vandalized and my car damaged. But the worst thing that happened was to my dogs."

"Your dogs?"

"My wife has raised Portuguese Water Dogs for years. It's a fairly rare and expensive breed. The dogs look like big poodles, but poodles' coats are curly and the Portuguese have wavy coats. The Obama family got two Portuguese a while back and their dogs attracted some publicity."

"Yeah, I remember the pictures. Good-looking animals."

He stopped, took a deep breath and continued.

"We had three full-grown Portuguese that were our family's pets. One morning, I found them dead in our back yard. Their throats had been cut and their bodies mutilated. My wife and daughters – well, all of us – were devastated."

"That's horrible," Annie said, noticing that Sam's eyes had grown wet. She felt shaken. She loved her cats and felt that people who abused animals were twisted in some unspeakable way.

"Was anyone arrested?"

"No, they were careful not to leave evidence." He was quiet for a moment, trying to regain his composure.

"Since all of this happened, the Fredericksburg police have kept an eye on things as best they can," he said. "We're moving ahead to formally open our campaign for German Texas soon. But I'm worried about what might happen next."

"Why do you think the secessionists see German Texas as a threat?"

He trained his eyes on the sidewalk outside the restaurant for a moment. Finally he spoke again.

"The German Texas culture emphasizes military weapons and marching. One of our major proposals is to develop an active gun club in each county whose members could serve as auxiliary police.

"That's designed to help short-staffed departments, but a lot of the hate mail focused on how wrong it would be to arm the filthy Nazis." He shook his head.

"Isn't that a fairly controversial idea?" Annie asked. "The Nation of Texas always bragged about creating its own militia, which made people nervous. Aren't you suggesting the same thing?"

"Not necessarily," he said. "We see German Texas as a special enclave inside our state. We could help make it safer. We're not suggesting that our territory be independent of state control."

Wurzbach looked at his watch. Annie wondered if he wanted to short-circuit the interview.

"I didn't realize how late it's getting. I need to get to my other appointment," he said. "Shall we go?"

"Sure. One of my reporters heard something about your German Texas campaign," she said as they walked out. "Maggie Mahaffey's tied up with the legislature right now, but she plans to contact you for an interview."

"I'll be more than happy to talk to her," he said. "Why don't you come up to Austin? I'll bet Jake would enjoy seeing you."

"I'm not so sure about that," Annie said. "But I enjoyed our lunch and want to keep in touch. One thing – please don't underestimate the Nation of Texas. Those folks may have gone underground, but they're still ruthless and could be deadly."

"I promise I'll be careful, Annie," he said, grasping her hand. "I'll keep you posted."

She walked the two blocks back to the office, oblivious to the heat that shimmered through airless caverns between the tall buildings. She usually enjoyed views of the skyline, but today she was distracted. She thought about the secessionist threats Wurzbach had described, but her mind kept coming back to Jake Satterfield's breakup with his wife. For a heady few months four years ago, she'd been the fulcrum of a love triangle involving Jake Satterfield and secessionist candidate Tom Marr. Marr had dazzled her with his looks, intelligence and charm, but she couldn't accept his secessionist views. She'd broken off their friendship and cemented her relationship with Jake Satterfield. She still wondered sometimes if she'd made the right choice.

CHAPTER 5

Kyle Krause sat with his laptop open on a polished-wood, round table at his Texas Girls strip club a few miles west of downtown Houston. He'd located most of his establishments farther north or east, out in the boondocks where the laws were ignored and the neighborhoods more acquiescent to the presence of adult businesses.

Krause stayed out late most nights visiting his clubs, so he'd slept in as usual. He'd eaten a light breakfast after exercising for two hours with his trainer at his condo. He'd put in a roomful of equipment when he bought the showy unit, including a stair stepper, treadmill and weights. He worried about pushing 40 and had stepped up his routine to shed weight.

He needed to look good to feel confident. He was lucky to be tall, but he disliked his big-boned structure and squared-off frame. If he gained a few pounds, he looked too much like the meathead bouncers at his clubs. Of course he'd started out as a bouncer in his early twenties in Houston, but he'd be damned if he ever had to make his living that way again. Growing up poor in the Hill Country was bad enough. He guessed that's why he could never fully embrace the University of Texas, with its deep-pocketed fraternity boys and pointless football rivalries. Dropping out and coming to Houston showed him a career path that was unorthodox but lucrative. He'd become a strip club manager in his twenties and bought his first club as he neared thirty. Houston still excited him. Like Las Vegas and a few other places in this country, it was a frontier for those who didn't mind taking chances. He'd return to the Hill Country some day when he had enough money. At this point, he wasn't sure how much was enough, but he knew he didn't have it yet.

He looked around, assessing the crowd. Crowd wasn't really the right word, since at 4 p.m., the Westside club had just a handful of customers. Everyone in the large room, including the staff behind the two bars and the woman dancing on the catwalk, knew that he was the club owner. He didn't mind that. He believed that owners should maintain a vigilant, noticeable presence and he liked the way he looked today. He could see himself in the stage mirrors and his brushed-back brown hair with its distinctive widow's peak looked professional. He was wearing a new custom-made, dark-gray suit, with a blue striped shirt and royal blue tie. He always dressed up for these outings, believing that it showed he took his ownership seriously.

Krause tapped into the late-afternoon stock closings on his laptop, checking on the NASDAQ results for Rick's Cabaret International Inc. He'd followed a pattern of buying failing clubs and turning them around, always using management techniques he'd copied from Rick's, Houston's hometown chain. One of just a few adult businesses traded on U.S. stock exchanges, it routinely drew praise from analysts as one of America's best small companies. Rick's operated about two dozen clubs and restaurants (breastaurants, some analysts leeringly called them) in large cities and had diversified into adult websites.

Damn, the stock had climbed again. Krause believed that his Texas Girls chain eventually could surpass the size of Rick's empire, but growing his adult business empire was just one of several goals right now. He had several secret businesses and a political agenda as well. Luckily, he had a willing partner in both his professional and personal life, his fiancée, Juliana Souza. He expected her to show up soon.

He wondered how much it would cost to update the big room's beige, brown and peach color scheme and change those gold chandeliers to more modern-looking bronze or pewter fixtures. Since this club was located in the business district off Richmond Road, it had to be a little classier than his others. He'd inherited, rather than chosen, the décor, and he noticed that it was outdated. He could visualize how much more sophisticated the room would look in shades of silver and black, with a touch of purple. He made a notation to ask Juliana to work on it, to get some estimates. He regarded himself as the idea person and his fiancée as the implementer.

Besides the main room with the stage and bars, there were a few, more secluded rooms where patrons could pay for a private lap dance. Lap dances were lucrative, though potentially troublesome. Bouncers had to make sure customers didn't get too carried away. Offstage, dancers also mingled with patrons in other ways, sometimes sitting down at tables, making conversation and accepting exorbitantly priced, watered-down drinks. This club also included a boutique out front, where patrons could buy scanty underwear and other flashy clothing for their wives or lovers.

Krause closed his laptop and sat for a moment massaging his forehead, but his solitude was short-lived. Club manager Tessa Rhodes came scurrying to his table. In her mid-forties, Rhodes had honey-colored hair and a pleasant face, but her thickening body had long passed prime time for the strip stage. He'd brought her into management ten years earlier and paid her well to keep trouble at bay when he wasn't around. She was more than grateful for the difficult but well-paid position, and constantly anxious that he'd change his mind. She was so overeager to please when he was around that it irritated him.

"I've got your Riesling cooling on ice, Mr. Krause," she said. "Can I bring it over and pour you a glass?"

"Bring it over, but I'll wait to drink it when Juliana comes," he said. "Who's the new girl on stage?"

"That's Carmen Silva," she said. "We're trying her out on the mid-afternoon shift. Remember, you said we could bring in a few fill-ins."

"Well, get rid of this one," Krause ordered. "She's not good enough for this club. You can see that nobody's paying any attention to her."

"Okay. I'll tell her at the end of her shift."

She left quickly and Krause watched the woman on stage perform what would be her last number, writhing a little too athletically to an oldie, Bruce Springsteen's "Dancing in the Dark." She had long wavy hair and a pouty red mouth, but those attributes were offset by chunky legs and lead-footed dancing. He thought that her breasts, partially concealed by blue pasties, were no better than average. All in all, she didn't live up to the standards he liked to enforce at his clubs.

Carmen exited the stage without a single tip from the audience, though there were now three tables near the stage populated by small groups of men. The after-work crowd – or more accurately, the leaving-work-early slackers – was thickening as 5 p.m. approached. The skinny deejay speeded up the music tempo and spoke in a more energetic voice.

"Give a big Texas Girls welcome to Huuunnnter," he said, drawing out the name in two long syllables as a tall blonde dressed in leopard shorts and a bra top danced down the catwalk. Now that was more like it. Krause smiled as she climbed the pole and shimmied down headfirst, with her twined legs supporting her lithe body. He occasionally worried that some woman would slide all the way down, fall on her fool head and break her neck, though he took comfort in the fact that as independent contractors, the dancers were responsible for their own medical costs.

Hunter was a big hit, capturing all eyes as she bent forward and gyrated her butt toward the audience. He supposed it was her version of twerking, but unlike some skinny pop singers who'd tried the move, she had a well-formed butt to shake. A few men stuck dollars into her waistband as the song ended. She was the type Krause liked best – young, blonde and very tall. He'd often thought of developing a specialty club called Tall Texas Timbers and hiring only dancers who were at least six feet tall and looked as good as Jerry Hall in her prime. That was the big thing these days, developing clubs that catered to different slices of the lubricious population. Rick's Cabaret was cashing in big time with its Onyx Clubs, which, as the company's prospectus said, catered to African American gentlemen. He'd thought about how he could do the same.

He toyed with the idea of introducing himself to Hunter and perhaps starting a secret fling with her. He'd done that a few times at his clubs in past years, but on the whole, he knew it was a bad idea. It gave a dancer too much power and created problems when other dancers and staffers found out, which they always did. And then there would be hell to pay with Juliana.

"Hello, darling. Enjoying yourself?" He heard a husky drawl behind him and whirled around to face Juliana, his fiancée. Speak of the devil, he thought.

Her mahogany-brown hair was parted in the middle and fell in thick waves past her shoulders. Her peachy complexion was enhanced by expert makeup and she wore a classic brown linen suit with a short skirt, long jacket and high-heeled sandals. He liked the fact that she cared about clothes and staying fit as much as he did. She was beautiful, though it came with a coldblooded approach to life that marred the overall impression. Sometimes she egged him on to more aggressive decisions than he would've made on his own. Her take on business was more tough-minded than his, but he'd had to admit more than once that her approach made more financial sense.

Krause had met Juliana as a teenager visiting his grandparents during summers in Copacabana, Brazil. Juliana was the daughter of their wealthy neighbors, a few years younger and a student at the best international school. She'd taught him how to surf and pressed him endlessly for details about life in the States. They'd kept up with each other and five years ago, she'd fulfilled her lifelong ambition by coming to Texas to live and work with him in his businesses. Her English was impeccable, if a little stilted. She spent much of her time in the Hill Country working with a risky venture he didn't like. He guessed, but wasn't really sure, that he loved her. For sure, he needed her.

He got up, kissed her and motioned to the seat beside him.

"Some wine, honey?" He said. "It's your favorite Riesling."

They clinked glasses, but he could see from her face that she wasn't feeling festive.

"How're things at the ranch?" he said. He left the operations there in her hands, just overseeing some of the finances.

"Everything's under control. We've got more clients than we can handle and the women are doing their part. I'm more worried about what's going on here in Houston."

"Aw, come on, Jules," he said. "Let's not get into this."

"We're not going to do business with Behar Zogu again," she said. "He's an idiot and now we're stuck with a huge problem."

"Hold your horses," he said. "We can wait a week or two to make that decision. The business at the ranch is more of a danger than Zogu."

"I don't think so. Somebody's going to get arrested," she warned. "And it better not be me."

CHAPTER 6

Dan Riggins woke up every morning in Mexico sorry that he was forced to live in a tawdry border town, longing to be home and knowing he could do nothing about it. So he mourned silently, knowing that his beloved Alicia wouldn't understand. But today was different – he'd cross that border and damn the consequences.

He tried not to worry as the moment approached. His faked passport and identification papers, including a driver's license in the name of a deceased shopkeeper from Laredo, were impeccable. He'd paid a premium through his underground sources and changed identities often during his four years on the run.

His stomach lurched as he reached the checkpoint between Ojinaga, Mexico and Presidio, Texas, but when he stopped at the roadside cubicle, the Customs officer waved him through. Once again, it was a smooth passage into the interchangeable arid lands on the United States side of the border. He could feel his body slacken as he swallowed the last of a lukewarm can of Coke.

He stopped at a gas station, got out of the car, took out a new cell phone and called a number about sixty miles away. Tom Marr answered.

"Howdy, cowpoke," Marr said, using the clichéd-by-design code words they'd agreed upon earlier. "Coming to the ranch today?"

"On my way. Should be there in a couple of hours."

"We'll have lunch by the pool. Staying the night?"

"Probably not. See you later."

He clicked off, noticing a malnourished, gray-striped cat rubbing against his pants leg. He guessed the animal had emerged from the tall weeds that surrounded the station. By God, he hated cats, always begging for food or attention, especially mongrels like this one with a torn ear and patchy fur. He wondered if the creature had mange.

"Get away from me," he said in a low but audible voice, stepping aside quickly so the ugly creature wouldn't deposit any fleas in his pants cuff.

"Sorry, mister."

A stubbly young guy in a short-sleeved plaid shirt that failed to hide a hideous full-arm tattoo picked up the cat and chucked it under the chin. The tattoo, complete with dragons and shamrocks, apparently was a paean to Ireland.

"She kind of lives here. Hasn't got a home."

"You should keep it away from paying customers," Riggins said, climbing into his car before he'd be forced into more inane conversation. He drove through the godforsaken town of Presidio, still shuddering from his encounter with the cat. Part of his dislike of cats came from his certainty that they brought bad luck, a superstition he'd picked up from his father, a hard man who'd trusted neither man nor beast.

At least a few times a year Presidio made the news as the hottest place in the country. Temperatures of 104 degrees or higher weren't uncommon. Today, the thermometer in Dan Riggins's car registered a mere 99. Riggins lived on the outskirts of Ojinaga, a sluggish Mexican city of 22,000 across the border, his most stable address in the last four years. He'd fled Texas to avoid the federal indictment accusing him and three others of drug trafficking and plotting two murders. He'd gone first to Peru, where Alicia Perez joined him after he'd engineered her escape. They'd spent two years in Peru, but the lure of West Texas and the remnants of their secessionist cause had proved irresistible. They'd moved to Ojinaga, where they could slip across the border.

Karen Riggins, his estranged wife in San Antonio, had divorced him and he'd lost contact with his grown twin sons, but he was philosophical. When the time was right, he'd reconnect with them. Alicia and the Texas secessionist movement still ruled his life and he was deeply worried about both.

He drove past Presidio, thinking how much it depressed him. Most of West Texas was magnificent, but much of its beauty and charm depended upon its mystical emptiness. The craggy mountains of Big Bend National Park and the cloud-dappled skies of the scrublands revealed their splendor in their raw, natural state. What man touched in West Texas, he usually despoiled.

Presidio was the classic example. Its dusty streets were lined with clunky auto-repair businesses, battered retail stores and dilapidated government buildings. The residential areas weren't much better. Houses of ancient stucco or weathered wood stood close together, yards laden with broken-down bicycles and discarded toys. He wondered how many of the town's 5,000 residents, mostly working-class Hispanics, had pickup trucks. Old, rusting but dependably sturdy, they cluttered the streets.

He drove as fast as he dared and it didn't take long before he hit the wide-open spaces. His spirits rose again with the sight of the brilliant sky and the shifting shapes of cottony clouds. Peru had majestic mountains and stunning scenery, but he never felt deeply connected to the land like he did here.

Riggins felt a rare burst of happiness. It had been four years since he'd seen his best friend. He was still ashamed of destroying Marr's campaign for governor and ending his political life. The only thing he'd done right was to keep his friend insulated from the worst of the fallout. Marr hadn't been indicted, but he'd been fined for campaign violations. He'd retreated into the quiet life of a rancher raising his daughter and sworn off the secessionist movement. He hadn't been in contact, but Riggins had called him yesterday. The upshot was today's clandestine reunion at Marr's ranch.

Riggins knocked on the door and Marr appeared. They leaned together, almost embracing. Riggins walked inside Marr's stucco two-story home, past the living room with its upright piano and formal portraits, and the dining room with its faded Persian rug and sturdy wooden sideboard. He followed Marr into the pine-paneled den with its leather sofa and chairs and windows that stretched across the back of the house. Hell, he thought, the house looks and even smells the same. It was an ineffable old-house aroma that blended fireplace ashes, boot polish and solid walls baked by decades of dry heat.

Being in Marr's house flooded him with memories. At odds with his own family in San Antonio, he'd come to the ranch with Marr on holidays from the University of Texas. The ranch was where they'd first hatched plans for Texas to secede. Knox Marr, Tom's iconoclastic rancher father, would spend hours brainstorming with them. Riggins had loved the nights of political plotting and whiskey drinking, stoked by fires in the cozy den's stone fireplace. Days were even better. He rode horses, branded cattle and helped with other ranch chores that were routine for Tom, but exotic for him.

Around the time of their senior year, Riggins's visits tailed off because Marr's campus romance with Elizabeth Barnard, a willowy philosophy major, had blossomed. He'd take her to the ranch often and they'd married on its patio one evening soon after they graduated. When Knox Marr died the following year, Riggins had helped the couple pack up their grad school apartment in Austin to return. Riggins came back for the christening of their first child, Betsy. Just four years later, Marr called him to come for Elizabeth's funeral after breast cancer ended his young wife's life.

Riggins joined Marr on the stone patio with its outdoor fireplace, pool and seclusion. He sat down across from Marr at a teak table shaded by a green-striped umbrella.

"Tell me more about Alicia," Marr said. "What happened?"

As Riggins thought, he noticed how much thinner and older Marr looked than when he'd last seen him four years ago. The tall rancher always was deeply tanned, which contrasted with his light hair and pale blue eyes. But Riggins detected more weariness in Marr's face.

"Gone off the rails again," Riggins said. "Disappeared early this week and isn't answering her cell phone."

"Did you have a fight?"

"No, but I think she got agitated after overhearing me talk about some problems and decided to take things into her own hands. Think she's headed either to the Hill Country or to Houston."

"That's a lot of territory to cover," Marr said. "Shouldn't we wait a few days, see what happens?"

"Nothing else I can do. Long as I stay in West Texas, I'm pretty safe. Kind of dangerous for me to travel anywhere else."

"You look a lot different than four years ago, Dan. So does Alicia. You might not be recognized."

Riggins could feel his friend staring at his shaved head, graying moustache and gaunt figure. He knew his aged appearance was probably as shocking to Marr as Marr's was to him.

"Her hair has turned completely white, good for disguise," he told Marr.

"But people have a way of remembering her."

Riggins smiled, thinking of Alicia. At 54, with her mane of thick hair, shapely body and ferocious energy, she was still youthful and sexy. But he'd suspected for a while that something terrible had gone wrong with her brain. In the last year, she'd become increasingly erratic and unpredictable.

"She gets irrationally angry sometimes," he said. "She always had a temper, but now it's over things that shouldn't matter. She was driving near our place in Ojinaga last month and shot holes in the tires of a driver who was going too slow."

"I guess we've all wanted to do that," Marr smiled.

"It wasn't funny," Riggins said. "I had to pay the man off to keep him from going to the cops. Not the kind of thing you want when you're in hiding."

"Third time she's disappeared, you said? Have you taken her to a doctor in Mexico?"

"She refuses to go, says she's perfectly fine. And she is, most of the time."

"What do you suppose is going on?"

"Best guess, a brain injury. Violence was a way of life in Peru. You know she was captured by the Shining Path when she was just 16. I think those damn thugs knocked her around."

Riggins changed the subject. "Tell me what's going on with you. You said you'd explain when I got here."

"I'm worried to death about Betsy."

"The world's sweetest kid?"

"Not so much lately. Since she turned sixteen, seems like I can't do anything right. Now she's gone."

"Gone? When?"

"We found her room empty three days ago," Marr said. "She left a note saying she wanted to be on her own for a while and not to follow her."

"Does your housekeeper know anything?"

"She says she doesn't, and I believe her."

"How about her friends?"

"I talked to two of her best friends. They said they didn't know anything at first, then one confessed that Betsy had fallen for a rock guitarist she met in El Paso after a show."

"El Paso – that's awfully far afield for girls their age."

"The three girls spent a weekend there with the cousin of one. Betsy was all excited about it."

"Is there any trouble between you?"

"She hated the whole secessionist thing and all the publicity when it blew up," Marr said. "Even after the media left us alone, kids teased her. That's one reason I got out for good. I thought things would get back to normal, but Betsy has never seemed the same. She's become rebellious, especially where boys are concerned."

"My boys sowed a few wild oats when they were teenagers," Riggins said. "I was gone so much. Karen usually ran interference."

"Yeah, I probably shouldn't have tried to raise Betsy on my own. She was so young when Elizabeth died."

"I'm kind of surprised you haven't remarried. Aren't there any attractive women in this neck of the woods?"

"Lord, yes," Marr said. "Even with my tarnished reputation, people try to fix me up all the time. But I haven't met anyone I really liked since Annie."

"Annie Price? Didn't she do enough damage to last a lifetime?"

"Dan, we need to stay away from this subject," Marr said with a firmness that surprised Riggins. "I don't blame Annie for anything that happened. Let's talk about something else."

"Okay, sorry."

"Betsy might have gone to Houston," Marr said. "Her friend Carly admitted that the band was from Houston."

Riggins thought of a horrible possibility and struggled to keep his face impassive. But Marr could read his changing expression. He grabbed Riggins by the shoulder.

"You know something you're not telling me?"

"I read something in the *Houston Times* online today about a body found floating in the Ship Channel," Riggins said. "It was an unidentified young woman, but likely it's not Betsy."

"Lord have mercy," Marr said.

"It's probably a stowaway from one of those big ships," Riggins said, regretting that he'd worried Marr about something that was probably farfetched. "We'll get to the bottom of it."

"I need to get to Houston. It's my best chance of finding Betsy."

"We'll leave in the morning. I'll get a few of my security guys looking into it tonight. While we're on the road, I'll just stay in the car and wear sunglasses."

"Dan, I don't want to get involved with your secessionists or blow your cover."

"I'll be careful. And I'll deal directly with my guys. They have ways of finding things quickly that you and I don't even know about."

"What about Alicia?"

"She may call within a day or two. She hasn't stayed gone for more than a few days at a time," Riggins said with a degree of hope that he didn't altogether feel.

CHAPTER 7

Kyle Krause steered his Porsche into the old strip shopping center off the Gulf Freeway southeast of downtown Houston, parking in the VIP spot at his original Texas Girls Club. The place wasn't much to look at, just an anonymous beige storefront wedged between a Korean nail salon and Vietnamese café.

"Ugh, I hate this place," Juliana said, refreshing her coral lipstick in the passenger seat mirror. "Let's not stay any longer than we have to."

"As soon as the meeting's over, we're out of here," Krause said.

The club catered to eastside refinery workers who were known to get rowdy, especially on Thursday or Friday nights when they'd gotten their fill of cheap beer and a grinding week of repetitive work. It was one of his working-class, no-frills establishments, but since it was the first business he'd owned and still made decent money, he felt sentimental about it. He resented Juliana's prissy snobbery. She was far more tolerant of the upscale clubs on Houston's tonier Westside, with their more elaborate furnishings and well-heeled customers, places that Krause felt were pretentious. Despite his custom-made suits, expensive haircuts and showy cars, he didn't feel too far removed from this club. He was far more at home in the cowboy atmosphere of the lower-rent joints. They reminded him of his first few heady months in Houston when he worked 12-hour shifts as a bouncer, flexing his muscle with dirt-bag customers, and banging as many strippers as he wanted.

He and Juliana walked in, past the well-lighted stage where a skinny woman was warming up to Robin Thicke's "Blurred Lines" and a few early patrons were drinking longneck beers. Krause unlocked the door to a cold interior office featuring a desk, a dark green leatherette sofa and a few chairs. This was the unwelcoming place where he often held tough conversations with employees and contractors. The chairs were hard and uncomfortable, and the mismatched look, plus the bare-bulb ceiling light, gave the space the atmosphere of an interrogation room.

He punched in the number of the front desk and the manager on duty answered quickly.

"Yes, Mr. Krause?"

"You know Behar Zogu, the scrawny guy with a moustache and greasy hair? The one who delivers stuff sometimes? Send him to my office when he gets here."

"Sure. Can we get you any drinks or food?"

"We'll take two diet Cokes, with ice cubes and twists of lime."

"Right away, Mr. Krause."

Soon he and Juliana were sipping their drinks and a few minutes later, the manager knocked. Krause tried not to grimace when he saw Zogu, who looked rattier every time they met. Thin and scruffy, he was dressed in a worn black leather jacket, threadbare jeans and scuffed, industrial-looking boots. He also had a hangdog look that Krause, who prided himself on his proud posture and commanding attitude, held against him. But Zogu had performed some valuable services for the business and didn't ask pesky questions, so Krause tried to overlook his shoddy appearance.

"Hello Ms. Juliana and Mr. Kyle," Zogu said. He extended a hand, but Krause didn't shake it, just waved him into a chair across his desk. Zogu sat beside Juliana, who glanced at him and looked away.

"The girls they are here, all nine," Zogu said.

"You told us you'd arranged for ten," Krause said.

"No, only nine," Zogu said. He smiled nervously and avoided Krause's eyes. "They are resting at the motel, waiting for you and Ms. Juliana to bring them to the clubs."

Juliana looked at Zogu and spoke in a disgusted tone. "Didn't you understand what I said yesterday? Those girls look like hookers."

"No, Miss. They are the most beautiful flowers of Albania," Zogu tried to smile. "My brother Bujar personally picked them out from the finest families of Tirana."

"More likely he got them off the streets," Juliana said. "They don't look like the girls we hire, even at this location."

"They hide on a ship many, many days. They need, how do you say, the beauty sleep."

"You promised us tall, beautiful blondes like the Ukrainian or Russian women you see at Rick's clubs," Krause said. "We said we'd give you one try."

"Mr. Kyle, I do good work for you for five years, always pleasing you. You will like these girls when you meet them. They love Texas already."

"Juliana wasn't impressed," Krause said. "I do rely on her judgment."

"The girls, they need better clothes and a few good meals," Zogu said. "They'll look so beautiful and dance so sexy, they'll shine like stars when they come to your clubs. The men will be, how you say, busting the doors down."

Krause and Juliana looked at each other silently. She still had her nose in the air about the whole deal, and he didn't want to give in just to please her. He made up his mind.

"We'll give them two weeks to rest up and a little money to get them fixed up. The three rooms at the motel are paid for, but you have to feed them."

"Thank you," Zogu said, smiling at Juliana. She stared back stonily and he looked away. Krause thought he'd have hell to pay the rest of the day and she probably would give him the cold shoulder tonight. It was tough being with a hard-ass woman like Juliana sometimes, but she, like Zogu, was entrenched in his businesses. Not that he'd ever seriously considered getting rid of her.

"You must keep them out of sight," Krause said. "They mustn't be seen or connected with our clubs until this unpleasantness dies down."

"Zogu will make sure it works out," he said. "You'll see."

He made a slight bow and left quickly. Neither Krause nor Juliana bothered to get up to say goodbye.

"I told you this wasn't going to work," Juliana said. "We should have paid the Russians what they wanted, instead of depending on this fool."

"Jules, you know that Zogu's solved some sticky problems for us and kept his mouth shut. We need him – and we really need his silence."

"I still think he's a loser. We'll probably have to send some of his girls to the ranch. They'll make us more money there."

"Well, that won't be the end of the world. They're young and healthy, and they don't have to be beautiful," Krause said. "Was the tenth girl the one who drowned in the ship channel?"

"What do you think?" Juliana said. "Not our problem. We need to stay away from that kind of trouble. I don't want to know what happened – and you shouldn't ask questions."

"Zogu knows how to keep quiet," Krause said, tapping his iPhone for messages. "If he doesn't, he knows there'll be a second body floating in the ship channel."

CHAPTER 8

Annie sat in her office, reading the depressing quarterly report from the McKnight Corporation, the company that owned the *Times* and a couple of dozen other newspapers. Because its newspapers' website advertising wasn't rising as fast as print advertising was plunging, the report forecast drastic cutbacks, including freezing salaries and hiring, and a second furlough before the year's end. She'd have to take another week without pay before Christmas. She wouldn't have enough money to go anywhere interesting. She'd probably just stay home and work on her house, which needed it. But she didn't look forward to the prospect.

Her desk phone rang and she noticed with surprise that the caller was Matt Sharpe. She hadn't seen the Houston police detective since they'd had breakfast a week ago at the ship channel cafe. She was pleased but puzzled to see his name and number come up. Maybe he had big news.

"Hey, Matt," she said. "What's up?"

"Are you about done for the day?" he asked. "I'm knocking off early and I'd like to buy you dinner."

"Sounds like fun," she said. "But I need to go home first and feed my kitties."

"How about meeting me at 7 at the Pappadeaux at Richmond and Kirby?"

"Great. See you there."

She sat thinking for a minute, mystified by the invitation. She'd had coffee and lunch with Matt many times when she was a reporter and he was her biggest police source, but never dinner. Of course, the situation was different now. She knew he'd separated from his wife months ago and was headed toward a divorce, so it didn't seem improper. Also, she was editing now, rather than reporting, so he wasn't a source she needed to keep at arm's length. But she'd never thought about going out with him. She'd considered him more as a mentor and teacher. She told herself to stop worrying about the implications of a casual invitation. After all, they were longtime friends. A dinner out in the middle of the week wasn't a gift to be spurned, given the state of her refrigerator and her dislike of cooking for one.

Pappadeaux was part of a locally grown chain, one of the Pappas family's portfolio of restaurants. The Pappas brothers also had Mexican, Italian and Greek-themed eateries among their hundred or so restaurants in Texas and other states. The Pappadeaux on Kirby a few miles west of downtown Houston served large portions of spicy Cajun seafood at reasonable prices. Annie had eaten there and enjoyed the ambience of its outside patio.

She drove home, showered and washed her hair. It had been a sticky day with shimmering heat, but the evening was supposed to be cooler. She put on a little J'adore, her favorite French perfume, and tried to decide what to wear. She didn't want to look too dressed up, lest she give Matt a too-eager impression that she regarded the evening as a date. She settled on a short black linen skirt, a white sleeveless blouse and gold sandals. She pinned her hair back from her face and let it hang softly below her shoulders.

The restaurant was just a few miles from her house and she opened the car window to enjoy the tiniest hint of a breeze. She pulled into the parking lot and saw Matt waving from his table on the patio. Between the potted plants and the ceiling fans, a full complement of trendily dressed customers ate, drank, flirted, talked and drank even more. The police detective looked cool and freshly shaven in jeans and a black polo shirt. She'd never seen him in jeans, but he looked good – trimmer, younger and relaxed. He hugged her and she sat down at their coveted outdoors table, lit with a citronella candle.

Annie always thought of Houston as a city that celebrated the night. People who had shut themselves in air-conditioning all day wanted to party after dusk, so the atmosphere at bars and restaurants was happy and loud. Even if the weather had cooled only into the low 80s, Houston evenings enticed hordes of city-dwellers to patios and porches. Annie could remember her first summer in the Bayou City, when she relished walking barefoot on neighborhood sidewalks that warmed the underside of her feet. Of course, the hot weather also brought out other night creatures, including giant cockroaches, which had to be kept at bay with frequent extermination visits. She'd never forget the night she was watching a movie on TV and a roach landed on the screen and flew out at her, as if part of the film's action. She let out a scream that sent her cats flying. Now she had mostly acclimated to large insects and sultry heat and relished getting out at night with a diverse mix of fun-seekers.

She chatted with Matt briefly about their respective workdays until a waiter appeared. They conferred about drinks, both deciding on Blue Moon beers with plenty of orange slices.

"Aren't you a chardonnay drinker?" he said. "I didn't think you liked beer."

"Who doesn't love beer on a night like this?" she said. "I love my chardonnay, but I'm trying to cut back."

"You journalists and your bad habits," he teased. "What would a newsroom be without alcohol? Do you keep a flask in your desk?"

"Isn't that the pot calling the kettle black?" Annie said. "Ever been to a gathering of cops that wasn't swimming in booze?"

He held up his hand. "Point taken."

The light mood continued as they dissected police department politics and high-profile cases. He ordered each of them another beer and shrimp and grits for his entree and grilled Redfish for her. When the waiter brought their meals, Matt put his finger to his lips.

"No more shop talk tonight," he said. "We both need a break. Can we just have a relaxing evening?"

"You bet, Matt," she smiled. "What's going on with your personal life?"

"Sue and I have been separated for almost a year," Matt said. "I expect she'll file for the divorce soon. It's all very civilized."

"How old are your kids now?"

"My daughter's still in high school, but the two older boys have finished college and are on their own. They're too busy with their jobs and friends to be traumatized."

"So they're okay with the divorce?"

"Yeah. I see all of them at least once a week," Matt said. "They were sad at first, but now they seem resigned."

"What happened, if you don't mind my asking?"

He leaned back, sighed and drank deeply before answering.

"Same old stuff. Sue thought I worked too much and didn't pay enough attention to her. The last few years haven't been good for either of us. Can't blame her. I've always been a workaholic."

"Yeah, me too," Annie said. "Aren't you close to getting your thirty years in? Still thinking about doing something different?"

"I expect I'll retire sometime this year. Then I'll look for some kind of business opportunity. I'm just about done with my master's in business from the University of Houston."

"I didn't know you'd gone back to school," she said. "Good for you. But wouldn't you miss police work? You're so good at solving crimes."

"To be honest, I'm a little burned out," he said with a wry smile. "And I'd like to make some money before I get old. What's going on in your personal life?"

"Nothing special. I've dated quite a bit since I broke it off with Jake Satterfield, the state senator. I think I told you we were engaged. But I haven't met anyone lately that interested me."

"How's the job?"

"Not very satisfying," she said. "Being a low-level editor means lots of responsibility plus lots of blame when things go wrong. I don't feel like I have much power, and I miss the fun of reporting."

"You were always such a natural reporter," he said. "When I met you ten years ago, you were smart and cute, but green as a cucumber. Last week when I saw you, you seemed so poised, confident and even more attractive. Houston has really ripened you."

She was touched, but a little embarrassed by his unexpected compliment. She didn't know where he was heading, but wanted to play it cool.

"Thanks, Matt. Houston has definitely ripened me. Soon I'll be so ripe, I'll be rotting before your very eyes."

He roared with laughter and put his big hand lightly on her arm. His touch felt warm and protective. They finished their entrees.

"How old are you, Matt? I've forgotten."

He looked chagrined, but didn't dodge the question. "I'm fifty-two, getting old. You're about forty, right? Still got a few years on you, Annie Girl."

"You look different – and better – than you did ten years ago," Annie said. "You've taken off some weight, haven't you?"

"Yeah, I started running again and gave up sweets," he said. "Speaking of which, would you like to order dessert, or would you rather have a quiet nightcap on my balcony?"

"Where's your balcony?"

"Just a few blocks from here. I have a garage apartment in Montrose."

"Okay, I'll follow you there," Annie said.

Fifteen minutes later, they were sipping scotch and looking at the stars on the narrow balcony of his apartment in the urban, tree-lined Montrose area. With its ancient oaks and solidly built old houses, Montrose was a haven for well-heeled hipsters and upstart millennials. It wasn't far from her Heights cottage, but his neighborhood was more upscale and sophisticated. Matt didn't fit the profile of the average Montrose dweller, but had found a great efficiency apartment. His place consisted of one large room above a garage that encompassed a kitchenette, a living space and a bedroom area with an adjoining bathroom. She liked its almost-military compactness and order, and the balcony was a big plus.

"This place is wonderful," she said. "I'm impressed that you keep it so neat."

"I like living alone, surprisingly. Sue and I got married too young. Had to, with a kid on the way. So I never had a place of my own, or the freedom of a bachelor's life."

He returned to the kitchen, brought out the bottle of scotch and poured more into the heavy tumblers.

"I don't usually like scotch, but this stuff just slides down your throat," she said.

"Thanks. I bought it on the Isle of Skye, off the Scotland coast," he said. "I went there by myself a few months ago and spent a week walking, reading and thinking about life."

"Why'd you choose the Isle of Skye?"

"My mom's family emigrated from there way back when," he said. "I always wanted to see it."

She was intrigued with their conversation. He'd surprised her all evening, showing a reflective side she'd never seen. Now he caught her off guard again, leaning over her chair and kissing her lightly on the lips. She kissed him back and after a while, he led her inside to his bed.

A few hours later, she woke and wondered briefly where she was. She heard Matt's even breathing and tried, but failed, to go back to sleep. She'd always found it difficult to actually sleep with someone she'd had sex with for the first time. It always felt suffocating. She'd rather digest the experience alone, without the laden expectations sex inevitably carried on the morning after. As he slept soundly, she got up quietly, put on her clothes and wrote a note to leave on his bedside table.

It was close to 2 a.m. as she drove her Camry along the flat, lighted and mostly empty streets from Montrose to the Heights. She was glad she didn't have to worry about getting on a freeway, that she could just glide along, lost in thought. Suddenly, she sensed a dark SUV following a little too closely for her comfort. She looked back a few times, but couldn't see inside the tinted windows. She pulled off in the parking lot of an all-night service station and the big vehicle kept barreling along the street. Shaken, she waited a few moments before getting back on the road and driving the mile or so home. Thankfully, she didn't see the SUV again. She parked in the driveway, let herself into her bungalow, threw off her clothes and fell asleep.

She slept later the next morning and dawdled over breakfast, thinking about her evening with Matt. It was almost 9 a.m. when she walked out her back door, opened the patio gate and saw her Camry parked in the narrow driveway. She uttered a low moan. Someone had slashed all four of her tires and dumped the contents of her trash containers all over her car. She'd been followed, as she'd suspected, but she thought she'd shaken off the tail. Who had it been and why did someone want to hurt her?

CHAPTER 9

Juliana Souza kissed Kyle Krause goodbye at the door of the three-story condominium they shared in southwest Houston. Located in a fashionable area on the Westside, the street consisted of rows of similar-looking condos with balconies, two-car garages and minuscule patios in the back. She didn't much like his place, but it was convenient for Kyle and he wouldn't hear of moving. She favored the multi-million-dollar Memorial area a few miles away with its mid-century spacious homes on large, pine-shrouded lots. Memorial offered a shaded retreat that felt respectable and established. But he liked his kitted-out third floor gym, the incurious neighbors and the anonymity that went with condo land, as she thought of it. However, since she was clearing excellent profits at the clandestine venture in the Hill Country, he'd given in to her desire to buy a beach house on Galveston Island, about forty-five miles southeast of Houston. She wanted a hideaway where they could relax and enjoy a romantic weekend once in a while.

Their kiss was perfunctory, as was his goodbye on this sun-soaked Saturday. He was headed out for a business trip and had no interest in checking out real estate on the island with her. She dreaded his road trips, always suspecting they came with nights fueled by plentiful drugs and pliant women.

"Jules, you can buy anything you want, as long as you stick to the budget we've agreed to and pay cash," he'd said. "You don't need me along. Lila Jo Lemmons is a pro and she'll know how to handle everything."

Juliana hadn't met Lila Jo, but knew that the real estate broker had sold Kyle his condo a few years ago. He'd liked her for finding what he wanted quickly and quietly, and carrying out his instructions without asking unnecessary questions.

"Okay, but you'd better be prepared to like it." She heard the unattractive edge in her voice and hastened to sound more agreeable. "Be careful driving to San Antonio and don't run over any of those hideous creatures."

She succeeded in getting a laugh out of him. She'd been horrified the first time she'd seen a dead armadillo, feet up and scaly shell glistening in the sun. He referred to them, as other natives often did, as Texas speed bumps. They weren't quite fast enough, or smart enough, to avoid mortal injury while crossing the state's highways. But she was superstitious about killing them and wondered why they were so creepily drawn to their certain death on the roads.

She stood there a moment flooded with mixed feelings, annoyed that he'd left, but anticipating a satisfying day without having to please him. Juliana loved looking at real estate and she'd sold high-end beach houses in Brazil for a time before she joined Kyle in Texas. She still checked out the online Brazilian listings for fun. But she hadn't wanted to study to get a real estate license in Houston and be forced to deal with Texans who had the money, but not the rarified taste of her customers in Brazil. She also liked flying under the radar and didn't want to call attention to her immigration status, which was unsettled at the moment. She was angry with Kyle about that, too.

She saw a battered red Mercedes hurtling down the street and figured that it must either be Lila Jo or a crazy teenager seeing how much speed he could get away with in his dad's old car.

The car stopped on the street in front of their condo and a middle-aged woman jumped out and waved vigorously. Lila Jo had the look of a housewife who'd ceased caring about her appearance and did just enough to pass muster in public. She had messy hair, overdone makeup and wore faded black jeans and a white T-shirt, which she attempted to gussy up with a flowing tropical print jacket. Her sandals were glorified flip-flops. Juliana, who prided herself on her put-together designer ensembles, had chosen white ankle pants with a lacy camisole and an electric blue blazer.

"Juliana, right?" Lila Jo said brightly. "Honey, we're going to have a good time today. Hop in and let's get going."

Lila Jo kept up a constant happy patter as she expertly navigated out of Houston to the Gulf Freeway heading southeast. Juliana thought the scenery outside the window spotlighted the ugly side of Houston, flat and featureless, except for junky, dated commercial areas. They passed the tired-looking Baybrook Mall and signs to Clear Lake, where extensive NASA operations and facilities had put Houston on the map decades ago. Clear Lake City was nice enough, she thought, but most of the other suburbs on the Eastside consisted of blue-collar housing close to refineries, beat-up stores and bars. The only time the area exhibited its own spooky charm was at night, when the big refineries were lit up as festively as Christmas trees.

Finally, they reached the bridge that heralded their entrance onto Galveston Island and Juliana's spirits rose at the sight of the open water. She'd only been to Galveston a couple of times and wasn't overwhelmed by its beauty, but she longed for access to a beach again. Since she'd grown up on Brazil's Copacabana Beach, she'd missed the Atlantic Ocean with a longing she couldn't quite explain to Kyle. Galveston's Gulf of Mexico beach wasn't nearly as attractive as coastal beaches on the ocean, but she was willing to give it a chance.

They drove down Broadway, the six-lane road that bisected the island, past Victorian houses and the old Bishop's Palace residence, now a museum. Juliana remembered what first attracted her to Galveston, the wide, colorful median planted in long rows of deep pink Oleander bushes. They looked so perky and festive, making up for the occasional slatternly convenience store or gas station perched between the majestic old houses. Lila Jo told her the island's population of about 50,000 included poverty-level old-timers and working-class families interspersed with affluent Houston residents seeking a weekend escape or retirement lifestyle. It definitely could use more gentrifying.

Lila Jo drove down the old commercial area called The Strand, which Juliana remembered that she'd strolled along during the past Christmas season, when she and Kyle had gone to a faux-Victorian festival called Dickens on the Strand. The older buildings housed a decent number of upscale shops and businesses. But she was eager to get on with the house hunting.

"Why don't we get a bite to eat at Gaido's and look at the listings I printed out?" Lila Jo said. She turned right to the Seawall area and soon they were sitting in the venerable restaurant looking across the plate-glass window at a view of the Gulf.

They ordered shrimp salads and Lila Jo continued to talk nonstop, this time about Galveston and its luckless history. Pirate Jean Lafitte haunted the island in 1817 and just after the Civil War, about 1,800 died in an outbreak of Yellow Fever. But that was just a prelude to the terrifying number of casualties the island suffered in the great hurricane of 1900.

"The Galveston hurricane killed between 6,000 and 8,000 people – still the biggest natural disaster in the United States," she said with a certain relish Juliana noticed when Texans gloried in the awfulness of Texas. "Historians say that the drowned bodies just kept surfacing and floating back after the city flooded. Absolutely ghastly."

Juliana felt nauseous and put down her forkful of shrimp salad. "Lila Jo, can we talk about the listings?" she said.

"Oh honey, I'm sorry," Lila Jo said. "I was just getting to the happy ending. The Seawall was built after the great hurricane. It's seventeen feet high and runs for ten miles. Now the island mostly doesn't flood."

Juliana didn't want to consider the implications of the "mostly" caveat when she was determined to buy a beach house, so she changed the subject. "Did you meet Kyle when you became his real estate agent?"

"No, we met long before that, when he played poker," Lila Jo said. "He doesn't play any more, but he recognized the potential early on. We're sort of partners now. He gives me seed money and I set up games around town. I guess you're the reason he stopped playing."

"We're very busy with our businesses," Juliana said. "He works a lot at night, visiting our clubs."

"Yeah, I know," Lila Jo said. "I told him he should buy a condo before prices went up the last time. He listened to me and I found him that awesome place you're in now."

"It's very nice," Juliana said. "But I love the water, so I'd like to be here on the weekends."

"Does Kyle want to spend his weekends here?"

"Not as much as I do," Juliana said. To her horror, tears began to leak from her eyes and suddenly she was sobbing. She muffled her sobs into a tissue and wiped her eyes, but not before Lila Jo bobbed up, ran around the table and enveloped her in a hug so tight it took her breath away. She hated the attention Lila Jo's impulsive gesture was getting from the curious diners, but despite herself, she was grateful for the woman's sympathy.

"What's the matter, sweetie? A pretty lady like you shouldn't have any reason to boohoo," Lila Jo said, returning to her seat.

"I came from Brazil five years ago to marry Kyle, but he keeps putting it off," Juliana said in a tremulous voice. "Now my parents and sisters and cousins are all laughing at me. They say I should come back to Brazil and find a good man. And he has other women sometimes. I can feel it."

"Well, he does seem to have an eye for the ladies," Lila Jo said. "But I don't have to tell you that all men stink like polecats. I left my husband when I found him screwing the twenty-year-old tart doing the filing at his office. We're not divorced yet, but I'm holding that over his head until our settlement, believe me."

Juliana nodded, still embarrassed that she'd shown her emotions in public.

"The thing, Julie Girl, is to bide your time till you can get even," Lila Jo said, pointing her magenta-colored fingernail theatrically. "Now let's look at these listings. I'd suggest something at the higher end. Make that boy pay."

Juliana and Lila Jo looked at five listings on the island's fancier West End that were adequate, if not spectacular. Then, prompted by Lila Jo's additional iPhone search, they looked at four others that were more elaborate. Juliana agreed with the real estate broker that a four-bedroom, four-bath house facing the Gulf with a pool and spacious grilling deck was the best. By the time they left the island, close to dusk, Lila Jo had put a contract on the half-million-dollar beach house. It was about 20 percent more than the upper end of the budget Kyle had suggested, but Juliana, egged on by Lila Jo, decided that she deserved it.

CHAPTER 10

Kyle Krause careened down Interstate 35 toward Laredo, giddy at the thought of being on his own for a precious few days. Juliana had been impossibly crabby for weeks and it would do her good to look at weekend houses in Galveston with the perpetually upbeat Lila Jo Lemmons. Maybe she'd catch some of Lila Jo's happy spirit. It wouldn't do their finances any good if the real estate agent found something Juliana wanted to buy, but that was another story.

Krause was using a low-key gray SUV for this trip because he was picking up three Salvadoran immigrant women and ferrying them to the ranch in the Hill Country. It was an onerous chore, but his good deed for Juliana might cancel out the bad behavior he was planning at the end of the trip. He missed driving his Porsche, not the least for the envious glances it drew from male motorists and admiring looks from female drivers and passengers.

He'd left early enough so that with luck, he'd make it to the ranch of his friend Spud Jarvis by late afternoon. The three Salvadorans were temporarily housed there, so he'd spend the night with Spud and his wife Daria before leaving for the Hill Country with the women. After dropping them off at Krause Ranch, he'd swing over to San Antonio where he was looking forward to a layover at his business, the Texas Gas Emporium. Bonita Vasquez, a manager at the gigantic travel mart, was also his lover. But he wouldn't see her until tomorrow night, so his mind flicked past her and on to nagging worries.

He mostly kept out of Juliana's secret business, though he'd given her the go-ahead to base her operations at the ranch they'd bought three years ago. She was devoted to the clandestine enterprise but he wasn't enthusiastic about it. He'd rather focus his energies on expanding his topless empire and avoiding unnecessary risks. Juliana had argued that her family had made big money from a similar business in Brazil, so as usual, she got her way.

Like many self-made Texans, he'd wanted a ranch to prove to himself and the business world that he'd arrived. But once he'd acquired the Hill Country property, he wasn't sure what to do with it. So using it for her business made sense, at least for a while. The massive ranch, fenced in and located in a fairly remote area, would increase in value and could be used for a number of purposes. If he and Juliana didn't fancy it as a weekend getaway, they could turn it into a dude ranch, or raise emus, ostriches or even something as prosaic as cattle.

His thoughts drifted to other Hill Country interests. He'd recently invested in the fledgling campaign to create a German Texas after his childhood friend, Sam Wurzbach, had sold him on the plan. Sam had kept up with him after he left the Hill Country for Houston's more lucrative business climate. Krause appreciated that Sam retained old friends, even one who'd excelled in the strip club business. Krause guessed that Sam knew he'd be interested in his concept of German Texas because he knew the truth about Krause's origins.

Krause's grandfather, a low-level leader in Hitler's Nazi regime, had been smart enough to flee to Brazil at the frenzied end of World War II. Juliana's wealthy grandparents, along with several other right-wing Brazilian families, had helped Rudolf Krause conceal his identity. Rudolf's son, Frederic, was ashamed of the family roots, wanting a fresh start in the United States. Frederic started a produce farm in the Hill Country, but soon ran it into the ground. He killed himself, leaving his wife and two young sons nearly destitute. Kyle Krause's success had helped to preserve the small farm for his mother and brother.

Krause liked Sam's German-Texas quest partly because he wanted to reclaim the German heritage his father had tried to escape. He had no love for Nazis or any use for the Old Country, but he'd always felt at home with the German-Texas flavor of the Hill Country. And he'd quite liked his pirate of a grandfather, who'd died a decade ago. Krause couldn't find it in his heart to condemn the old man for something he'd gotten caught up with in his youth. Besides, the concept of German Texas made a lot of entrepreneurial sense. Krause could see himself expanding his strip club empire there, especially if he helped set up more lenient rules.

He shifted mental gears, relaxing in the freedom of the road, even this pallid stretch of interstate with its predictable scenery. On a clear, bright day, the heat shimmered in ribbons on the asphalt as he flew past low-lying brush. He turned up the air-conditioning, though he'd dressed for the weather in cargo shorts, a threadbare T-shirt and a Texas Girls cap pushing back the hair he hadn't bothered to style. He played his favorite country music CDs, Brad Paisley and other crooning pseudo-cowboys as loud as he wanted, since Juliana wasn't around to criticize his taste. She never could get into country music, preferring Brazilian and American pop, which he hated.

He consulted scribbled directions from Spud Jarvis and turned off the interstate to a farm-to-market road. He drove for a few miles and turned again, this time to a dirt road. A faux-rustic wooden sign identified the property ahead as the Jarvis Ranch. The main building was a low, dirty-white stucco house with a few outbuildings behind it. He knew Jarvis had acquired the foreclosed property recently at a courthouse-steps sale. Spud had described it as his first and last Texas home. To Krause, it looked like a far cry from paradise.

As he drove into the rutted driveway, he could see the balding figure of Jarvis puttering in the front yard. His elongated arms and legs always hung out of clothes that weren't quite long enough and he had an old man's protruding belly. Krause wasn't sure why he'd been nicknamed Spud, but knew it had something to do with an impoverished childhood on an Iowa potato farm. He'd come to Laredo as a young man and quickly perceived that it needed a dose of fun. The first of his topless clubs was a hit and he followed up with several satellites, quickly saturating the small city. Across the Rio Grande, virgin territory beckoned and he was eager to plumb its heights – or depths – with adult entertainment. Nuevo Laredo was more than twice the size of Laredo with an even higher quotient of fun-loving visitors, so it was easy to establish outposts there. But the growth of violent drug organizations along the border had stopped Jarvis's Mexican expansion. He'd reached a détente with several groups in the mid-1980s, and in a grudging sign of respect, they even paid him some go-away money.

Krause had sought out Jarvis's advice more than a decade ago after acquiring his first Texas Girls club. He'd gone down to Laredo to visit Jarvis's Triple-X Clubs and adopted some profitable practices, including bringing in live bands on weekends and offering a premium menu to attract a higher class of customers. When Jarvis confided a few years ago that he was unloading a few clubs, Krause bought two, glad to get a foothold in South Texas. By then, the Laredo entrepreneur was pushing seventy, had met the love of his life and wanted to spend his declining years with his beautiful Salvadoran dancer. Daria del Fuego, now in her late thirties, remarkably had reciprocated his affection. They'd married and moved to the ranch.

"Welcome to Paradise," Jarvis said.

"Thanks, guy," Krause said, squeezing his liver-spotted hand. "Great place. All you need is some Longhorns."

"Got me a half-dozen of those babies. We'll drive out to the pasture to see them later."

Krause thought his friend looked more ancient and cadaverous than ever. Jarvis had always reminded him of a sad mortician until something struck him as funny. Then he'd erupt in maniacal laughter that went on a shade too long for Krause's comfort.

The interior of the ranch's house was almost as plain as the exterior, with a motley collection of furniture that looked like somebody threw it in with the sale of the property. But Krause was surprised to see that the landscape outside the back door was fancy. The newly constructed patio area was paved in multi-colored stone with an outdoor kitchen. A large, custom-built pool included a float-up, thatched bar at one end and several lanes for swimming laps at the other. A sprinkler system nourished palm trees, red-flowering plants and St. Augustine grass, the only variety hardy enough to flourish in the torrid climate.

"Fantastic patio," Krause said, settling into a shaded chair. "Never pictured you as the sort of guy who'd hang out by the pool. Must be Daria's idea, right?"

"Yeah, that girl loves her swimming and grilling. Whatever Daria loves, Daria gets."

As if on cue, his wife opened the back door, carrying a tray of beers and snacks. Through her lacy black cover-up, Krause could see a white bikini on Daria's well-toned body. But he knew not to look for long, because Jarvis could turn jealous.

"Hola, Kyle," she said, extending her cheek for a kiss. "Thank you for coming to pick up my women. Juliana will like them."

"Where are they?"

"Enjoying dinner and TV in the guest house," she said. "That's where our visitors stay, so that no one will see them. They're recovering from their long journey."

Daria's family in El Salvador ran a high-end coyote business, bringing mostly women up through Mexico and into Texas. When women came to Daria, she would find places for them, mostly in the topless clubs or restaurants in South Texas. More recently, she had placed a select few at Juliana's ranch.

"You'll meet them tomorrow morning," she said. "I have explained Juliana's business to them. They are eager to join her for a year, or however long their services are required. They want to make money to bring their children and relatives to Texas. When they complete their deal, she will pay them $1,000 each. She has already given me their transportation fees."

"All that's between you and Juliana," Krause said. "I'm just taking them to the ranch."

She nodded and the three of them chatted until dinner was served. After a meal of roasted fish with black beans and rice, Daria brought liquors and cigars and said good night.

Krause and Spud talked about their businesses for a while, but the conversation took a more philosophical turn as the light dimmed into a quiet starlit sky.

"This is a damned fine piece of Texas," Spud said, puffing on a particularly odoriferous cigar. "But it's getting ruined like everything else."

"What's getting ruined? Laredo, Texas, the United States or the world?"

"All of the above, though I mainly meant Texas," Spud said. "A man can't create anything great like we did. Too much interference by government bureaucrats."

"You sound like those secessionists," Krause said. "Don't tell me you've joined the Nation of Texas."

"Them folks had the right idea, but messed up everything with that stupid shootout. Got themselves in a peck of trouble that will never be put right."

Krause smiled and leaned forward, emboldened by the brandy. "I just joined a group in the Hill Country that has a better idea. They're going to turn the Hill Country into German Texas."

"German Texas? What the hell is that?"

"You know the Hill Country is the prettiest part of Texas," Krause said. "But it's always been underdeveloped."

"That's true. Never been any good clubs up there," Spud said. "Probably have more cows than girls."

"That's going to change," Krause said. "If we get our way, we can make it a huge tourist attraction – kind of like a Vegas in Texas."

Spud reacted with one of his odd outbursts. His entire body shook with soundless paroxysms, followed by cascades of braying laughter. Krause found it irritating and kind of scary, but didn't say anything.

"Are you smoking the peyote again?" Jarvis said. "Vegas in Texas ain't going to happen."

"It'll be better than Vegas," Krause said. "You'll see. You and I could go together and create something big. Clubs, gambling ranches, all kinds of German-themed stuff will be up for grabs."

"Do your German-Texas buddies know about your Vegas dreams? Bet they're counting on cute little Alpine villages, not strip clubs."

"Maybe, but they'll see it my way," Krause said. "Money talks."

Jarvis leaned back in his chair, puffed on his cigar and looked at the stars. Krause thought he'd gone to sleep before he finally spoke.

"You're still young enough for big dreams. But I'll stay here and enjoy my piece of Texas until it's spoilt."

CHAPTER 11

The next morning, Krause left early after packing the three Salvadoran women and their sparse belongings into the SUV. The women seemed in good spirits, preferring to sit together in back and talk. That was fine with him, because he never had much to say to strangers, even less if he had to speak in another language. Like most Texans, he spoke some Spanish, but the women's rapid-fire conversation daunted him.

He was relieved to find that the women, introduced as Angela, Sara and Isabel, were older, perhaps in their mid- to late twenties or early thirties. They looked more Spanish than Indian, with light skin, nice faces and well-padded bodies. As Daria had observed, Juliana would applaud her choices. He couldn't remember their last names, but knew that Angela and Isabel were sisters and Sara their cousin. Perhaps because they were older, they seemed more at ease with themselves than the young, high-strung women who auditioned at his clubs. He was glad Daria had talked to them about the workings of the ranch because he didn't want to have to explain anything – in English or Spanish.

The morning passed quickly and Krause pulled into a rest stop for lunch. The women looked pleased when they saw the voluminous basket of food Daria had packed. He took out the sandwiches, drinks and cookies and everyone picked out what they wanted and ate in contented silence. They piled back into the car and lapsed into an afternoon torpor. Krause drove steadily and by mid-afternoon, he'd reached the guard gate of his ranch. He spoke briefly to the man on duty and drove inside.

Something about the place, which they'd called Krause Ranch in the absence of a clever name, had always made him uneasy. He couldn't quite put his finger on it, but the ranch had never felt welcoming. Perhaps he and Juliana had snapped up the densely wooded property too quickly. It had been listed at a good price, but he wondered now if the previous owners had just been in a hurry to get rid of it. The trees and heavy underbrush were thick and gloomy, especially after Juliana had installed fencing and barbed wire. He didn't much care for the people Juliana had hired either, especially Maria Espinosa, the part-time director who worked when Juliana couldn't be there. Espinosa, a heavyset Hispanic with a broad forehead and grayish skin tones, came up to meet them. She looked and acted like a prison matron.

The modest assortment of one-story buildings looked as innocent as a summer camp, but Krause could sense that the Salvadorans also felt the odd chill of the place. They'd stopped talking and all three seemed reluctant to gather their belongings. He wanted them to hurry up so that he could leave, but he tried to hide his eagerness to get away. The three women stood together, as if supporting each other from unseen dangers. He introduced them to Espinosa in his limited Spanish and handed her a stack of paperwork Daria had sent. Espinosa began talking with them in Spanish and they nodded in comprehension. He smiled, waved, got back in the SUV and drove without stopping through the guard gate. He felt sorry for the women who watched him drive off, but after all, they'd known what they were signing up for when they agreed to come to the ranch.

After a few minutes on the open road, he was breathing easier. For the first time all day he relaxed. He deserved his treat, so he headed toward San Antonio.

Six years ago, he'd built his first Texas Gas Emporium off I-10 outside the Alamo City and had been astounded by its immediate success. It was his iteration of the gigantic places that had sprung up in recent years to attract hordes of gas-guzzling motorists and truckers. The emporium boasted twenty-five gas pumps and a glittering convenience store that offered everything from warmed-up hotdogs and burritos to Mexican pottery and flavored condoms. There was an ice-cream counter and a game room to entertain the kids and a motel behind the convenience store where truckers could rent showers, rooms and if they went about it discreetly, women. Krause's business concept was designed to fill every need of the modern road warrior.

When Juliana joined him in Houston, she'd been so impressed with the Texas Gas Emporium and its profits that he'd built three others, one off I-10 near Beaumont and two off I-20 near Dallas and west to Odessa. But since she didn't particularly care about cars, gas or truckers, she didn't interfere in the management of those businesses. So he used them as an excuse to get out of Houston and to skim off money to stash in a secret account. He thought about his growing funds with satisfaction. He wasn't about to ask Juliana's permission for all of his purchases.

There were a few women stationed at each emporium to give in-room massages and other, tip-worthy services as well. Some of the women had drug and alcohol habits that kept them mired in prostitution. Others would rather work for big tips from long-haul truckers than eke out meager salaries clerking at the nearby Wal-Mart. As business accelerated or dwindled, he could move the women between the Gas Emporium locations. He mostly left management of the massage business up to Bonita Vasquez, the Mexican-American woman he'd hired five years ago to run those services. She'd done well and always took time to make Krause's visits pleasurable. He'd called earlier and told her he was an hour away.

Now, as he pulled into the emporium, he could see Bonita on the porch of the motel-style building in back. In her mid-thirties with long, dark hair and almost-black eyes and lashes, she was attractive without being beautiful. She dressed professionally enough that she didn't look like a madam and was a shrewd businesswoman. She and Krause shared a long history and he'd come to value her problem-solving skills as much as her willing body.

"Kyle, *mi amigo*, welcome," she said, kissing him softly on the cheek. He smelled her musky perfume and it brought back memories of happy encounters. She led him inside her unit, which consisted of a large living room leading into a kitchen with a bedroom and bathroom in the back.

"Hi, beautiful," he said, looking around. She had apparently redecorated since the last time he'd been here, with furniture and fabric in gaudy reds and yellows. She had also added some Mexican velvet paintings of mountains and deserts that he hated, so he refrained from comment on the new décor. He never spent more than a few hours there and didn't really care if it was wall-to-wall polka dots.

"How's business this week?"

"Good here," she said. "Not so good at the Odessa store. Had to get rid of two of the women. Too drunk to work their schedule and stealing money from the truckers. Very unprofessional."

"I'll go over the figures with you later," Krause said. "Now I just need to rest."

He leaned back in the leatherette chair and sighed. She came around behind him and started massaging his neck and back. Her skilled hands felt heavenly and he began to unwind from the stress of the trip.

"Had to get away from Juliana for a few days?" she asked. Bonita had met Juliana once, and the two women had immediately sized each other up as dangerous rivals. He cursed himself for being so open with Bonita about his frustrations with Juliana.

"She went to Galveston with a real estate broker," he said. "Wants to buy a beach house – the last thing I want or need."

"You sure she's not making love to a beach boy?" she teased. "Maybe she needs a change."

Her instinct for the jugular roiled his temper. "Cut the crap, Bonita, and bring me a beer."

She poured two Coronas into frosted glasses from the freezer and added limes. He smiled and touched glasses with hers, trying to make amends for his cross words. After a while, she led him to the bedroom, unbuttoned his shirt and eased him down on her king-sized bed. For a few minutes, he relished being fully in the moment, as he almost never could in his problem-plagued life. It was as if time stopped – and then in an instant, it all went sour. He heard the walls shake and felt a huge explosion that definitely wasn't the orgasm he'd hoped for. Something terrible had happened.

He leaped off the bed, wrapped a towel around his lower body and ran ahead of Bonita to the door. The scene in front shook him almost like a second explosion. Part of the convenience store was gone. The left side of its roof had a gaping, smoking hole and the walls on that end had caved in. He knew that if he didn't get help fast, the gas pumps in front would be next. If they blew, the entire property would catch fire.

"Get me a phone, quick," he yelled at Bonita. "If those gas pumps go up, we're goners."

CHAPTER 12

Annie was running off the tension of her workday when her cell phone rang in the pocket of her shorts. She noticed it was Matt Sharpe and picked it up quickly. It had been four days since they'd been together at his apartment. Though they'd traded flirtatious texts, she'd begun to wonder whether their night together was the latest mistake in her star-crossed love life. She knew that her judgment about men was often flawed, especially when alcohol was involved. She hadn't meant to sleep with him that night and was embarrassed that she'd succumbed so easily to his scotch and flattery. She tried to reassure herself that he was a decent man, but she knew that the sex would change the friendship. So she was glad that his tone of voice sounded warmer, but otherwise normal.

He'd come by the morning after her car was vandalized and searched the area for clues. But he didn't find anything and asked if she was certain she'd been followed home from his apartment. She knew she hadn't imagined the dark SUV behind her in the predawn hours, but couldn't say for sure if it had meant harm. But she felt uneasy, remembering how Alicia Perez had stalked her four years ago. Could it be Perez, risking recapture by showing up in Houston in a revenge move? That seemed unlikely, but she found herself searching online more often for signs of new secessionist activity and looking in her rear-view mirror more frequently when she drove.

"What's up, Matt?" she said, slowing to a walk.

"Want to go to a porn star show at a strip club tomorrow night?"

"Now that sounds romantic," she joked. "What's the deal?"

"The Texas Girls Club on the North Freeway is hosting Carla Carmine, who's billed as one of the busiest porn stars in California."

"Another feather in Houston's cap. Is that unusual for a strip club?"

"It doesn't happen every day in this area, but it's not uncommon for porn stars to make public appearances at clubs to extend their fan base," he said.

"Usually the vice squad is there, too."

"Why is that?"

"Obviously, we don't want them to step over the line of what's legal," Matt said. "Also, it could be rowdy, with too many people drinking even more than usual. I'll just be there as an extra pair of eyes and hands for the vice squad folks."

"Well, as it happens, one of my reporters has been investigating the Texas Girls clubs' mogul, Kyle Krause, so I'm curious enough to go."

"Holding out on me?" Matt asked. "Give me the scoop."

"Please keep it under your hat. It's early in his investigation."

"Think I'd go running to Kyle Krause with that news? Hardly. I'll pick you up at 7."

Annie was intrigued. She'd been researching Houston's troubled history with strip clubs to help Nate with his project. The city currently was home to at least one hundred clubs, more than most other metropolitan areas, though it was hard to definitively keep track because they opened and closed with regularity. There were many theories about why Houston was such a magnet for topless entertainment, but Annie thought one reason was the proliferation of conventions Houston hosted that attracted large numbers of men, including the giant OTC. As a center for energy production, the city yearly welcomed more than 50,000 participants in the Offshore Technology Conference. The OTC was always a headache for the *Times* to cover, but it was a huge boon for bars, restaurants and strip clubs. Annie personally knew one local woman who broke off her marriage after a picture of her husband cavorting with a prostitute surfaced online.

Also, though she thought of strip clubs as a sort of a hangover from the 1960s – prior to the feminist movement, when men were less evolved – the businesses were actually flourishing worldwide.

She'd learned that Houston had tried for years to put too-exacting regulations on the clubs, such as trying to specify the number of inches dancers should be separated from customers – only to be sued by large chains. Now, the regulations had been simplified, and the largest clubs, or their chain ownership, paid into a special fund that supported the vice squad. It was a way to self-police that had both critics and supporters. The mom-and-pop clubs were usually the ones that would flout regulations with impunity. They tended to move out of the city to locations in the counties that were beyond policing. Overall, it was a strange system, but it seemed to work.

Matt showed up at her door the next night, gave her a kiss and whistled appreciatively at her outfit – a short white denim skirt, a figure-hugging black top and white bejeweled sandals.

"Wow, Carla Carmine will have nothing on you," he said.

"Thanks, Matt," she smiled. "No badge or uniform?"

"No, we need to blend in with the best of Houston's lowlife."

The Texas Girls club fronted on the North Freeway, the section of I-45 that wound through downtown north to Houston's George Bush Intercontinental Airport and on up to Dallas. The big airport was named for George H.W. Bush, the much-beloved longtime Houston resident, not his less-esteemed son, who'd chosen to relocate to Dallas after his presidency ended. The 23-mile stretch from the airport to downtown vexed some city boosters with its low-rent billboards, sagging businesses and wilder-than-usual traffic. It seemed to showcase the worst of Houston for newly arrived visitors, but nobody did much about it. The Gulf Freeway, which led from the south side of downtown to Houston's smaller Hobby Airport, was even tawdrier. When she first moved to Houston, Annie had been appalled by the city's haphazard, anything-goes development, but after ten years, she had an unreasonable affection for it. Houston had resisted zoning for decades and wasn't likely to ever embrace it. Now, she believed, along with other Houstonians, that market forces, not zoning, mostly dictated what a place looked like. Houston, by and large, didn't look that much different than big cities with more conventional zoning laws.

Matt drove around the jammed parking lot of the strip-center club and finally located a space. He opened the car door and took her arm, steering her toward the booth just inside the Texas Girls entrance. A meaty, shaved-head bouncer with a ZZ-Top-style beard and a cobra tattoo on his neck demanded their IDs. He looked at them closely and frowned when he saw Matt's police identification.

"What are you doing here, Mr. Detective? Trying to get your jollies?" He sneered in a belligerent tone. "We follow all of the rules."

"I expect you'll see plenty of cops here – in uniform and civilian clothes," Matt said in a neutral tone.

A striking woman with long brown hair and a glittering outfit stepped out from the ticket booth and said, "Bobo, what's wrong?"

"Nothing, Miss Juliana," he said with a chastened air. He walked outside.

She looked at them as if memorizing their faces, examined their IDs and led them to the front of the large room, where some tables still remained empty toward the stage. She showed them to one with a forced smile and swept out.

"Who's that babe?" Annie wondered. "She acts like she owns the place."

"It must be Juliana Souza, girlfriend of the owner," Matt said. "She helps Kyle Krause run the clubs, I hear. Bobo the bouncer has a reputation as a really bad dude, though he certainly minds Juliana. Did you ever see a big man slink away so fast?"

Annie laughed. "You seem to know an awfully lot about the clubs. Didn't think that was your specialty."

"I've just been helping one of the vice cops who's looking at Krause's whole operation. She's here tonight," he said, beckoning to a corner table. A woman came over, wearing a black slacks outfit rather than a uniform. She was in her thirties, Annie guessed, and attractive, with thick, curvy eyebrows and curly dark hair.

"Hi, Monica," he said. "May I present my friend, Annie Price? Monica Gardiner is a colleague of mine who's here to see that Carla Carmine behaves herself."

"Seriously?" Annie asked. "How does a porn star behave herself in a strip club?"

"We just want to make sure there are no sex shows," she said. "We'll shut them down very quickly if that happens. They can strip all they want, but they have to obey the public decency laws."

"My goodness," Annie said. "You have your work cut out for you."

"Indeed we do. Can you excuse us for a moment? I need to talk to Matt privately," Monica said. "See you, Annie."

He went to Monica's table and the two of them talked for a while with a man Annie assumed was another plainclothes officer. She looked at the strip clubs' magazine she'd picked up at the entrance. It was glossy, with big photos of women in lacy underwear and flashy ads for local clubs. She noticed a two-page feature previewing Carla Carmine's appearance.

The feature story noted that Carmine had worked for "major XXX film companies, including Bang Brothers, Naughty America and New Sensations." The tall blonde's shapely body was praised as "all natural" and her interests were described as "men, women and threesomes." Some day she wanted to run a cupcake shop.

Annie put the magazine down, annoyed that she was wasting time reading such inanities. She guessed there was a market for that sort of thing, but it sounded so phony. She hoped that she'd never be reduced to writing PR for sleazy enterprises.

She saw a familiar-looking man stopping at the table and smiled, trying to remember where she'd seen him. To her surprise, she recognized State Senator Sam Wurzbach, the champion of the German-Texas movement.

"Hi, Annie," he said, looking sheepish.

"Hey, Sam," she said. "What're you doing here?"

"Last week, you asked me whom I was seeing in Houston," he said. "Now you know. Kyle Krause and I were high-school wrestling buddies in Fredericksburg."

"The plot thickens," she said. "I'd heard he might be a supporter of the German-Texas movement."

"Kyle is a terrific businessman and really believes in what we're doing," Wurzbach said. "So I support his ventures whenever I can. I was in town today, so I decided to stop by. My wife even knows I'm here."

"How're things going in the Hill Country? Any new threats?"

"Nothing of a serious nature," he said. "Hope you and your reporter can come to Austin soon. We'll be having our first German Texas fund-raiser."

"Sounds interesting. We'll call you," Annie said.

Matt returned to the table as the lights went down and they drank their $7.50 beers in silence. The crowd grew hushed as a breathless-sounding deejay ran through Carmine's resume from California.

"She's a native Texan who loves horses, ranches and longneck beers," he added. The deejay put on music, some hard-rock anthem Annie recognized from the 1980s.

Carmine came out, tall, blonde and natural, and twined her legs around the pole on stage. She looked pretty good, Annie thought, and seemed to know how to dance. After the first two numbers, though, the novelty of her performance wore off. Annie chugged the rest of her beer, feeling restless.

The tempo sped up, Carmine smiled knowingly and a man in a leopard bikini danced on to the stage. He looked handsome but seedy, like Matthew McConaughey in the strip-club movie, *Magic Mike*. The man moved closer to Carla Carmine and they began dancing together.

Suddenly the lights went out and Annie heard worried murmurs. After a few minutes of uncertainly, a stage light went on and Monica Gardiner, the policewoman she'd met earlier, spoke briefly.

"The Houston Police Department is closing this establishment for the rest of the night," she said. "Please leave by the normal exits in an orderly fashion."

Annie got up with Matt and they began walking to the door.

"What happened?" Annie asked.

"The man on stage with Carla Carmine is also a porn star," Matt said. "We agreed that if he appeared, we'd have to shut down the show. Heard rumors that there might be a sex show in the making. Houston ain't New Orleans, you know."

CHAPTER 13

Annie sat in her glass cubicle office editing one of many stories she needed to send over before the afternoon news meeting. Her day had started off with a couple of editors' meetings, lagged until after her solitary lunch at her desk, and gathered speed as the afternoon wore on. Assigning editors always had to wait for reporters to file their daily stories, some at the last possible moment. Annie couldn't begrudge their last-minute work because as a reporter, she'd done the same thing, hoping for one last phone call to be returned. But her tension would mount as the stories piled up, and today she felt winded, as if she was running a race she couldn't possibly win. She wondered if she ought to have her blood pressure checked. She looked up and saw Travis Dunbar standing outside the door.

"Hey, boss," he said. "Can I come in?"

"Sure, Travis," she said, trying to sound welcoming. "What's going on?"

"You remember the floater in the Ship Channel? Finally got Sharpe to talk on the record about what they found."

"Was it a Russian Mafia smuggling deal?"

"No," Travis said, plopping his bulldog body into a creaky chair. "He thinks the body is that of a young woman from Eastern Europe. They found a label in clothes fragments that they traced to a shop in Tirana."

"Tirana? Where's that?"

"The capital of Albania. Has about a half-million people. Not a common hot spot for trafficking, though the Russian Mafia has tentacles everywhere in Eastern Europe. But Sharpe doesn't think it was the Mafia."

"Why not?"

"The body was basically in good shape. Some of the girls who get tossed overboard have broken bones and worse. The Mafia treats them like garbage and throws them away."

"So how does he think the girl got here?"

"A stowaway, perhaps a girlfriend of a seaman. He's trying to trace the ships that have moved in and out of the port in the last few weeks."

"Doesn't sound like big news," Annie said. "Maybe a six-inch story?"

"All right," Travis said. "But I think there's something bigger behind it. It smells rotten to me."

"Keep tabs on it, but you've got lots of other things going. What about that drug lord from the Valley who landed in jail here yesterday? Can you get his lawyer to talk?"

"I'm trying. I'll write the other story and send it to you. Then I'll head over to the courthouse."

She resumed her editing, noticing it was almost 4 p.m. She'd be here really late if she didn't hurry, but it was hard to concentrate with the interruptions. She noticed Maggie Mahaffey tapping on the glass. Drat, she thought. Maggie wasn't exactly her favorite reporter and she tended to be longwinded.

"Come in, Maggie," she said, mustering a smile. "What can I do for you?"

The reporter sat down, smoothed her hot pink skirt and crossed her legs, showing off high-heeled ankle boots that encased tiny feet. Petite women who dressed like Barbie dolls had a tendency to raise Annie's hackles. She felt guilty for hoping that Maggie wouldn't prolong the interruption, but she couldn't exactly tell her to state her business and go away.

"I'm giving you my two-week notice," Maggie said. "I'm moving to Austin for a new job."

"Oh? What's the job?"

"I'm going to be a morning anchor on WFAB-TV, the Fox station. I'll make almost twice what I'm making here and won't have to worry about these stupid layoffs."

"Congratulations," Annie said, resenting her triumphal air. "We'll miss you, but it sounds like a good opportunity. You haven't done TV before, have you?"

"No, but Senator Jake Satterfield thinks I'm a natural," Maggie said. "He knows the station's owner in Dallas and put in a good word for me."

Annie felt as if she'd been slapped, just hearing her former fiancé's name come out of the mouth of the preening prima donna. She kept a neutral look on her face and tried to sound normal.

"Jake knows practically every big donor in Texas. He's hit up most of them for money."

"I know you and he were an item once," Maggie said. "How could you give up that gorgeous guy?"

Annie bristled, angry with the reporter for trying to make it personal. Why was Maggie tormenting her? Annie vowed to remember this encounter if she ever had to write the self-obsessed sexpot a recommendation.

"That's a rather rude question, Maggie. Why are you asking?"

"Sorry," Maggie said. "I just wondered, since he's a free man again. Says he's getting a divorce."

"I've heard that before. But it's really not my business or yours, is it?"

"You could say I'm making it my business," Maggie smiled. "Jake and I are seeing each other. That's one reason I'm moving."

Again, Maggie's words felt like a sucker punch to her chest, but she wasn't going to give her the satisfaction of a reaction. She couldn't resist a barb.

"Well, best of luck. You'll need it with Jake."

Annie got up and extended her hand across the desk, wanting to end the meeting and lick her wounds privately. Maggie stood and shook her hand daintily.

"You're not upset, I hope?"

Talk about twisting the knife, Annie thought. What an obnoxious bitch she is. Don't stoop to her level.

"Of course not," she said. "As you said, there's probably another layoff coming. It's good that you're leaving – you'll probably save someone else's job."

"That's one reason I've been looking. This is such a depressing place and newspapers are a dying industry. Television is a much better platform for me."

"You're probably right," Annie agreed. She walked Maggie to the door. "It's getting late, so I'll catch up with you next week on the details."

Annie shut the door more emphatically than she'd intended. She sat quietly, giving herself time to calm down. She felt like putting her head down on her desk and wailing like a kindergartner deprived of a nap. But she resisted, knowing that any change in her behavior would stir gossip among the reporters on the other side of the glass wall. That was the down side of having a fishbowl office – lower-level staffers were always watching, trying to decipher the office politics.

Just the mention of Jake had made her chest tighten. She was furious that he was seeing Maggie, but she hoped she'd masked her feelings.

She walked out with a smile, her back ramrod straight, and looked for Greg Barnett. Formerly her investigative editor and still her boss as managing editor, he'd need to know the news about Maggie right away. She spotted his lanky frame leaning into a reporter's desk, discussing a story. She stood nearby and waited.

"Want to get a cup of coffee in the tunnel?" She asked him in a low voice. They smiled their way through the newsroom, got on the elevator and descended to the row of shops underneath the building before he turned to her. "What's going on, Price?"

"Maggie Mahaffey is leaving for Austin. Going to be the Fox station's next blond It-Girl."

"I should have guessed. She's always been too much of a diva. Newspapering's not quite glamorous enough for her."

"She's not a bad reporter," Annie said. "When she's not worrying about her hair or her manicure, she can turn out a halfway decent story."

"Meow, Annie," Greg smiled. "That's the cattiest thing I've ever heard from you."

"Guess I have my reasons," Annie said.

"We'll need to think about this," he said. "Obviously, we don't have the money to replace her, but since you'll be down to three reporters to supervise, we may have to change your job description."

"Are you trying to tell me my position's at risk?" Annie said.

"You know as well as I do that we're all at risk. I hope you'll have a job here as long as you want," Greg said. "But you'll need to take on some reporting responsibility, as well as supervising the three reporters."

Annie looked at Greg for a moment, thinking. Her lips curved into her first genuine smile of the day.

"Promise?"

CHAPTER 14

Annie poured herself a glass of chardonnay. She needed a drink, and after her day, she deserved one. But just one, she said to herself, putting the cork back into the bottle and easing it to the back of the refrigerator, hiding it behind the milk carton. She no longer kept screw-top wine around because it was too easy to open and polish off the whole bottle.

She scooped out a can of smelly cat food for Marbles and Benjy, who thumped across the hardwood floors like baby mountain lions. She enjoyed watching them gobble their food while she sipped her wine. Her cats were good therapy after a tense day. Her parents were not, but she decided to call them anyway. Her father answered at their home in Blacksburg, Virginia.

"Dad, are you there by yourself?"

"Yeah, your mother's gone shopping. What's going on with you?"

"How's your column going?" Jeffrey Price, who'd retired five years ago, confined his journalistic efforts to a twice-a-week column for the *Blacksburg Sun*, the newspaper he once ran for a rapacious chain. Even though the newspaper business had changed drastically since he'd left it, he was the person she turned to for advice. She admired his passion for improving his community.

"Just wrote a pretty good one for Sunday on pollution in the New River," he said. "What's happening in your newsroom?"

"One of my reporters just quit to go work for a TV station in Austin. Greg wants me to add some reporting to my editing job, since I'm losing someone."

"How would that work?" She heard the skepticism in her father's tone.

"I'd keep editing my reporters' stuff, but also team up with them on bigger stories, to deepen the reporting. To tell the truth, I'm excited."

"Honey, I know you've missed reporting, but can you do justice to essentially two jobs?"

"Don't think I'll have any choice, Dad."

"I don't want you to overwork," Price said. "You need balance to stay healthy."

Annie knew that her father was obliquely expressing worry about her tendency to stress out and drink too much. She'd confided in him about her periodic efforts to cut back on alcohol and he kept that information confidential.

"Don't worry about me. I'm doing fine," she said. "Reporting will get me out of the office, which will be great."

She spent another ten minutes talking about her brother and sister and their children and her mother. She hung up the phone, took another gulp of wine and tried to quiet her racing mind. Her doorbell's retro chime startled her.

Who'd be ringing her doorbell at 8 p.m.? Her 1920s Heights neighborhood, still a little raw around its edges, was pretty safe, but occasionally things happened. She went to the craftsman-style door and peered through its four decorative panes at the top.

She was shocked to recognize the handsome, white-blond head of Tom Marr. What would bring this West Texan – cattle rancher, disgraced secessionist candidate for governor and almost-boyfriend – to her front door? She hadn't seen him for four years.

She opened the door and he reached out to her, holding her tight against his tall torso. She basked in the thrill of his long arms, solid chest and clean Ivory-soap smell for a delicious half-minute before she broke away.

"Tom," she said. "What're you doing here?"

He smiled, but his face looked drawn, as if he'd been driving a lot and sleeping little.

"Annie, can I come in a minute to explain?"

"Sure." She peered out in the dark and saw an SUV parked on the street.

"My driver's parked out front. He'll wait while we talk. Is that okay?"

She stepped aside and he moved into the house with curiosity, surveying her cozy living room with its red and green patterned Indian rug, cherry and maple flea-market finds and tiny fireplace.

"I've never seen your house. Looks like you. Pretty and not so fussy you don't feel at home. Nice."

"Thanks. Want some chardonnay? I just got home a little while ago and afraid I don't have much to offer in the way of food." She could use another slug or two of wine herself.

"No, don't worry about me. I won't impose on you long. I'm in Houston to look for Betsy. She's run away."

"Oh my gosh. She's about fifteen by now, right?"

"Just turned sixteen, but she thinks she's twenty-five and unfortunately, looks it," Marr said. "She's almost six feet tall, like you, but rounder, with blonde hair and blue eyes."

"Hard to believe," Annie said. "Seems like yesterday she was showing me her American Girl doll collection."

"The good old days," Marr said. She saw tears in his blue eyes.

"Tell me about it."

"She went to see some rock bands in El Paso with a few girlfriends and apparently met a guitar player with a Texas group. Saw him a couple of times on the sly. We think she's run off with him and could be here in the Houston area."

"What can I do?"

"A friend of mine saw a story on your website about a young woman found in the ship channel…" He stopped, unable to continue. Annie saw his hands quivering. She put a hand on his shoulder.

"It almost certainly wasn't Betsy. The police said today that they think the dead girl was from Eastern Europe, probably Albania. How she drowned and ended up in the ship channel, we don't know yet."

Marr's face lit up several hundred watts. He grinned, grabbed her shoulders and hugged her so hard that she winced in pain. Poor guy. She'd never been a mom, but in the brief time they'd been around each other, she'd felt close to Betsy.

"Thanks," he said. "I can breathe again."

"It's okay. Have you hired a detective, talked to the police?"

"I've got friends working on it. To tell the truth, I'm keeping it kind of quiet, hoping I can get her back before the media finds out. Hate to see her harassed again by reporters."

"I understand," she said. "It's between you and me until you tell me otherwise."

He looked at her, touched her cheek softly and walked with her to the edge of the front porch. She liked his gentleness and remembered how gallant he'd been around her. He paused to say goodbye.

"My driver's waiting, but can I get back in touch with you about Betsy?"

Annie hesitated, not sure what to say. She wasn't sure she trusted him and he could see it.

"I'm not a secessionist anymore," he said. "I cut my ties with those folks four years ago. I'm just a plain old cattle rancher now."

"I'm glad to hear that, Tom. I'd like to hear from you."

CHAPTER 15

Betsy Marr heard her cell phone ringing, but she couldn't place where it was, or where she was, for that matter.

She opened her eyes, took in the beige motel room and the bearded, sleeping face of her boyfriend, Patrick Costas, lying next to her in bed. Her cell phone rang from her purse that she'd carelessly thrown on the stained carpet.

She grabbed it just before it stopped ringing. Patrick turned over in bed, murmuring sleepily. She took the phone and padded in bare feet to the bathroom, her naked body shivering in the too-cold air-conditioning. She wrapped a towel around her torso as she tried to focus on the excited tones of Carly Adams, talking in her usual exclamation points.

"What's up, Carly? Slow down, girl."

"I heard my mom say that your dad went to Houston to search for you," Betsy heard her friend say. "Just thought you should know."

"Does he know Patrick's name?"

"I told him I didn't know his name or which of the bands he played with."

"Good girl."

"When are you coming back?"

"I don't know. I can't stand being home and arguing with my dad all the time. And I love being with Patrick. You'll see when you fall in love, Car. It's awesome."

"Wow. He's gorgeous, for sure. But school starts in a month."

"I don't care. I'm sick of school, sick of Marfa, sick of living on a cow farm in the middle of nowhere."

"You can't stay gone forever."

"Maybe, maybe not. Patrick might take me to California. He says he's going out there soon to make a demo." She was about to expand on his plans when she heard a voice in the background on the other end of the line.

"Bets, my mom's yelling for me to get downstairs for breakfast. Got to get off the phone. Call you back soon."

"Later, Car."

Betsy looked at herself in the mirror with curiosity. Shouldn't she look different, now that she'd done it with Patrick? But her thick, tumbled honey-colored hair looked the same and her curvy body wasn't any different either. She smiled to the mirror, and thought she looked older around the eyes, maybe a little sexier. She'd met Patrick three weeks ago and since then, he'd been all that she could think about. He'd come to Marfa to see her and she'd sneaked him into the guesthouse for a couple of days. No one knew, because she often hung out there watching TV, reading and just chilling when she wanted to get away from her dad's prying questions. He'd been a royal pain for the last six months, since she'd gone to a dance with a senior and come home a little buzzed. He didn't realize that just because they lived in Hicksville, kids still smoked a little pot and drank whenever they could get hold of beer or liquor from their parents' stash. He'd cracked down on her hours, especially on school nights, and lectured her about her grades. Admittedly, her once-perfect grades had slipped, but it was only because she was so very bored at school. Her high school was small and rural and she'd known most of the boys all her life. Dating them was almost like going out with her brother, though she'd never had a sibling.

"Baby," she heard from the next room. "Come back to bed."

She bounded into the room, jumped into the queen-sized bed and covered Patrick's bare chest with kisses. He kissed her back, grabbed her breasts and the next half-hour went by in a delicious blur of sex. She'd been traveling with him five days now, in three different motel rooms, and the novelty hadn't worn off. Yeah, the motels had been a little cheesy, not like the places she'd stayed on a few trips with her dad, but that was exciting too, like she was seeing a new piece of the world. She traced the outline of the ship tattoos on his neck and left arm in blue and green ink.

She licked the inked likeness of a tall sailing ship on his neck, which tasted salty with sweat after the frenetic activity of the previous half-hour. He was so beautiful, even though she didn't normally think of a guy as beautiful.

She loved his tattoos and the multiple piercings in his ears. His sparkly blue eyes reminded her of Bradley Cooper in one of her favorite old movies, *The Hangover*. Her dad gave her corny lectures when he spotted someone on the street with lots of tattoos, which happened occasionally, even in rinky-dink Marfa. He'd go absolutely nuts if he ever met Patrick. Not that she'd ever let that happen.

"Where'd you get that one?" she said.

"On Mykonos, when I visited the family last year," he said sleepily.

Betsy was fascinated by Patrick's independent life. He thrilled her with tales of his second-generation Greek parents, who'd worked in the Galveston shipping industry for two decades, but returned to Mykonos three years ago to help the large extended Costas family run a hotel. Patrick could have gone too, but preferred his music and the laidback Texas lifestyle to the grungy work he said he'd have to do at the Costas hotel. He'd hooked up with several different bands while he lived on his own, and when he ran out of money, he'd spend a few months working on a rig out in the Gulf. Betsy had almost never been out of West Texas, except to Disney World when she was eight. She'd been so sheltered during childhood after her mother died. Her father rarely left the ranch since he'd parted ways with the secessionists four years ago. She'd hoped he'd marry Annie Price, the reporter who'd visited the ranch twice when he was running for governor. She'd loved Annie, the way she talked to her like Betsy was a real person instead of a kid, and thought the reporter loved her and her father. But Annie ended up writing the stories that destroyed her dad's career and she never came back to the ranch. And her dad had become an old man who hardly went out and even stricter – it was suffocating and hateful.

She drifted off to sleep, waking up only when Patrick shook her gently.

"Baby, the band has a gig tonight that might become a big deal. We could get asked to play regularly, for decent pay. Want to come?"

"Sure," she said. "Is it a bar?"

"Kind of," he said. "It's actually a strip place in Pasadena called the Texas Girls Club. Ever been to a topless bar?"

"Are you kidding?" She said with excitement. "West Texas doesn't have that kind of place, at least not in the boonies."

Her mind was whirling. She knew he thought she was 18. If he found out she was only 16, she didn't know what he'd do. She was afraid he'd dump her and then she'd have no choice but to go back to Marfa with her tail between her legs. She had a good fake ID that gave her age as 21. It had worked for her before – she hoped it would tonight.

CHAPTER 16

Behar Zogu drove to the budget motel near his home on the Eastside, his mood swinging between anticipation and dread. The Albanian girls were interesting but unruly, and he wasn't sure he'd be able to keep them in line for the next week or two. They reminded him of a basket overflowing with puppies – lively and fun to watch, but likely to pee on the carpet the minute you turned your back. The girls were loud, profane, asked a lot of questions he couldn't answer and were already straining at the bit to break out and explore the big city. He was regretting his offer to smuggle them to America with the help of his relatives in Albania.

He'd filled the back of his battered pickup with groceries, mostly cheap American foods that would be easy for the girls to microwave in their motel rooms – where he hoped they'd stay. He'd picked up lots of frozen pizzas, ice cream, breakfast bars, Cheetos and other junk he knew they'd love. He included some PBR beer, but no vodka. Those women were rambunctious enough without hard liquor.

The meeting with Krause and his girlfriend hadn't gone well. He knew it was a mistake for Juliana to see the girls yesterday when he'd just deposited them at the motel, but she'd barged in without warning. She'd looked at them with scorn and they sensed her hostility. Luckily, he'd gotten rid of her quickly, saying the girls needed to rest from their stressful journey as stowaways. Zogu wasn't alone in his dislike of Juliana – most of the strip clubs' employees couldn't stand her either, and he sensed that even Krause sometimes got fed up with her bossy personality. But Zogu felt relatively secure with his place in the business. In the five years he'd worked for Krause, he'd taken on increasingly unsavory and clandestine tasks. He felt confident that his services were valued.

He thought about the life he'd made since landing in Houston seven years ago with little English and no money. He'd quickly disappeared into the Eastside's gritty working-class neighborhoods and cast about for his best opportunity. A small but tight Albanian community had welcomed him and he'd fallen in love with Genta, his Texas-born sweetheart from a big Albanian family soon after he arrived. They'd married and in short order, produced his beloved son and daughter. He'd begun looking harder for a job where he could make more money than the day-laborer shifts he'd worked in the past. Luckily, Genta's ambitions matched or surpassed his and she was thrilled when he got work at the Texas Girls clubs. They both could tell that Krause's business was thriving – and expanding. He worked late nights and early mornings and showed himself willing to handle any kind of task. Soon the owner was tapping him as a courier and fixer, delivering sensitive packages to different club locations – usually drugs, he suspected – and looking after girls who'd gotten knocked up or knocked around at the clubs.

He felt fortunate, knowing he had a legion of relatives in Albania who'd jump at the chance to escape their beautiful but poor country for the promised land of Texas. He'd occasionally used his family's connections in the shipping industry to hide people aboard ships bound for the Houston port, where they could slip into the country without papers. Those experiences had emboldened him to propose to Krause a shipment of girls who'd become cheap, pliant workers in the topless clubs. His boss, knowing that Eastern Europeans often stood out for their tall, blond beauty, was intrigued. He'd paid the necessary money to hide ten girls aboard a cargo ship, and Zogu's brother Bujar made the arrangements in Tirana. As the middleman, Zogu stood to make enough money for Genta to stay home while their children were small.

But now he worried that he'd given too much leeway to his brother, who'd assembled a motley group he feared wasn't attractive enough to pass muster with Krause and his girlfriend. Some of the girls were pretty enough, but generally they resembled diamonds in the rough instead of the perfect polished solitaires that Krause and Juliana seemed to expect. He knew that these girls came from poor families without much chance to wrest their way up from poverty. If they'd been born luckier, they wouldn't have had to risk being stowaways to a new country. He didn't allow himself to dwell on the unfortunate fate of the tenth girl, which nearly had scuttled the whole deal. And now he'd have to work fast to get the Albanians ready for the spotlight.

Zogu parked his pickup, started unloading the groceries and knocked on one of the motel doors. Leka, the self-styled leader of the group, answered and his heart sank when he saw her again. Leka was strong and strapping, but she'd never be a beauty. She'd dyed her hair blonde, but it was a brassy gold that didn't mesh well with her thick black unibrow and muddy complexion. She had a square face and a decent figure, except for thighs that jiggled when she walked.

Still, he liked her because she was smart and sassy, and he sensed that the eight other girls would follow her lead. He would work through her to get them to accept the makeovers he planned before presenting them to Krause.

"Zogu," Leka shouted, enveloping him in a bear hug. "You brought American food for us?"

"I brought things that you can cook in the little kitchens," he said, matching her rapid-fire Albanian. "Can you go to the other rooms and get all the girls so we can have a meeting?"

She bounded out and two of the other women, who introduced themselves as Ardita and Edona, took over, settling him into a worn easy chair, massaging his back and bringing him a motel glass filled with Albanian vodka they'd apparently smuggled in airplane-style bottles. He hoped they didn't have much of that strong liquor left. The room stank of cigarette smoke, clothes were piled carelessly in a corner and raucous laughter rang through the closed door of the bathroom. He wondered just what they were doing in there.

Leka returned with the five Albanians he'd assigned to two adjacent rooms. Again, their appearance filled him with dismay. Though it was early afternoon, no one was dressed for prime time. Two wore jeans with printed tops that looked like pajamas, and the others wore beat-up workout clothes with torn tights. Several looked like they'd just gotten up, and one bleary-eyed girl looked like she'd been up all night drinking. All nine sprawled on the lumpy double beds with the shabby gold bedspreads, or sat on the floor with their backs to the wall. They chattered about him and the groceries he'd brought, though Zogu had signaled for quiet.

Finally, Leka stood up with him and whistled through a gap in her front teeth. They turned silent right away. Leka spoke quickly and persuasively, explaining that Zogu would help them get ready for their new jobs and lives in America.

"We'll be able to afford new clothes, nice apartments and as much food and vodka as we want," she said.

The girls applauded enthusiastically and Zogu felt better. He promised to bring them groceries every other day and told them that his wife and her friends would start visiting them daily to begin cutting, dyeing and styling their hair and help them with their clothes. Brunettes must dye their hair blonde, he emphasized, because the owner of the club where they'd work – if they were lucky – desired blondes above all.

"All blondes? That seems strange," Ardita, a petite brunette, said. "Doesn't he know that many Albanian girls have dark hair?"

"No, he doesn't know much about Albania," Zogu admitted. "He thinks Albanian girls look like the tall, blonde Russians on TV in the vodka commercials."

"Will he like us?" she said, suddenly worried.

Zogu felt pity for the girls. Who knew what they hoped? Who knew what sort of families they'd left behind? He thought they were either brave or desperate – probably both – to undertake a dangerous trip, hide out in three crowded motel rooms and still be optimistic as they confronted an uncertain future.

"We will make sure that you all look beautiful when he meets you," he smiled, hoping he sounded more convincing than he felt.

They shouted with pleasure when Zogu said each girl would get one new outfit Genta would help pick out. He asked them if they had questions – a mistake, he realized right away.

"What happened to Arlinda?" Edona asked. The image of the dead girl came into his mind. She'd been pretty, but not smart or cautious. She'd paid for her carelessness.

He shifted uncomfortably, wondering if he should tell them the truth. But he decided that he couldn't chance it.

"We must never speak of your time hiding aboard the ship," Zogu said, raising his voice dramatically. "It would bring terrible trouble from the American police. They could send us all to Texas prisons, where we'd probably die."

"Can't you tell us where she is?" Ardita said.

"She's gone, but that's all I can tell you. Arlinda didn't follow the rules and because she didn't obey, she got into trouble."

They digested this soberly, their earlier rowdiness gone.

Leka came to his rescue again, stepping forward, clapping him on the shoulder and looking intently at each girl. She had an uncanny way of commanding their attention.

"Zogu is not to blame for that girl's foolish mistake," she said. "Trust him and his wife and they will help us with our jobs and perhaps with finding good husbands."

The Albanians erupted into raucous laughter and Zogu felt the stirrings of alarm. Who'd told them he'd find them husbands? Was that really part of his responsibility? Then he reflected on the single men he knew and decided not to worry. They might indeed be interested in meeting at least some of these girls.

"Tell us about the American clubs," Edona said when the cheering died down.

"Some are very beautiful places, with big mirrors, fine liquors and elegant stages for you to dance on and show off your beauty," Zogu said. That was stretching it, for they'd probably go to the older, redneck clubs. He decided he'd better draw the question-and-answer period to an end.

"You must try to become your most beautiful self by the time we take you there," he said. "Rest up, watch the American TV and swim in the pool. But stay in the motel rooms. Remember that you don't have documents yet. The fat policemen would kick you with their sharp cowboy boots and throw you in their jail."

The Albanians looked properly chastened, but Zogu worried that they could turn mutinous after he left.

"For how long?" Leka asked, looking crestfallen.

"Just a week or two."

CHAPTER 17

Nate Hardin nursed a Dos Equis at his table in Ninfa's on Navigation, his favorite café in a funky industrial neighborhood east of downtown. He liked being early for social engagements, enjoying the ambience of a busy place and thinking about the evening ahead. It was Saturday night and he and his best friend, fellow *Times* reporter Travis Dunbar, were meeting for a quick Tex-Mex dinner, as they often did. But tonight was special. Travis was bringing his poker-playing girlfriend and Nate was eager to meet the woman his friend had been keeping under wraps.

He loved Ninfa's with its famed Ninfaritas (impossibly strong margaritas), its cilantro-laced green salsa and sizzling meats. He'd seen pictures of the chubby-cheeked Mama Ninfa Laurenzo, who'd founded the restaurant a half-century ago, as an outgrowth of her struggling tortilla factory. The cafe had become the founding outlet in a popular chain of Mexican restaurants in the 1980s before the enterprise changed hands. But the original Ninfa's near the Ship Channel remained and its clientele still gathered for Tacos al Carbon. He enjoyed a few moments of high-level people watching, especially the romantic intrigues at the crowded bar, as he waited for Travis and the mystery woman.

He sopped up the last warm chips from a basket into the peppy green sauce and signaled the waiter for a fresh basket. He could eat his weight in chips, but was a dedicated enough runner that it didn't show on his lanky frame. He checked messages on his iPhone and finally spotted Travis heading toward the table hand-in-hand with his woman.

He was a little surprised. Lila Jo Lemmons looked at least ten years older than Travis, even with reddish-magenta hair curling toward her shoulders. She wore a black skirt with a green jacket, a bejeweled sunburst necklace and red cowboy boots. She and Travis were both short and squat, but Nate thought they looked good together. Her brown eyes were warm in a face that, like most Texas women of a certain age, was heavily made up. Nate stood up and extended his hand. Lila Jo gripped it with a surprising strength.

"Hey, Nate. Glad to finally meet you," she said in a slow, pleasant drawl that sounded to Nate like East Texas, possibly Tyler or Nacogdoches. The young Hispanic waiter brought more beers and they munched on chips and salsa.

Soon Nate was laughing at Lila Jo's salty real estate stories about a Houston barge owner who paid cash-in-hand for a drug lord's abandoned mansion, but was shocked by the variety of sex toys he'd found in the master bedroom's closet.

"Honey, I could fix you up with a nice two-bed not far from downtown if you have $7,000 for a down payment," she told Nate.

"I don't know, Lila Jo," he said. "Not sure I'm ready to tie myself to Houston yet. How about you, Trav?"

He was sorry he brought it up as Travis squirmed uncomfortably.

"I'm a bit financially challenged at the moment, I'm afraid. Got to start winning at poker again."

"Baby, your luck will change," Lila Jo said, putting her hand over Travis's chubby mitt.

Conversation slowed as they focused on the steaming plates. Nate polished off a plate of green chicken enchiladas, mopping up the last of the sauce with a flour tortilla as he listened to Travis rant about the downfall of the newspaper industry and the dark fate of the *Houston Times*.

He and Travis had been inseparable since Annie Price hired Nate a year ago, luring him to Houston from a paid internship in the newsroom of the *Corpus Christi Post*. He'd been thrilled to leave Corpus, which had a scenic waterfront with beautiful homes for the wealthy but offered few opportunities for young people, especially cub journalists. He'd worried about what he'd do when the newsroom stint ended, but luckily didn't have to face the ignominy of returning to Waco to live with his parents. Annie had seen some of his stories on the Associated Press wire and had actually called him for an interview. Nate at twenty-five was the youngest reporter on the *Times* staff and the last person hired before the freeze imposed by the newspaper's struggling owner.

Nate's attention wandered as Travis bemoaned the paper's inability to seduce Houston's privileged army of white-collar workers into subscribing to the *Times*. Some of the city's well-heeled downtown workers read the paper, but the younger they were, the greater the odds against their subscribing. Circulation of the paper continued to sink like a rock, especially among workers in their twenties and thirties. The *Times* did a lot of newsroom brainstorming about improving the website to make it irresistible to young people, but clearly the middle-aged editors leading the effort hadn't come up with the magic formula. Those older print fossils didn't understand websites and likely just wished they'd go away, Travis said.

Nate, bored with the subject, agreed that falling readership showed a regrettable lack of civic curiosity among the city's young workers, but what were the reporters going to do? Force people to buy the paper instead of trolling free entertainment sites on iPhones as they sipped their morning lattes? At least some would check out the headlines online.

Lila Jo, who'd eaten a plateful of steak fajitas with big dollops of guacamole, paused to speak.

"Sweetie, the daily paper's all but dead. Your folks need to figure out how to make the website a lot more fun. What do you think, Nate?"

"I'm afraid I have to agree," he said. "When I was at Baylor just a few years back, I was shocked at how few people read the college paper."

"Well, that's Baylor for you. They just read the Bible," Travis cracked, referring to the university's Baptist origins.

Nate looked at his iPhone and saw it was close to 10 p.m. The Saturday-night crowd crackled with alcohol and rising hormones, and the vibe was happy, but Nate was ready to move on. He'd been hanging out at the Texas Girls clubs a few nights a week, trying to figure out what made Kyle Krause and his strip club business tick. He was gathering intelligence on Krause for the profile he planned to write. Soaking up the ambience of the clubs had been an education and he'd made plenty of valuable contacts. In the last few weeks, he'd talked to strippers, bar employees and club patrons, but Krause was still eluding him.

His attention drifted back to Travis, who'd moved into the familiar territory of dissecting newsroom machinations. Both reporters knew that their colleague Maggie Mahaffey had resigned and that the loss of a reporter meant that Annie would take on some reporting duties.

"What's Annie saying about that?" Nate asked, knowing that Travis had more of a relationship with their boss – strictly professional, of course – than he did.

"She wants me to take over Maggie's reporting on the German-Texas movement. She may team up with me," Travis said with an air of importance.

"Now that will be a hardship. I know you can hardly stand the thought of working closely with her," Nate said. Travis's worshipful attitude toward Annie was a running joke.

"I'm dying to meet Annie," Lila Jo said. "She sounds like my kind of gal. Speaking of women, look at those two blondes at the bar – they're staring at you, Nate. You should go over and say howdy."

"Uh, thanks, Lila Jo, but I'm not interested."

She clapped her hand over her mouth and patted Nate on the shoulder.

"Sorry, honey. I forgot. How about that cute waiter? Bet he could use a friend."

"Appreciate it, but I'm headed over to another of the Texas Girls clubs. Going to check out the one on the Gulf Freeway."

"Are you still stalking Kyle Krause?" Travis said.

"Kind of. Just haven't been to that location yet."

"Hey, I know Krause," Lila Jo said. "Sold him a condo. Is he in any kind of trouble?"

"He's into everything – strip clubs, gambling and maybe even prostitution," Nate said. "He'll be a big story for us before long."

He felt gratified at the shocked look on Lila Jo's face. Part of the delight of being a reporter was finding out things other people didn't know and dribbling out the juicy bits.

"Well, get a life," Travis said. "You're off-duty tonight, remember?"

"Trav, you know a good reporter is never off-duty," Nate said, only half-joking.

"You'll get over that in a few years, dude."

CHAPTER 18

Nate parked his dirty blue Toyota pickup in a crumbling and poorly lit parking area behind the Texas Girls Club. There wasn't room in the front because it was prime time for the bar crowd. The Korean nail salon had closed hours ago and the Vietnamese café was winding up its business, but Texas Girls and two other bars in the dingy-looking strip center off the freeway were hopping. He saw one tipsy young couple and three middle-aged men headed drunkenly toward the door of the strip club. He knew that this Texas Girls location was Krause's first, and rumored to be his favorite, so he hoped to spot him there on the biggest night of the week. He didn't see Krause's Porsche, but he knew the owner drove several different vehicles and also used a chauffeur. He'd heard that a decent local rock band, Hands on Deck, might play at the club tonight and he was looking forward to hearing it.

He thought about Lila Jo and Travis. He'd liked her East Texas friendliness and was relieved that she accepted his sexual orientation. You never could tell about native Texans. Some were perfectly okay with gay men and women, but there were still plenty in the Lone Star State who would view him as God's abominable mistake.

He wondered briefly if he should've spent the rest of Saturday night relaxing with friends instead of trying to track down the strip club king. Travis kidded him about being too serious about his work and he guessed Travis had a point. But Nate regarded his twenties as a time to work hard and lay the groundwork for a good career, rather than getting drunk every night. He'd gone to Baylor as an Eagle Scout and semi-devout Baptist, but had come out as a gay man midway through college. He rarely went to church any more, but some of his core Christian values had stuck. He'd never say it to his more cynical friends, but he felt he'd been put on earth to do something worthwhile. He'd settled on journalism as his way to make a difference. He couldn't help but being repelled by all of the nubile flesh he was seeing in the strip clubs. He thought women who stripped in the clubs probably made decent money, but felt sorry that they had to endure crude advances, crass owners and a seamy industry.

He walked into the front foyer, handed a ten-dollar bill to the curvy woman with the punked pink hair at the counter and slid through the black curtains to the main bar and stage area. He took a seat near the front, where a gawky blonde with crooked yellow teeth and a sparkly silver halter was writhing to the end of the band's cover of Justin Timberlake's "Sexy Back." The five-member band, playing at the far left of the stage, was energetic and good enough to play in a better venue than a strip club.

The crowd, mostly young blue-collar workers in jeans and T-shirts and a sprinkling of better-dressed older men, was mildly appreciative, but not bowled over, by the dancer, he deduced from the paltry amount of bills left on the catwalk or tucked into her bikini bottom. The band's guitar player, a tall, muscular guy with a pirate-like black beard, announced a fifteen-minute break.

Nate ordered his fourth Dos Equis of the night and took stock of the increasingly ebullient crowd. To his surprise, he honed in on the unmistakable widow's peak and cold eyes of Kyle Krause, talking intently to a young blonde at an unobtrusive corner table. Nate had spotted Krause with his girlfriend, Juliana Souza, from a distance over the last few weeks and he knew that the woman at the table wasn't her. The blonde had on heavy eye makeup, tight jeans and a clingy red top, but somehow she still looked awfully young to be inside a strip club. Nate saw that she was tall and solidly put together, with large breasts that looked real – instead of the enhanced bosoms he mostly saw on the clubs' catwalks. Who was she? Juliana's replacement or was Krause interviewing new topless talent?

He decided he'd better take advantage of his luck at finding the mogul. He walked casually over to Krause's table and caught his eye. The blonde's big blue eyes widened in surprise – and something like fear.

"Good evening, Mr. Krause," he said, putting out his hand. "Nate Hardin from the *Houston Times*. I've been trying to catch up with you."

Krause's stare flicked over him dismissively. He ignored Nate's outstretched hand and Nate saw a menacingly large bouncer headed their way. The employee had a shaved head, long scraggly beard and a snake tattoo crawling up his neck.

"It's all right, Bobo," he told the bouncer. "I'll handle this."

Bobo walked away, but stood at the black curtain watching.

"I know who you are," Krause said. "Seen you at a few of my clubs and I'm tired of you stalking me."

"I'm just another curious customer," Nate said. "I want to interview you about your clubs and their place in Houston's topless industry. I've left three messages…"

"Why would I talk to you? The *Times* hates me and my clubs."

"I don't think that's true," Nate said. "The paper's written about a couple of police actions involving your clubs. But that's just normal police beat coverage."

The girl hastily got up from the table, avoiding their eyes. She murmured an excuse and headed off in the direction of the restroom. Nate thought she looked like she was about to throw up.

"That's not Juliana, your girlfriend," Nate said. "Seems a little young to be in a strip club. Who is she?"

Krause stood up. His muscled body loomed over Nate, who held his ground.

"Listen up, Hardin," Krause said. "You're welcome to look around all you want, but don't bother my friends or employees. If you still have questions, you can call me during office hours. Understand?"

"Yeah. I still want to interview you," Nate said. "We're writing a story about your clubs and you'll be in it – one way or another."

"I'll think about it," Krause said. He handed Nate a business card and sat down again.

"Hey, just call me," Nate said. "I'll make sure you're treated fairly."

He walked out of the crowded room, back through the dark curtain, and into the foyer. The club had a glassed-in store and he decided to duck in for a while to think about his next move. He pretended to study the penis-shaped vibrators in pink and black, the metal handcuffs and other ridiculous-looking sex toys under the glass counter, and slowly sifted through racks of flashy lingerie.

"Girls really like those red teddies," the middle-aged, chunky woman behind the counter said. "Looking for something for your sweetie pie?"

"No, ma'am. Just browsing. What does Kyle Krause buy?"

"I've never seen him buy anything," she smiled. "But you'd better believe his girlfriend is the one who decides what to order."

He chatted with the friendly woman for a while, trying to learn something more about Kyle and Juliana, but although she was eager to talk, she didn't have much to reveal. He looked at his watch: it was getting close to 1 a.m. Might as well go home.

Outside, the strip center parking lot had mostly emptied. Should he hang around and hope Krause and his mystery girl would come out in a friendlier mood? Probably not, he thought. It wouldn't do to press his luck. He'd call him on Monday.

He walked behind the strip center toward his car parked in the shadowy overflow lot. He leaned over his car door as he searched his pockets for his keys. As he fumbled, a hand came up noiselessly behind him brandishing a long metal tool. The tool struck the back of his head a few times, its metal flashing in the dim light. Nate felt the first blow, but couldn't do anything before the second one came. He went down heavily and knew nothing more.

CHAPTER 19

Annie was lost in a dream, or so she thought. She heard a buzzing and a rackety clattering that wouldn't stop. She opened her eyes cautiously and spotted her cell phone vibrating on top of her antique cherry bureau. She sprang up quickly and winced as she rushed to catch the phone. Her head was vibrating too, from too many glasses of chardonnay she'd drunk with Matt last night. He'd come over for dinner, but it had turned into an extended cocktail hour that had led to her bedroom. He'd left around midnight because he was on duty early today.

"Hello. Hello?" She said into the phone, hearing breathing and what sounded like a suppressed sob. "Who is it?"

"It's Travis," said a voice so low that she hardly recognized the *Times'* police reporter.

Wide awake now and alarmed, she said, "Travis, what's wrong?"

"I'm calling about Nate," he said in a quavering voice. "He's dead. He was found in a parking lot at a Texas Girls club on the Gulf Freeway."

"No, that can't be true," she said, her mind reeling. "What happened?"

"I don't know much yet, but Matt Sharpe is headed out there. Can you come?"

"I'll meet you there in twenty minutes."

She put down her phone, sat on the bed unsteadily and burst into tears. She'd loved the energy, intelligence and go-for-broke enthusiasm of the skinny reporter with the wild curly hair. He was only twenty-five. How could this have happened? Was she to blame for assigning him to investigate topless clubs? How would she ever tell his parents?

She swallowed three aspirins, her signature cure for a bad hangover, and got into the shower. She didn't bother to wash her hair, just toweled off quickly and threw on jeans, a black T-shirt and sandals. As promised, she got to the club's parking lot in twenty minutes. Since it was barely 7 a.m. on a

Sunday morning, there were no customers around, just a few blue-and-white police cars. She'd tried Matt on his mobile before leaving the house, but it was busy.

Travis, disheveled in shorts and a wrinkled shirt, was waiting when she opened the car door. He hugged her closely for a moment and she could feel his body trembling. At twenty-seven, she thought, he'd never experienced death, especially of a beloved friend. Unfortunately, she had.

"The cops are in the back parking lot," he said.

They walked behind the building and ducked under the yellow crime scene tape. Matt was at the scene, as she expected. He stood in front of the covered gurney writing on a notepad. Several other officers and technicians were talking and writing. They looked askance at Annie and Travis until Sharpe acknowledged them with a solemn nod. Annie saw Nate's mud-spattered blue pickup parked in the lot and had to blink back tears. The young reporter always said he'd never seen the purpose of a carwash, arguing that because of Houston's weather and pollution, his pickup always would be dusty or caked with mud.

While technicians strapped the gurney into the hearse for transport to the county's morgue, Matt stepped away. He hugged Annie and clapped Travis on the shoulder. His professional behavior gave no indication that he and Annie had spent most of the previous evening together.

"Terrible," he said. "Met him a few times when he subbed for you, Travis. Seemed like a decent reporter and a real good kid."

"What can you tell us?" Travis said, flicking on his IPhone's tape recorder.

"We think he died early this morning, maybe about 1 a.m. Clobbered in the back of the head two or three times with something heavy, maybe a lug wrench. Probably looking for his car key when somebody sneaked up behind him."

Annie, queasy and weak, could barely get the words out. But she had to know.

"Do you think he suffered?"

"Doubt if he knew what hit him," he said. "Don't dwell on that, just focus on what we can do to get to the bottom of it."

"Of course, Matt."

"What was he doing here, other than the obvious?"

"We'd eaten at Ninfa's on Navigation and he said he wanted to check out this club," Travis said. "He was investigating the topless industry, especially Kyle Krause's clubs."

Matt knew that, of course, but he didn't let on. He nodded and took notes.

"Nate wanted to profile Krause, but hadn't been able to pin him down for an interview," Annie said. "He'd been leaving him messages, but also hoped to run into him at one of the clubs."

"A janitor who came in an hour ago called us when he found the body," Matt said. "Said he'd also called Krause. He let it slip that the big man was here last night."

"What're you going to do?" Travis said.

"He's coming down to headquarters in a few hours to talk to us," Matt said. "Of course, he denies knowing anything about it."

He flipped through his notes quickly as Annie and Travis waited. She looked around, taking in the tawdry setting of Nate's killing. The back parking lot was separated from a neighborhood of dilapidated, one-story houses built in the 1950s by a wooden privacy fence with some slats missing. The fence stretched across several of the strip center's businesses with room for about fifty cars. Banana trees grew above the fence and several large trash bins behind the club overflowed with beer cans and kitchen garbage. A morning breeze rippled through the air and she nearly gagged from the combined odor of rotting food and refinery gases, making her sick headache more miserable.

"Don't jump to conclusions," Matt said. "We found his wallet beside him with his ID intact, but no cash. Maybe he was jumped by a drunk, or someone hanging around looking for easy money."

Annie could feel him looking at her.

"Did he have any enemies?"

"I don't think so," Annie said, tears welling up again. "He was so young and he'd barely lived here a year. I don't think he had any serious attachments, do you, Travis?"

"No," Travis replied in a wavering voice. "He went to some of the gay bars occasionally to meet people, but he rarely went home with anyone. He was really serious about his work. Wanted to do big stories. He was one of the most dedicated reporters I've ever met."

"Anything else?" Matt said, closing his notebook. "Got to get back to the office."

"Can I call you later?" Travis asked. "I'd like to hear what Kyle Krause says for himself."

"May not be able to tell you much, but sure. Call me."

"Travis, I'll see you back in the newsroom," Annie said. Matt took her aside, squeezed her hand and said he'd call later.

She stopped on her way to the newspaper office to get a sausage biscuit and coffee at a drive-in restaurant, hoping that a full stomach would make her head feel better. But she couldn't keep the food down, vomiting in the grass beside her car in the parking lot. She wiped her mouth and gargled some ice water from a plastic cup. That awful day when she found out her friend Maddy had been killed the night before in a car wreck came back to her in a rush. They'd thought briefly that it was a terrible accident, but soon suspected that she'd been murdered. In Nate's case, there was no doubt. A promising young reporter's life had been snuffed out in the back of a tawdry strip center. She had no idea why.

She shuffled disconsolately into the office. In the cavernous newsroom, it was mercifully quiet, as it usually was on a Saturday morning. She was able to unearth a personnel file on Nate. She looked through it for a few minutes, stopping in the middle of reading his personal essay to go to the ladies room and wash her tear-stained face. He'd had such great potential as a reporter and the right kind of ambition, to do stories that would change lives.

She picked up the phone with a trembling hand, willing herself to remain calm. Then she dialed the number she'd found for his parents in Waco. It rang three times and a female voice came on. She swallowed hard.

"Is this Mrs. Hardin?" She asked. "This is Annie Price, Nate's supervisor at the *Houston Times*. I'm very sorry to have to call you. Can you put Mr. Hardin on, too?"

CHAPTER 20

Kyle Krause sat in a glassed-in interrogation room at the downtown police station waiting for Matt Sharpe, the detective he'd been told was assigned to the case. With him at the table was his high-priced lawyer, Ben Bauer. Despite charging what Krause considered exorbitant fees and a glib slickness that irritated him, Bauer had helped him out of plenty of messy situations, and he appreciated that Bauer, like him, was of German-Texas stock.

Krause couldn't believe his bad luck. Why had he picked last night to go to the Gulf Freeway club after successfully avoiding Nate Hardin for two weeks? He hated reporters and tried to dodge them, though Juliana had nagged him about learning to use the media. He was convinced that the newspaper was out to destroy his clubs, always picking at some niggling violation, like the bouncers being too rough, or the dancers not always wearing pasties to cover their nipples. The night that the cops closed down Carla Carmine's show at the North Freeway club was the latest outrage. He'd probably have to pay a $10,000 fine for that clear case of police overreaction. He believed that some prohibitions in the strip club world were necessary, but he rarely passed up a chance to flout what he considered the stupid rules. The state's Alcohol Beverage Control officers had it in for him, he was sure. Rick's Cabaret never seemed to get bad press – his swaggering competitor was regarded as a hometown hero just because it was listed on the NASDAQ.

The recent explosion at his San Antonio gas emporium was another piece of rotten luck. His friend Sam Wurzbach was convinced it was payback from the secessionists for giving money to the German-Texas movement. Sam was probably right, though he tended to overreact at times. Luckily the two of them had managed to hush up key details of the explosion, with the local authorities blaming the significant damage on a simple gas leak. His insurance would cover most of it, but it was still a setback. Business would suffer while the building was being repaired. And he wondered whether the loony secessionists would attack his clubs next, or his home. Who knew what they were capable of? But he wasn't backing off his support of German Texas. As his mother used to say, in for a penny, in for a pound.

Still he was nervous, jiggling one foot as he and Bauer waited for the tardy detective. His restlessness wasn't lost on his disapproving lawyer, sitting beside him in a fresh-looking seersucker suit.

"Kyle, do yourself a favor," Bauer said. "Don't act hostile when Sharpe questions you."

"Are you kidding?" Krause said. "I can't believe I'm even here. Why do I have to put up with this?"

"A kid died in the parking lot behind your building. You'd better come across as cooperative. Think about acting like you're sorry."

Krause opened his mouth to say something, saw a big man in a well-worn navy sports jacket and khakis striding toward the glass door, and lapsed into quiet. He thought he recognized the cop from the night Carla's show was busted. Damn, he just couldn't catch a break.

Matt Sharpe settled himself across the table from Krause, stared at him for a few measured beats, then took out a folder containing a fresh legal pad and starting writing. He switched on a tape recorder.

"Mr. Krause, we appreciate you coming in. I'm taping this interview for clarity. Understand you were at the Gulf Freeway club last night?"

"Yeah, I visit all my clubs at least once a week," Krause said, trying but failing to sound friendly.

"Several people saw you talking to Nate Hardin, the young reporter found dead early this morning."

"He stopped by my table and we talked a little."

"Was this the first time you'd met him?"

"Uh, I guess. He'd left me some phone messages."

"Did you call him back?" The cop's eyebrows had flown up a notch.

"No, I didn't know what he wanted," Krause said, regretting he'd let slip about the messages. "I don't talk to reporters much."

"Can you describe your conversation last night?"

"He wanted to interview me about my clubs. I told him I didn't see the point."

"Several people we talked to from the club said it looked like a tense conversation."

Krause wondered who'd squealed to the cop. "I said he was welcome to look around the premises. I just asked him not to bug my employees and friends. I told him to call me back during business hours."

"Did you tell him you'd throw him out of the club?"

"Not at all. If anyone says that, they're lying."

"Did you see him again?"

"No." Krause looked at the officer without wavering.

"Can you describe what you did after that conversation?"

"I had a drink or two, talked to some of the dancers and left when the club closed at 2. Went back to my apartment. My girlfriend was there."

"Can I get her name, address and phone number?"

Bauer broke in. "We'll provide anything you want."

"How about your employees? Do you know what they were doing during the time the reporter was there?"

"It was an extremely busy night," Krause said. "Everyone was stretched thin. I'm sure they had better things to do than talk to a reporter."

The cop's eyebrows went up again and he looked at them both for a moment.

"We'll be back in touch with you, Mr. Krause, but you're free to go for now. Just don't leave town without notifying us. Thank you for coming in."

The detective gave Krause and Bauer his card. "If you have any questions or remember something that might be relevant, don't hesitate to call me."

After the cop left the room, Bauer looked at him.

"He doesn't have anything on you yet, but if I were you, I'd lay low," Bauer said.

"How do you know what they have?"

"If he had any physical evidence, like fingerprints, you'd know it by now. But they're still investigating."

"Nothing will turn up," Krause said. "Nothing that incriminates me, that is."

"That's certainly what I hope for," Bauer said. "In the meantime, don't do anything dumb."

CHAPTER 21

Betsy Marr held hands with Patrick Costas across the booth of the packed pancake house in Pasadena. Despite the chattering early Sunday afternoon crowd, the high-backed wooden booth gave them the illusion of privacy. They'd finished their blueberry pancakes and sausage, lingered over coffee and now touched delicately on the question before them. It was about as sticky as their syrupy plates, Betsy thought, but Patrick was persistent.

"Bets, I'm down to my last hundred," Patrick said. "Our motel room is paid up for two more days. Then what?"

She squeezed his hand and looked into his almost-black eyes for something, but she really didn't know what she was looking for – reassurance, trust, love? Maybe all of those things.

They'd gone last night to the Texas Girls Club for Patrick's gig and she had to admit, it had been kind of fun. She'd been sitting at a table by herself, watching the band when a nice-looking older man – probably in his forties, she guessed – walked up and asked politely if he could sit down. She was about to say no when he'd extended his hand and introduced himself as Kyle Krause, the club's owner. She'd told him about the band and her boyfriend, and he'd waved to Patrick and told her how much he was enjoying the music. He asked her about herself and she didn't flinch as she said she was Betsy Taylor from Dallas. The name came from her genuine-looking fake ID, which he'd asked to see. She could see him computing her birth date in his head, looking relieved that it showed her as twenty-one.

"Just checking," he said pleasantly. "We don't want to get into trouble."

They talked until the band's break, when he walked with her over to meet Patrick. She could see that Patrick liked him, especially when Mr. Krause asked if the band was available the next few Saturdays.

He led her back to the table after the break and they continued to chat about the club. She was glad for his company, because it meant that other, not-so-attractive men would stay away from the table. There were so many guys in there, older and kind of dangerous-looking, like they'd stopped by for a beer after robbing a gas station. She'd also noticed a couple of younger dudes with scruffy hair and bad teeth looking at her, and she'd been nervous about them. She routinely attracted male attention – she wasn't completely sure why. Patrick said it was because she was beautiful. But who knew what went through men's minds?

Then there were her breasts. She'd developed early and by the age of twelve, her breasts were as full and round as those of grown women. For a few years, she'd been embarrassed when she had to buy 36D bras and bikini tops when other girls her age still had small, graceful buds. By fifteen, she'd discovered their power. She could get a boy to do most anything she wanted just by wearing a tight top and flirting a little. But it caused problems with her dad, who seemed embarrassed if she wore something low-cut or form fitting. She heard him telling their housekeeper, Maria, to talk to her about what kind of clothes proper young ladies should wear, especially to school. She'd felt sad that he wouldn't talk to her himself because they'd always had such a close relationship. She'd taken to studying old pictures of her mother, who'd died of cancer when she was four. She looked like her mother in the face, but her own body was much rounder than her mother's slender frame. She guessed her dad was disappointed with her looks.

She'd been alarmed when she heard he was coming to Houston last week. She'd called Maria and told her to let her dad know that she was okay, but didn't want to be followed or contacted just yet. Maria had been her confidant, so Betsy had told her about traveling with her boyfriend. She'd threatened to hide if her dad came looking and left open the possibility that she'd be back soon.

Now, as she sat in the booth with Patrick, she realized that he really was counting on her to start dancing at the Texas Girls club. Krause had offered her three shifts a week and said she could easily earn up to $1,000 in tips for just a few hours of work. He said that if she were a good dancer, she wouldn't have to strip entirely. She could still wear modesty pasties, blue glittery pieces that would adhere to and cover her nipples, and tap pants, which offered significantly more coverage than bikini bottoms. She wouldn't have to mix with the clientele much either, he said. She could dance on the main stage, have a drink or two if a customer approached her nicely and wouldn't be expected to do lap dances in the VIP room. That was important because the VIP room was off by itself and Betsy knew that couldn't be a good thing. Also, Krause said she could coordinate some of her shifts with Patrick's band appearances. She'd listened to it all carefully, because she felt guilty about money. After she'd run away, her dad had frozen her bank account and cancelled her credit cards. She wasn't contributing anything to their expenses.

When she told Patrick about Krause's offer, she was slightly surprised that he seemed excited about it. She'd assumed that he might not want her to dance on a stage nearly naked in front of other men. But that didn't seem to bother him. It gave her a funny feeling, but she supposed he was raised with more liberal parents than her stuffy old dad. She knew Patrick loved her and just wanted the best for them.

"Think about the money we'd have, baby," he said. "We could get a really nice apartment, eat out all the time and go to fun places."

"Do you really think I should?" She said, sipping the hot chocolate she'd ordered to top off her pancakes. She always ate too much sweet stuff when she was stressed.

"Your body is gorgeous," Patrick said, squeezing her hand. "What's wrong with making a little money off the way you look? You're luckier than most girls. You've got everything – legs, boobs, a fantastic ass and a beautiful face."

She flushed with pleasure. Nobody had ever complimented her the way he did. It made her feel like a real woman, not a stupid high school girl.

"It seems kind of creepy," she said. "What if men grab at me?"

"That won't happen. I'll be around, and they've got bouncers."

"Maybe I should try for a waitress job."

"You'll have bad hours, crabby people and you won't make any money."

He dug in his back pocket, took out some folded bills and put a twenty down on their grease-spotted ticket. The plump waitress in a too-tight pink uniform picked up the bill and went away to make change.

"She'll get two bucks from us, which doesn't add up to much in this old town," Patrick said. "Do you really want to work that hard for so little dough?"

"Not really," Betsy said. "Will you still love me if I'm dancing up there on a stage for other guys?"

"You'll be dancing for me, baby, and don't you forget it," he said with a wink.

The waitress brought back the change and he slapped two dollars on the table. They walked out hand in hand and he kissed her at the door of his black pickup.

"Let's go have some fun. I want to take you to Galveston where I can show you off in your little red bikini."

CHAPTER 22

Annie got to the office on Wednesday with eyes that felt like they'd been rubbed with sandpaper. She'd lain awake most of the night after returning from Nate's funeral in Waco. It had been one of the most wrenching experiences of her life. She had gone with several of the paper's top editors and a handful of the younger reporters, including Travis. Nate's mother, father and younger sister had behaved with quiet dignity and didn't say anything to reproach her or the other *Times* editors, but she'd felt unreasonably guilty and helpless since Nate's body had been discovered.

In the last decade, U.S. newsrooms had shrunk by tens of thousands of journalists and their numbers continued to drop off each year. There were fewer reporters working on big, controversial stories, so the profession overall should be safer. Or so Annie tried to tell herself. But she also knew from her own experience that reporters would always risk danger when they asked questions people didn't want to answer. Still, Nate's death made no sense to her. He'd been investigating Kyle Krause's clubs, but police insisted that there was no hard evidence to point to Krause, and employees had backed him up. They'd seen him leave at the front entrance of the club about 2 a.m. Was it possible for Krause to sneak out before he left without attracting attention and kill Nate in the back parking lot? Maybe, she thought, but that seemed like an unlikely scenario when he'd just talked to the reporter. Annie wished that she could think it all through with more clarity, but right now she was too emotional.

She saw Travis come from the newsroom elevator and head toward her. His face was drawn and he walked more slowly than usual. She knew that as one of the last people to spend time with Nate, he felt as anguished as she did.

"Did you sleep any last night, Travis?"

"Not much. You?"

"No, but today's the day we need to start going through all of Nate's computer notes and notebooks. Can you spend a few hours doing that with me?"

"Where do we start?"

Before the funeral, Annie had gathered the personal items from Nate's workspace, including his Baylor mug and pens, a ratty denim jacket and some college textbooks on investigative reporting. She'd piled it all into a box and had given it to Carolyn Hardin the day of the funeral. They'd both cried and she'd held Carolyn for a long moment before promising her that she'd get to the bottom of his death. Annie knew that the Hardins were coming to Houston over the weekend to clean out Nate's tiny studio apartment near downtown. She could not even imagine how difficult that would be for them, but they'd declined her offer to help.

"I took Nate's personal stuff to the Hardins yesterday. I'm going to start going through the paper files in his desk drawers. Do you happen to know his computer password?"

"Yeah," Travis said. "Try 123Bearsjourno. He was still a Baylor fan, you know?"

They worked quietly for a few hours, with Travis sitting at Nate's computer and printing out files while Annie went through his desk and read through paper files he'd stowed in drawers. Nate, like most journalists, was a pack rat and took voluminous notes in telephone interviews that he later printed out and saved in his own idiosyncratic filing system. It didn't look like he'd thrown out anything during his stint at the *Houston Times*.

Travis took a break to check in with some of his police sources for news of the day, which was light. He'd offered to go out and bring back some lunch. He took his time, driving to a deli near downtown and getting something special. He and Annie went to a small conference room and he offered her a muffaletta with chips, sweet tea and a peanut butter cookie. She was touched that he'd remembered her fondness for the Cajun-style sandwiches on fresh-baked round bread.

"I haven't been able to eat much, but this is wonderful, Trav," Annie said, biting into her sandwich.

"Thanks. I feel better just getting back to work." Travis gave her the ghost of a smile and handed her a bunch of napkins. They ate in silence for a few minutes.

"I know you spent a lot of time with Nate. How much did he tell you about his research?" Annie asked.

"We'd joke about his visits to the topless clubs, but he seemed really interested about finding out how they operated. He'd definitely honed in on Kyle Krause. I think Krause's background fascinated him, especially his involvement with the German-Texas movement."

"Yeah, it's a shame Maggie left before doing anything on that story," Annie said. "Now we're starting at ground zero."

"I don't think so," Travis said with a triumphant smile. "Look at this memo."

He handed Annie a printout he'd made from Nate's computer. She read it in silence.

"Wow," she said. "If Nate was right, Kyle Krause is the biggest backer of Sam Wurzbach's campaign to grab a piece of the Hill Country for German Texas. That might give him a motive to kill Nate."

"Seems unlikely," Travis said. "Krause's contributions are legal, as far as I know. He's strange and shady, but I don't think he'd kill anyone to keep his political contributions secret."

"That's true," Annie conceded. "I ran into Sam Wurzbach at the North Freeway club and he told me Krause was a big supporter. I just didn't know how big – he's contributed close to a half-million dollars, according to Nate's calculations."

"Was Wurzbach there the night the cops shut down the Carla Carmine show?" Travis asked. Annie had assigned him to follow up the raid and he'd written a story about that incident.

"Yeah, he seemed a little embarrassed to be seen at a porn star show," Annie said. "He made a point of telling me that Krause was an old high school friend who believed in the campaign for German Texas."

"You never did tell me how you happened to be there," Travis said. "Researching the porn industry for your next career?"

"Hardly. A friend who's a cop took me with him," Annie said. She was quiet for a moment before deciding to be candid. "I might as well tell you, but please keep it under your hat. I've been seeing Matt Sharpe."

"You and Sharpe are dating?" Travis said. "Isn't he a little old for you?"

"Travis, how could you say that?" Annie said. "I suspect that Lila Jo has a good ten or fifteen years on you."

"That's true," Travis said. "I just didn't picture the two of you together. I'd heard that since he separated from his wife, he's quite the bachelor about town."

"What do you mean? Let's not even go there," she said. "I assume he's dated other women. Should we get back to work?"

"Okay, sure. Nate traced all the campaign money given to Wurzbach during his last legislative campaign. Some of it came from Krause's strip club managers."

"I'm impressed, but not surprised," Annie said with another wave of sadness. "Nate really used his investigative skills."

"I helped him a little with the money trail," Travis said. "But he spent hours on this stuff in his free time."

"I'm still not sure what to make of this German-Texas campaign. What do you think?" She frowned as she underlined key phrases in Nate's notes.

"It seems different from the Nation of Texas. They're secessionists who want to turn this state into a separate country, to break up with the United States," Travis said. "The German Texans say they want an enclave where they can celebrate and keep their heritage alive. It looks like they're talking about including land west of Austin and north of San Antonio, taking in towns established by German immigrants."

"That would include New Braunfels, Fredericksburg, Boerne and Comfort, for sure. What about Kerrville?" Annie thought out loud, running through her mental map of the Texas Hill Country.

"You're wondering if Kerrville's very own state senator, Jake Satterfield, is in on this?"

Annie frowned. How much did he know about her past history with Jake?

"I don't think Satterfield's involved," Travis said. "But obviously, we'll have to find out what he knows."

"What do you think they mean by a German Texas enclave?"

"We only know what they've been asking for publicly. German language taught in schools, road and street signs in German as well as English and a big museum and tourist center," Travis said.

"My hackles went up when Wurzbach talked about training German Texans to help low-staffed police departments," Annie said. "He seems like a great guy, but what does he really want? Arming German Texans sounds about as bad as arming the Nation of Texas secessionists."

"Yeah, I agree. It doesn't seem like a good idea."

"What else do you see in Nate's records?" she asked.

"Kyle Krause owns a lot of Hill Country land, including a huge, fenced-off ranch," Travis said. "Nate thought he might be using his managers and girlfriend to buy property."

"Wonder what that's all about?" Annie said.

"The secrecy seems odd," he said. "Wonder what they're doing there?"

"Something else we'll need to check out."

They spent all afternoon reading through Nate's stuff and making notes before Annie looked at her watch. It was nearly 5 o'clock and they needed a break. But they also needed to talk this through while it was fresh in their minds. It might be a good time to pick the brain of Brandon McGill, the *Times* reporter who covered the secessionist movement. She hoped he was still at his desk.

"Let's find Brandon and get his take on this," she said. "I'll buy you both a beer at La Carafe."

CHAPTER 23

Annie walked the two blocks from the newspaper office to La Carafe with Brandon and Travis. She knew that this early on a weekday, happy-hour customers wouldn't be there yet. They could find a secluded table before it got crowded. She wanted the three of them to take their time to brainstorm, away from the late-afternoon bustle of the newsroom.

La Carafe was the favored drinking establishment of *Times* reporters and lower-level editors. The higher-ups generally would go to fancier watering holes, like the Petroleum Club, an exclusive members-only place. Located on Congress Street in Houston's oldest commercial building, La Carafe wasn't sufficiently upscale to attract high-salaried bankers or white-collar oil company staff. But its exposed brick walls and seedy air of permanence felt like an anchor in the increasingly fragile newspaper world. Journalists loved its disreputable air and eclectic jukebox.

She found a rickety table and chairs in an upstairs corner and asked Travis to fetch beers from the bar. After her chardonnay-soaked Saturday night and the nightmare aftermath of Nate's death Sunday morning, Annie had vowed not to drink wine again for a while. She could handle beer because she'd sip it slowly and be satisfied with one or two. It didn't slip down the throat with the ease of her favorite Chardonnay or Pinot Noir.

Travis brought three frosted glasses with Coronas and limes and a bowl of peanuts as she finished briefing Brandon on everything they'd learned from Nate's notes.

"Yep, I've been hearing a lot of chatter from sources close to the Nation of Texas," Brandon said. "Those secessionists think the German Texans could ruin their political scheme to convert the state into a republic under their control. They want all of Texas and they view the German-Texas movement as a dangerous rival for territory."

He studied Annie through his square black-framed glasses, stopping to chug his beer with a handful of peanuts. Born in West Texas, Brandon understood the remote parts of the state better than anyone on the staff. His wide network of sources there was unsurpassed. Annie appreciated that he always measured his words carefully, avoiding exaggeration and bombast.

"Four years ago, your stories came close to destroying the secessionists' statewide network," he said. "But they've built it back amazingly fast."

"Are they as strong as they were when Dan Riggins was running it?"

"No, but they're getting there, and Riggins is still very much involved. Lately I'm hearing there's a mystery person at the helm who's really good at carrying out his orders and keeps a low profile."

"That's intriguing. Any guesses?"

"Not yet, but it's obviously somebody Riggins trusts."

She shuddered, thinking about Riggins and his deadly mistress.

"You said you'd heard that he and Alicia slipped across the border into West Texas a while back. Have they been seen again?" she asked.

"Not recently. Far as I know, they're hiding out somewhere in Mexico. But Riggins still keeps his foot soldiers spread across Texas – hundreds of loyalists working for security companies or, rumor has it, in law enforcement."

"Guess they were shocked to find out about the German-Texas movement," Annie said, sipping her beer.

"Stunned and furious is the way I'd characterize it," Brandon said. "If the German Texans end up controlling the Hill Country, that would be a huge political loss for the Nation of Texas. As I said, the secessionists want every bit of Texas under their thumb."

"But the German Texans don't want an independent country, just a cultural enclave, right?" Travis said. "Are they a real threat to the secessionists?"

"The secessionists, rightly or wrongly, view them as deadly competition," Brandon said. "They believe that the German Texans want more than a cultural enclave in the Hill Country. They fear that the German Texans are positioning their movement to take over the whole state."

"I guess they're projecting their own ambitions and paranoia on the German Texans," Travis said. "Makes sense, in a twisted kind of way. But what can the secessionists do?"

"For now, they'll do whatever they can to undermine the German Texans politically," Brandon said. "But as Annie knows, violence is always on the table."

"That's certainly evident in their campaign against Sam Wurzbach," Annie said. "Sabotaging his bakeries wasn't enough. They had to make it personal by killing his family's dogs."

"Sounds like their tactics," Brandon said.

Annie swallowed the last of her beer. She felt lucky to have skilled reporters like Brandon and Travis to work on this. But their three-person team would be stretched to the bone to unravel these complex threads. She was pleased to see Travis focused and thoughtful, putting aside for the moment his sadness over Nate. She felt much the same. A setback in her personal life usually meant increased intensity to work so that she could feel a sense of control over something.

"Guys, one more?" she said. "I'm buying."

"What's next?" Travis asked.

"I suspect we'll spend the rest of the week getting our ducks in a row. Brandon should take over the investigation into Nate's death while you and I head to the Hill Country next week," she said.

She'd enjoy her second beer and their companionship. Then she'd go home, clean her house and wash her clothes, things she hadn't done in a week. It would be good for her and Travis to get out of town for a few days. She felt comforted just thinking about being on the road and working as a reporter-editor instead of sitting in the newsroom waiting for something to happen and feeling bad about Nate.

CHAPTER 24

Dan Riggins heard his nephew's pickup banging down the rutted path that passed for a road outside Ojinaga, Mexico. The summer had been especially dry and hot and when the rare vehicle lumbered by, it was usually covered in dust by the time it passed his rented place. He could see the maroon truck coming now, navigating the curvy road with nothing on either side except for scrawny plants, sun-baked grasses and a few small houses in the distance. He mopped his face like a cowboy with the red bandanna he stuffed in his jeans pocket.

The pickup skittered to a stop outside his pink stucco house and Rob Ryland got out and hugged his uncle. Riggins hadn't talked to Rob for a few days, but he and his nephew were frequently in touch now. When Riggins and Alicia fled Texas, they'd left the Nation of Texas in shambles. Riggins had been reluctant to share power, and his deputies in the movement had scattered, fearful of being arrested after the shootout on the Interstate 10 freeway. They mostly went back to their day jobs and waited to see what would happen.

After his impulsive, failed attempt to kidnap *Times* reporter Annie Price, Rob Ryland had landed in jail. Riggins regretted abandoning his nephew to the vagaries of the court system and secretly funneled money for his defense. Luckily, because of his youth and a lenient judge, Rob got off with probation and an order to stay away from the secessionist movement. Riggins had waited to see how Rob would handle his freedom before contacting him. He'd been impressed that his nephew had found a job with an Austin alternative paper and quickly put his fractured life back together. Last year, Riggins had contacted Rob to see if he was still interested in the Nation of Texas. Rob came to Mexico to meet with him and they talked for a long time. Riggins, acting on a combination of instinct and desperation, had given Rob a key role in rallying the secessionist leaders. But because of the court order, it had to be top-secret. Rob continued to work at the Austin newspaper and Riggins remained the group's leader. All directives that went through the underground network were issued in his name, but his nephew was helping him with steps to resuscitate the group. The recent rise of the German-Texas movement had caught Riggins off guard. He'd ordered some quick and dirty action while he mulled a more substantive plan.

However, Riggins was increasingly distracted with worry about Alicia's condition. His recent trip to Houston with Tom Marr had been fruitless. They hadn't found either Alicia or Marr's runaway daughter Betsy. But a few days after Riggins returned to Mexico, Alicia had come back to Ojinaga, exhausted, sick and rambling.

Riggins had asked Rob to come to the Ojinaga house for some planning because he hesitated to cross the border again so soon. He took chances, but they were always calculated risks, and his intuition told him not to try to sneak back into Texas right now. He'd also grown closer to Rob and welcomed the only family member with whom he was still in contact. He needed a sounding board for his latest round of troubles.

"Thanks for coming, son," he said. "Alicia wants to see you."

Rob walked through the living room of the small house. Riggins and Alicia had rented it for two years, but he'd never visited and Riggins could tell he was curious about it. His nephew looked approvingly at the cozy living room with Saltillo tile floors, decent furniture and a large TV. Its satellite dish lent a focal point to the barren back yard. Riggins needed to keep up with news across the border and was addicted to CNN International. A room air conditioner in the living area blasted cold air, a welcome respite from the 101-degree temperatures they routinely suffered in the Mexican scrub country.

Rob looked impressed. "Really nice for Mexico," he said. "Did you have trouble finding something decent? The town looks kind of awful."

"Our cartel sources have been pretty helpful to me and Alicia," Riggins said. "As you know, they're very interested in Texas secession and will support us all the way. They'd certainly like more access to large markets on the other side of the border."

"You haven't told me much about that," Rob said. "Which cartels?"

"Don't worry about that right now. The less you know, the safer you'll be. I'll brief you fully when you need to know. Want to see Alicia?"

"Of course," Rob said. He admired Alicia, but Riggins could tell he'd always been a little afraid of her. Her reputation as a skilled assassin with an unpredictable temper preceded her.

Riggins walked in the bedroom ahead of Rob to make sure his darling was still awake. The door was open and Alicia lay still – too still – in their king-sized bed under starched white sheets. Her round dark eyes with their thick lashes were open, but she seemed lethargic. Her long, thick white hair fanned across the pillow. She gave Rob a weak smile.

"Rob, *que pasa?*"

"*Hola, Tia Alicia,*" Rob said. He sat at the edge of the bed and gingerly squeezed her hand. "How're you feeling?"

"Not good," she said with a small sigh. "How is my little yellow house?"

Before she and Riggins had fled to Peru, she'd lived in West Texas near Tom Marr's vast ranch. Riggins had built a small home for Alicia where he visited her between foreign trips for the CIA. It was just a three-bedroom, stucco house painted a cheerful yellow, but both Riggins and Alicia had regarded it as their secret, treasured place. In happier days, she'd run a pottery business from the house, commissioning pieces to sell at San Antonio's Mexican Market. She'd leave the place only for her pottery business or to carry out assassination contracts.

"Your house is just the way you left it," Riggins said. "It will be waiting for you when we're able to come back to Texas."

"Do you want me to go there and pick up anything for you?" Rob asked.

"No, but please don't let anyone break into my beautiful house and steal my things," she pleaded. "All of my furniture and pottery and clothes are inside."

"*Mi corazon,* I pay someone to come by and check on it," Riggins said. She hadn't mentioned it much while they were fugitives, but he knew how terribly she missed the only home she'd known since the Shining Path terrorists captured her as a teenager in Peru.

She made an effort to talk to Rob for a few minutes, but Riggins could see that her energy was fading.

"Still so tired from the trip," she said. "I'm glad you came, Rob, but I think I will sleep now."

Rob kissed her cheek and walked out of the room with Riggins, who closed the door softly.

They went silently into the small kitchen at the back of the house. Riggins got two beers out of the refrigerator and handed one to Rob. They sat at the square kitchen table and clinked the glass bottles solemnly.

"To better times," Rob said. "I've never seen her so subdued. Have you gotten her to a doctor?"

"I paid a lot yesterday for a good doc to come across the border and examine her. He thinks it might be a brain tumor, but we won't know until she goes to a hospital for a head scan. I'm hoping I can get her to the Ojinaga hospital tomorrow. So far, she's refused to go."

"Do you know where she went after she disappeared?" Rob asked.

"She said she'd driven all over Texas, but I think she mostly spent her time in Houston," Riggins said. "I looked at the stuff in her car. There were a bunch of gas and motel receipts from the Houston area."

"Any idea how she spent her time?"

"God knows. I'm not sure I want to. She still hates your former newspaper colleague, Annie Price, and has vowed to kill her. That didn't happen this time, but I'm dreading the fallout from whatever she did."

They drank their beers in moody silence for a while until Riggins said, "Can I pick your brain about something else?"

"Sure, Uncle Dan."

"It's that Kyle Krause character and his relationship with the German-Texas group."

"The strip-club king in Houston? Didn't you say he wasn't much of a threat?"

"Yeah. I was wrong. He's a dangerous troublemaker." He got up, got two more beers and offered one to Rob as he thought out loud.

"Krause is especially tight with our German-Texan friend, Sam Wurzbach. He's given more money to those Hill Country Huns than anyone else."

"Our patriot members up in Fredericksburg have stirred up a lot of trouble for Sam," Rob said. "We hear he's been talking to the cops about the bakery break-ins."

"What did he do when his fancy dogs were poisoned?" Riggins asked.

Rob looked down, abashed. "I heard his little girls were awfully upset. Was that really necessary?"

"You have to learn, Rob, that a psychological blow is the most powerful kind of guerilla warfare," Riggins said. "It's a classic CIA move."

"Okay," Rob said. "Let's not talk about it. What do you want me to do about Kyle Krause? Our guys in San Antonio did a pretty good job blowing a hole in his gas emporium. Too bad they couldn't get to the pumps."

"Yeah, he was really mad, but he and his buddy Sam managed to get it hushed up. Let me think about it some more," Riggins said. "Hold on. Did you hear something?"

Riggins walked out the back door and looked across the arid yard and beyond, just to make sure nobody was there. Though he was stuck in the boondocks, the habits of a secretive lifetime conspired to keep him vigilant.

As usual, the back yard was devoid of human habitation, but he saw a coyote in the distance sniffing around. The nasty animal was another reason to hate this place. His nephew had become smarter, but Rob still needed toughening up. He shouldn't have been so troubled by the dog caper. But Riggins had to admit that he was glad for the company. Lately, he'd had to watch what he said around Alicia for fear she'd go off half-cocked again. She was brave but foolhardy and hardheaded, even at her best. What was wrong with her? What were they doing in this godforsaken border town? He felt impotent and miserable.

"What else do you need from me?" Rob asked. "I need to get to the other side of the border before dark. I'll have a long day tomorrow driving to Austin."

"Sam Wurzbach is still our biggest problem," Riggins said. "Without him, I think the German Texans might just fold their tents and slink away."

"What do you want our folks in the Hill Country to do?"

"Stand by, for the moment," Riggins said. "We'll watch his next moves."

CHAPTER 25

Zogu pulled into the budget motel's parking lot and pulled out the latest load of groceries for the Albanian girls. This time he'd purchased only items from the list compiled by his wife Genta and he wasn't surprised that it contained mostly low-calorie and healthy foods. Cottage cheese, yogurt, sacks of carrot and celery sticks, coffee and lots of Lean Cuisine dinners filled the plastic bags. Genta had forbidden him to buy pizza, beer, coffeecakes and other cheaper fare he'd brought at first, items he suspected the girls much preferred.

Genta and her two friends, all hairdressers and estheticians from Houston's Albanian community, were a force to be reckoned with. The beautiful mother of his children was taking her role seriously as housemother and stylist to the Albanians. She knew that as soon as the girls began working for Krause's businesses, Zogu would be paid many times his initial outlay for bringing them from Albania. Then Genta could cut back her hairdressing schedule and stay home, perhaps fulltime, until their children went to school.

He was pleased with the reports he was getting from her each night. For the past five days, Genta and her friends had gone each morning to the motel and spent whole days with the girls in what sounded like a quicker version of the makeover shows they'd watched together on TV. What were those shows called? The Fattest Loser? Big American Booty Camp?

The Albanian girls weren't all fat, however. Most were slim, bordering on skinny, as if they hadn't routinely gotten enough to eat in Tirana. A couple of them were a bit pudgy, but nothing like the extremely large American girls he'd sometimes see strolling with their chubby kids in the mall. The problem was more that the Albanian girls didn't know how to fix their hair, make up their faces or dress in clothes that were cheap, but stylish and flattering.

Genta, who'd grown up in Houston, had mastered all of those womanly arts, he thought proudly. Still, what could she accomplish in a week or so before Krause and his girlfriend demanded to inspect the girls?

He walked in laden with packages to one of the three rooms he'd visited a few days ago. Right away, he could see amazing changes. The room was neat and smelled clean, instead of encrusted with stale smoke from cigarettes. Genta hated smoking and had banned it from the rooms. There were no clothes piled carelessly in the corner like last time. He could see duffle bags stacked neatly in the closet and the beds were made.

Genta was trimming the hair of a girl sitting in a chair in front of the double mirror and sink outside the toilet room. It was Leka, with softer blonde hair and well-defined eyebrows. His wife had banished the brassy frizz and the awful unibrow. Leka looked almost pretty.

She squealed with delight when she saw Zogu, as did three other girls watching TV from the beds. Genta looked happy to see him, but reproved the girls for their rowdy greeting.

"Ladies, don't scream. Say hello in a polite, nice voice," she said in a mixture of English and Albanian she'd learned at home. They looked at the disgusted expression on her face and instantly complied.

"Hello, Zogu," they chorused in English, in well-modulated voices.

Zogu beamed fondly at Genta. He put the groceries on the counter of the kitchenette. Two of the girls jumped up to inspect the contents. They looked disappointed when they pulled out cottage cheese and carrot sticks.

"No cereal or ice cream?" Ardita, one of the girls he'd met last week, said with a pouty face.

"Ladies, don't forget that we're trying to lose a few pounds. Do you want to look like Russian pigs?" Genta said. "When we go out shopping tomorrow, we'll stop for frozen yogurt as our treat."

Ardita looked happier immediately. Genta had reported that the girls loved shopping, particularly at Target, Marshall's and other discount stores. The little shopping trips, supervised and scheduled late in the afternoons, relieved the boredom of being shut in most of the time.

"Can I go swimming in the blue pool?" Ardita asked.

"Sure, if you take a few of the girls," Genta said. "Take Afrodita and

Elvana with you. Those sleepyheads should be up now."

Genta had organized an exercise class by the pool each morning, leading the girls in stretches and dance moves that would be useful in their career as topless dancers. Truly, Zogu thought with renewed admiration, there was nothing his Genta couldn't do. She had the authority of a drill sergeant without so much as raising her sweet voice.

Ardita, who'd been lounging on the bed, got up and stripped down to her panties and bra. She started unhooking her bra right in front of Zogu, whose eyes unfortunately were riveted to the impromptu striptease. His wife gave him a dirty look.

"Ardita, take your bikini and change in the toilet room," Genta said in a furious voice. "Show some modesty in front of my husband, please!"

Zogu could imagine that most of the girls had been squeezed into tight living quarters with whole families in Tirana, and had never experienced the luxury of modesty.

Ardita came out of the bathroom wearing a faded, threadbare bikini and Zogu looked down this time, still embarrassed. She'd rolled up several white towels from the bathroom and carried them under her arm.

"Don't take so many towels," Leka said in her best bossy voice. "Selfish sow! We all need them."

"Sunscreen, please!" Genta said. "Houston is a very hot place and you will burn quickly at midday. Put it all over your body, especially your face. Stop by for the girls in Room 104. They need to get out, too."

Ardita relinquished some towels, throwing them at Leka, and slammed the door.

Leka, who'd dodged the towels, stood up proudly, her makeover complete. She twirled around so that the other girls could get the full impact of her hair and makeup. They whistled and clapped. She looked good and she knew it.

"Beautiful, Leka," Genta said. "Shoulders up and walk like you know you're the most gorgeous girl in the room. Edona, your turn now."

Zogu watched as Edona plopped into the chair in front of the mirror. Genta examined her hair with a professional's appraisal, shaking her head over the bad dye job that had left her curls shades of red, orange and yellow, not unlike a circus clown.

Genta held up two pictures from a hair-styling magazine. In one, the model's hair was an ash blonde shag. The other page showed a woman with a golden flip.

"Which one, girls?" she asked. All four, including Edona, pointed to the picture of the ash blonde.

Someone banged on the door, spoiling the rare moment of unanimity.

Zogu opened it and saw Ardita again in her sad bikini. She looked alarmed. He beckoned her in.

"Room 104 is empty," she shouted. "The backpacks have disappeared. Afrodita and Elvana are gone."

CHAPTER 26

Midmorning at the *Houston Times* office, Annie knocked on the door of Greg Barnett's glass office. He waved her in. She and Travis were headed to the Hill Country for a few days and she needed to brief her boss. She'd told him earlier about what they'd found in Nate's files.

"What're you hearing from the police today about Nate?" he said with an anguished look.

"Nothing new."

Annie knew he'd been almost as torn up by Nate's death as the reporters. Greg, formerly the investigative editor at the *Times*, had been promoted to managing editor three years ago and immediately named Annie to the job he'd vacated. In his mid-forties, Greg was a Boston-bred Harvard graduate who'd fallen in love with journalism working for the Crimson, the student newspaper. He'd shelved his plan – mostly the plan of his wealthy parents – to go to law school and eventually practice with his father's white-shoe firm. Instead, he'd bounced around at papers in the Northeast before ending up at the *Times*. Annie thought he'd brought fresh ideas and an outsider's perspective that had been lacking in the newsroom of Baylor and University of Texas graduates. Also, she loved his big heart and enthusiasm for complicated stories. He was divorced and available, as far as she knew, but she wasn't remotely interested in him. Why was she always attracted to the bad boys?

She snapped out of her reverie and tried to focus on the trip.

"Brandon can't go on the road right now, so he'll be handling Nate's death investigation and keep an eye on Kyle Krause," she said. "Travis and I will do as much reporting as we can on the German-Texas movement, first in Austin with Sam Wurzbach, and possibly in Fredericksburg before we come back."

"How do you feel about reporting again, Annie?"

"I can't wait," she smiled. "I guess I didn't realize just how much I was missing it. But I hate the circumstances."

"Yeah. With Maggie and Nate gone, it's just you with Brandon and Travis. But that's still a hell of a lot of reporting talent."

"Thanks. Do you think we can replace either of those reporting vacancies?"

"Sadly, no. The big bosses like the way the online revenue is trending, but it's still such a small percentage of our profits. Print advertising isn't holding its own, with national ad revenue going down each month."

"Pretty depressing."

"Yup. Rumor has it that the bosses are coming in soon to look at more cuts."

Annie's stomach lurched and she tried to swallow her fear. She didn't have much of a financial cushion and she would hate to have to leave Houston.

"Do you know where the cuts might land?"

"Wouldn't want to guess. I expect they'll still need a managing editor, as well as a gifted reporter like you. But your rise as an editor may be stalled for quite a while."

"I really don't care," Annie said. "Do you think I'll have to take a pay cut?"

"Well, I didn't want you to worry about that. But very likely, your salary will be cut by ten or fifteen percent if they decide to abolish the investigative editor job."

Annie winced, thinking of her bills, though she was trying to be thrifty.

"It's okay, Greg. I can manage."

"Thanks, I hate that, but I appreciate your flexibility. Tell me more about the trip. Will you see Jake?"

He looked at her and she could see compassion in his face. He knew that Annie had been devastated by her breakup with Jake.

"Yeah, he's one of the point men on this story. No way to avoid talking to him and I'm at peace with that. Time to face up to things and stop trying to drown my sorrows."

She could see Greg's approval. He'd been there for her in tough times and she knew he worried about her struggles with alcohol and depression.

"You're a big girl, Annie. But don't put yourself through unnecessary grief. If it seems too painful, let Travis talk to him."

"I'll be all right. Nate's death has made me think about what's important. Holding on to past grievances isn't doing me or anyone else a bit of good."

"What can I do for you while you're gone?" She basked in his support, in the open, easy way he smiled at her. She felt lighter, ready to find Travis and hit the road.

"Just be at the other end of the phone line when I call in. I trust your judgment with all my heart."

CHAPTER 27

Annie relaxed in the passenger seat as Travis drove out of Houston on Interstate 10. He whirled past Memorial, Spring Branch and other suburbs of West Houston and sped farther out toward the town of Katy. They passed the strip malls and housing developments that consumed increasingly wider bands of the flatlands stretching west each year. She'd always enjoyed seeing the tall, white rice dryers of Katy silhouetted against the sky, relics of the rice farming industry that had dwindled as Houston spread inexorably outward.

It was a beautiful late August day, with temperatures still in the nineties but the air feeling less sticky than the week before. The bright blue sky and hint of a breeze held the promise of autumn -- eventually. When Annie first moved to Texas, she expected the cooler, football weather by September that she'd enjoyed in her hometown of Blacksburg, Virginia. But to her dismay, September could be the hottest month of the year in Houston. October was often slightly cooler, and November usually turned mild, but Annie still missed the falling temperatures and bright colors of an early southern autumn.

She felt relieved to be on the road after the last traumatic week. She'd always liked going out of town on reporting trips, setting her own hours, pursuing her own agenda and relishing the freedom, even if it came with solitary restaurant meals. Traveling on business was a welcome break where she didn't have to worry about socializing and could focus on her work. She could indulge her inner introvert. She often did her best thinking on long solo drives to places she'd never seen. But she liked being with Travis this time – and leaving the driving to him.

After navigating the heavy traffic out of Houston, he'd relaxed his crunched-up posture and stretched his short legs. His cherry-red Honda Accord was comfortable and quiet. She'd asked him to drive because she knew that like most of the newsroom's reporters, he'd want the company's relatively generous gas reimbursement. It had been several years since the *Times* staff had gotten decent raises and money was tight for everyone. He'd eagerly accepted her offer.

"Feels so good to be out of the office – even if I'm taking along my boss," he joked.

"Just think of me as a very old reporting partner," she smiled. "I'll be really rusty, so you'll have to make allowances."

"I doubt that's going to be a problem," he said. "But are you sure you want to interview Jake Satterfield? We could switch, you know?"

Annie was stung. First Greg, now Travis, was trying to spare her tender feelings. Was her entire life an open book – a messy, predictable romance novel?

"Sorry, Annie," he said. "I didn't mean to pry, but I know that you and Jake had a falling out when you were covering the secessionists."

"Actually our falling out came after, when we were a couple," she said in what she hoped was a light tone. "We'd talked about getting married, but it didn't work out."

"Well, he's an idiot," he said with an emphasis that surprised Annie. She knew he liked her, but she hadn't considered that his feelings might be stronger. Was the road trip with him a mistake? She dismissed that thought because his relationship with Lila Jo seemed happy.

"That's kind of you, Travis, but don't worry about me," she said. "Jake's scheduler said he'd be free all afternoon and I expect it'll take that long. What about Sam Wurzbach?"

"He's eager to meet with anyone who wants to talk about the concerns of the German-Texas community, as he put it," Travis said.

"I'm sure you're one step ahead of me, but I'd like to know more about how he and Kyle Krause became friends in high school and what drew them together more recently. I believe they were on the wrestling team together, but they seem so fundamentally different."

"Yeah. Not much on the surface would seem to link the topless king of Houston with the bakery mogul of the Hill Country," he said.

"Hope Wurzbach's more talkative than Krause," Annie said. "I guess if he's a politician, he has to be."

As Travis drove farther west, she felt her tension sloughing off. The flat land began to slope gently, and pretty farms and pastures replaced the picked-clean blandness of new subdivisions. Rural Texas was so appealing. It was a shame that burgeoning cities were subsuming more of it each year. Was that really progress?

Travis, as usual, wanted to talk about the fate of the newspaper industry.

"Think the *Times* will still exist a decade from now?"

"I think the *Times* website has a decent chance of lasting," she said. "Not so sure about the daily paper."

"Never thought I'd hear you say that," Travis said. "Thought you'd be the last true believer in the future of the print product, as they call the newspaper these days."

She shook her head with a frown. "Five years ago, I would have been," she said. "I don't know any more. But you can always work for the website."

They rode a little longer in companionable silence before Travis said, "I never really asked, but what do you think about the concept of secession?"

"It's hard to separate my beliefs from bad reporting experiences, but I'm basically against it," Annie said, a little surprised by the conversational turn. "If things don't go their way, too many people in this country want to take their marbles and go home. Seems like we're becoming a nation of spoiled children."

She paused a moment. "You're a native Texan. What do you think?"

"I think the Nation of Texas folks that you wrote about seem selfish. They want to keep all the good stuff in Texas, like oil, just for themselves," he said. "It seems kind of unpatriotic."

"There are more secessionists in Texas than any other state in the country," she said. "But Texas isn't alone. Separatist movements are flourishing in other states, like Alaska."

"Yeah, Alaska's always struck me as a little wacky," he said.

"Texas is way up there on the wacky scale," she smiled. "But the drive for secession stems partly from its history. Texas was a republic for ten years between winning its independence from Mexico and entering the United States."

"So that's why the secessionists are always talking about creating a new republic?"

"I think people who are unhappy with the present always look to the past," Annie said. "But nothing much was accomplished while Texas was a republic. It was too big to govern effectively in the 1840s and almost got into another war with Mexico."

"I hope Sam Wurzbach isn't just another secessionist," Travis said. "It sounds like a different thing. Preserving the German heritage in Texas seems sensible – seceding from the United States just seems crazy."

"Yeah," Annie said. "But I'm skeptical about the German-Texas movement, too. What do they really want? We have to find out."

CHAPTER 28

"Hungry? There's a good little barbecue place up the road that might be quicker than trying to eat in downtown Austin," Travis said.

Annie had lulled herself to sleep in the passenger seat. She sat up straight and stretched her arms. Food would probably blast away her late-morning lassitude.

"Good idea."

Minutes later, he pulled into a rustic log building that Annie had noticed on previous trips. It wasn't quite noon, but already cars half-filled the parking lot of Stumpy's, a modest café on the outskirts of Austin. That boded well for the quality of the barbecue inside.

"There are picnic tables in back and a nice view of the creek," Travis said. "It would be fun to sit outside, if I can land a table in the shade."

They walked inside a rectangular dining room with old-fashioned knotty pine paneling and long communal tables. Two older women served customers behind a short cafeteria line and a muscled young man with dreadlocks tamed by a hairnet chopped beef brisket on a butcher-block slab behind them. The steaming meat looked dark and crusty on the outside, the way Annie liked it, and smelled smoky and peppery. The menu was short: brisket sandwiches and plates with baked beans, slaw and a few other sides. The restaurant also made its own pecan pie and served it in thick slices with ice cream, but she'd be good and skip it.

Annie and Travis got sandwiches and iced tea, paid at the cash register and walked their trays through the back door to the grassy picnic area. They selected a shaded picnic table with a good creek view, put their trays down and settled in, facing each other.

The back door opened again. Annie looked up and almost choked on her iced tea. She recognized Rob Ryland, a former *Times* reporter she had worked with four years ago with disastrous consequences. Dressed in dark jeans and a black T-shirt, he looked a little older, but still had the hazel eyes, longish brown hair and the deceptively wholesome looks of a young Paul McCartney. They'd worked together reporting on Tom Marr's gubernatorial campaign with its links to the Nation of Texas. She'd been Rob's mentor and they'd spent weeks working side-by-side on the big story. Then she found out the young reporter was the nephew of secessionist leader Dan Riggins and secretly had spied on her and jeopardized the newspaper's investigation. She had confronted Rob and he left the paper, but later threatened to kidnap her from a hospital's parking garage. A Texas Ranger had arrested him on the spot. He'd been lucky to get off with probation and a pledge to stay away from secessionist activities.

Darker memories surfaced as Rob stood at the restaurant's door with his tray. She remembered the night he'd brought her home from a bar and taken advantage of her weakened state. She'd been mourning the death of her best friend by drinking heavily with other *Times* staffers. Rob had spent the night, ostensibly to make sure she was all right, and had forced himself on her. She'd blamed herself afterwards, but his insistence that he'd done nothing wrong had shaken her. She'd kicked him out the next morning and they avoided each other until they were both assigned to the secessionist story. He'd worked with her cooperatively, until she found out about his betrayal.

She composed herself and spoke to Travis. "I just saw Rob Ryland, Dan Riggins's nephew who used to work at the *Times*."

"That scumbag who spied on your investigation and tried to kidnap you?" Travis asked. "What's he doing here?"

"I heard he was living in Austin," Annie said. "Not sure what he's up to. I think we should follow him."

Travis's eyes shone. He loved intrigue of any kind. "Let's do it."

Annie described Rob, and Travis took his half-eaten lunch inside to look for him. Annie finished her lunch quickly and walked around to Travis's car in the graveled parking lot at the side of the building. She waited until she saw Travis coming out behind Rob. Rob got into his pickup and she and Travis followed him. They drove a few miles into Austin and turned into a parking lot just after Rob. The building was one Annie was familiar with: the headquarters of an alternative paper called the *Austin Comet*.

Unfortunately, Rob had caught them and strode to Travis's car, where he tapped on the passenger side window. Busted! They got out.

"Annie Price, were you following me? Are you trying to harass me?" Rob was furious and loud.

"We didn't mean any harm, Rob," she said. "We saw you leaving Stumpy's Restaurant and needed to take the same route. Wondered what you were doing these days."

"I have a good job covering music and local politics for the *Austin Comet*. So now you know," he said. "It's a fresh start for me. I'd hope that you wouldn't deny me that."

"Of course not," Annie said. "Rob, this is Travis, my reporting partner at the *Times*. We're actually here on a story."

"And what would that be?" Rob said belligerently.

"Since you're working for a newspaper now, I'd better not say," Annie said. "Competition, you know."

"Does it have anything to do with the secessionist movement?"

"Can't talk about that," Annie said. "But since you mention it, we've heard that your Uncle Dan is still active in the cause, though he's a fugitive. Has he been back in West Texas? Can you tell us anything?"

Rob's face changed quickly, but Annie couldn't read it.

"I'd be shocked if he'd been in Texas," Rob said. "As far as I know, he and Alicia are hiding somewhere far away. Your guess is as good as mine. I'm just a law-abiding journalist these days."

"Do you keep up with the Nation of Texas folks? Or is that group more or less dead?"

"Are you kidding?" Rob said. "As long as Texans love their state, the Nation of Texas will never die."

"No, I'm prohibited from being involved in that group, as you may recall," he added. "But things are even worse now than they were four years ago – terrible leadership from the President, Congress and the courts. Why would Texans want to be part of that?"

"I don't know," she said. "Could it be they believe in something larger than Texas? After all, our ancestors fought for our independence. Could it be that most Texans still think the United States is a pretty good country?"

Rob shook his head and gave her a withering look.

"You could have been part of a historic new republic, but you chose to do everything you could to hurt Texas," he said. "I'll never understand that."

"Rob, we'll never agree on this, so there's no more to say," she said. "Are you enjoying your reporting job?"

"I love my job with the *Comet*," he said. "I'm doing exactly what I want to be doing. Sorry I sounded off, Annie."

"Bye, Rob."

Rob nodded to her cordially, but turned to Travis with animosity. "Follow me again and I can guarantee that you'll be very sorry."

He strode across the parking lot as they got back into Travis's car. Annie shook her head.

"Sorry, Travis. Bad idea. Following him didn't work out too well."

"What a nasty guy," Travis said. "At least we know what he's doing now."

"Maybe," Annie replied. "He's working as a reporter, but he still talks like a secessionist."

CHAPTER 29

Soon after the encounter with Rob, Travis pulled into their budget motel on the outskirts of Austin. In the spirit of economy, Annie had made reservations at the cheapest of the chains. Travis noticed the parking lot had cracked in several places, probably from truck tires beating it down for decades. He checked out his small single room, pleased to note that it was next door to Annie's. He sat on the double bed with its cheap floral bedspread, checking emails on his smart phone. She'd asked for time to freshen up, so they met twenty minutes later for the drive downtown.

He was annoyed to see that she'd dolled herself up, changing into a straight black skirt with a purple top that he thought showed too much cleavage, a black blazer with rolled-up sleeves and sexy, high-heeled sandals. She'd brushed her hair back from her forehead, put on mascara and eyeliner and outlined her lips with deep pink lipstick. Of course she'd want to shine for Satterfield, that hound dog of an ex-boyfriend. He felt protective of Annie and jealous of her attention to men who didn't deserve her. He admired her in so many ways and felt sorry that she carried the torch for that bastard politician.

"Nice outfit," he said. "Should I change?" He was wearing khaki shorts and one of his more subdued Hawaiian shirts.

"Thanks," she said. "I don't think so. You look fine."

She seemed preoccupied and didn't smile, staring ahead as they passed office towers, gas stations and chain businesses on either side of the freeway toward downtown. He drove quickly and stopped to let her out on Congress Street. She'd walk to Jake Satterfield's office from there. He'd park the car at a nearby garage before heading to his own interview with Sam Wurzbach.

"Bye, Travis," she smiled. "Check in with me later to let me know how things are going."

"Are we going to have dinner together?" he said, trying not to sound too hopeful.

"Let's play it by ear. See how long these interviews take. We shouldn't make definite plans yet."

Her noncommittal answer depressed him, but he tried to concentrate on his upcoming meeting with Wurzbach, the darling of the German-Texas movement. He arrived ten minutes early after exploring the Capitol and cooled his heels in the outer office. Wurzbach and most other legislators were housed in the fancy four-story underground extension to the Capitol. A fire in the 1980s had inflicted serious damage, and renovations included constructing a massive addition underneath and adjacent to the building. Located at the top of Austin's Congress Street, the Capitol set a dramatic stage for trendy businesses sloping down to Lady Bird Lake, renamed for the late, beloved first lady. At night, when the Capitol was lit up, Travis thought its elevated, bronzed exterior looked as majestic as anything he'd ever seen.

He didn't want to dwell on Annie's meeting with the fat-cat Satterfield, whom he'd heard was dating their former *Times* colleague, Maggie Mahaffey. The stuck-on-herself reporter and self-absorbed politician deserved each other. Travis had never gotten to know Maggie, so he hadn't exactly mourned her departure. He'd judged her as attractive but superficial, and knew she wouldn't waste her time on him when she could vamp a powerful player.

Travis was attracted to Austin for its quirky blend of music, youth-oriented nightlife and lucrative tech jobs. Many of his college friends had migrated there for high-paying positions, but he loved journalism, so he'd settled in Houston because of its larger newspaper. What if Annie was right that print journalism was destined to devolve into a bunch of competing websites? He loved technology, but a website without a newspaper would feel as empty as a world without trees. He wasn't sure why, but he guessed he had what the *Times'* geezer subscribers were always talking about – an irrational need to hold onto something tangible, to feel the carefully curated package of news in his hands as he sipped his morning coffee. Seeing his byline on a printed page always felt special. If the print edition disappeared, he guessed he could move to Austin and become a wealthy techie.

Wurzbach came out of his inner office to greet Travis, who warmed to his quick smile and open manner. After a few pleasantries, he led Travis to a conference room, closed the door and they talked for several hours.

Travis learned that Wurzbach was a native Texan a couple of years older than Kyle Krause. They'd both attended high school in Fredericksburg and bonded as hard-working stars of their wrestling team. While Krause had chased his fortune in Houston with the topless industry, Wurzbach had persevered in the small town with his burgeoning chain of German bakeries. He'd kept in touch with Krause over the years and recently had persuaded him to invest in German Texas.

"Doesn't the name Wurzbach come from the Old Country?" Travis said. "Is that how you got interested in the concept of a German Texas?"

"The name's about as German as you can get," Wurzbach smiled. "My ancestors came to Texas in the 1840s, part of the first wave of German immigrants. It wasn't an easy life for them. Farming in the Hill Country was tough."

He told Travis his ancestors had spread through the Hill Country and made a decent life for themselves until anti-German hysteria gripped the state during World War I.

"My great-grandfather was persecuted during the war," Wurzbach said. "He wasn't physically injured, but some of his friends were horsewhipped, and even tarred and feathered, by fellow Texans just because of their German surnames. It was a terrible time."

"I never knew that," Travis said. "Did it happen in other states?"

"Sure," Wurzbach said. "But it was worse in Texas because of the state's isolation and large population of German immigrants. Texans developed an unreasonable fear of people who'd been their friends and neighbors for decades."

By 1900, he said, Texas had become home to about 200,000 people of German descent. Most were settled in ten counties where German Texans composed as much as ten percent of the population. Those counties are still regarded as "German" counties.

"The German Texans loved their state, but desperately wanted to keep their old-country traditions alive – their German hunting and singing clubs, German churches, and German-language instruction," Wurzbach said. "They were very successful at keeping their culture flourishing until World War I."

One well-publicized incident showed how the hysteria affected Texans of German ancestry, he said. On Feb. 12, 1918, a young clerk for the Germania Club in Fayetteville, near Houston, raised the German flag to notify members of a social event that evening. It was an established way to communicate with club members, but on that day, led to unanticipated trouble.

"Law enforcement officers arrested eleven men and charged them with the federal crime of espionage – simply because they displayed the flag," Wurzbach said. "Charges were later dropped, but the incident terrified German Texans."

By the end of the war, few vestiges of the vibrant German culture remained.

"German language instruction had been outlawed in most high schools, German street and town names had been changed, citizens were afraid to speak German, cultural clubs had been disbanded and virtually all German-language newspapers closed," he said.

"It was a major blow to the German traditions in Texas that continued after the war – with the emergence of the Ku Klux Klan and other groups that detested 'foreign' influences," he added. "German Texans have vowed never to let these prejudices spring up again."

"That was a long time ago," Travis said. "Why would that be a concern now?"

"The modern-day secessionist movement shocked us all," Wurzbach said. "Four years ago, your paper published stories about the Nation of Texas and their ruthless quest to force our state to break away from the United States."

"But they've failed miserably," Travis said.

"It's a threat that's rising again," Wurzbach said. "We see signs they're regrouping, so we want to make sure our German culture and traditions are protected."

He showed Travis on a map the ten counties that still contain a significant population of Texans descended from German immigrants. Those counties -- Austin, Comal, DeWitt, Fayette, Gillespie, Guadalupe, Kendall, Lee, Medina and Washington – could easily revive German traditions.

"We want the legislature to designate these counties as the enclave of German Texas," he said. "Those counties would offer German-language instruction in schools, put up German signs and give German-oriented businesses incentives to locate there."

"But aren't we all Texans?" Travis said. "What about the border counties? The predominant language is Spanish and the majority population is of Mexican descent. Should that area be called Mexican Texas?"

"No, we fought and prevailed in the Texas Revolution against Santa Anna," Wurzbach said. "He butchered our brave men at the Alamo in 1836, but a few months later we won the Battle of San Jacinto. The Mexicans forfeited their rights to Texas forever."

"I don't see much difference," Travis said.

"We're not asking for the whole state – just a slice, where German Texans could be assured of maintaining and building on their culture," Wurzbach said.

"Do you have the support of the counties to create your enclave?"

"Definitely," he said. "People living there think it would be a great economic and marketing tool."

He looked at his watch, saying they needed to leave for his first major German-Texas fundraiser. He'd invited Travis to join him, so the two left the Capitol to drive to a restaurant in the countryside.

CHAPTER 30

"Mr. Satterfield should be available in ten minutes, Ms. Price," the middle-aged secretary told her. Annie nodded and shivered in her lightweight summer jacket. Why did Texas government officials always keep their offices so cold? You came in sweating from the summer heat and encountered a blast of frigid air that practically blew you out of the room.

She also felt chilled because she was nervous, and who wouldn't be? She hadn't laid eyes on her former boyfriend in three years, since he'd confessed weeks before his divorce was final that he'd gotten his estranged wife pregnant. Annie had been joyfully planning their wedding. She knew that Jake loved women and had a wandering eye. But the last thing she'd expected was for him to sleep with the wife he'd said he detested after her affair with one of his law partners.

Lately, after not dating anyone who interested her for a long dry spell, she'd begun to hope again. She was enjoying dating Matt Sharpe, though she couldn't visualize a long-term future with him. Tom Marr fell into a different category. The night he'd appeared on her doorstep a few weeks ago had seemed significant. Four years ago, he'd almost succeeded in wooing her away from Jake. But she couldn't go along with his secessionist philosophy. When Marr said on her front porch that he was finished with the Nation of Texas, she'd cautiously acceded to his request to call her.

They'd talked on the phone a few times and she'd enjoyed their wide-ranging conversations. But he seemed to be rationing the calls, moving slowly and deliberately to keep things on an even keel. He still was following leads on Betsy's whereabouts and believed that his daughter soon would return to the ranch of her own accord.

Annie didn't know when or if she'd she see Marr again. She had so much going on with her work that she couldn't worry about it right now. But somehow, just knowing that Marr was interested had given her the courage to see Jake, to try to put that disastrous experience into some kind of perspective. Of course, the meeting also had an official purpose. She wanted to assess how Jake, as the state's most powerful state senator, perceived the German-Texas cause.

The inner door burst open and she heard a familiar high-pitched female voice. It sounded like Maggie Mahaffey, but surely it couldn't be her former *Times* colleague. She listened a few seconds longer. Of course it was Maggie. That's the kind of thing that happened in her crazy love life.

She stood up as Jake followed Maggie into the waiting area. He undoubtedly knew that Annie would be coming for their scheduled appointment, but Maggie looked shocked, and none too happy to see her. At least there was that small satisfaction, Annie thought. The petite blonde as usual was decked out in pink. Maggie wore a pale pink knit dress with a hot pink bolero jacket and enough rosy lipstick and blusher to supply a department store cosmetics counter.

"Hi, Maggie. Hello, Jake," she said with what she hoped was reasonable poise. "How's the new job?"

"Annie, what're you doing here?" Maggie said. "Uh, the job's fine so far. Just finished my first week. Jake, shall I call you later?"

"Why don't I call you?" he said, steering her towards the door. Annie heard them talking in low voices in the hall. She couldn't make out what they were saying, but Maggie sounded angry. He seemed to be trying to calm her.

He came back in, moving with the confident, Elvis-like swagger that she'd always loved. He slowly looked her up and down, his smoky blue eyes crinkling, apparently happy with what he saw. He pulled her into a hug and before she could break away, kissed her lightly on the lips.

"Annie, you look gorgeous," he said. "Let's go into the conference room and catch up."

He seated her at a glass-topped square table and plopped down across from her. He leaned forward slightly, just the way she remembered he always did. He had a politician's knack of convincing the person before him that he or she was the most important person in the building.

He grinned and said, "What can I get you, a large chardonnay?"

Despite her vow not to depart from a businesslike demeanor, she laughed. The first time she'd talked to him was in an Austin bar during a crowded happy hour. She had too many glasses of Chardonnay after several days of intense reporting on state budget hearings. They'd tumbled into bed that same night. Separated from his wife, he'd visited her as often as they could manage during the heady days of their courtship. But hectic weekends between Austin and Houston coupled with his family obligations in Kerrville had taken a toll, even before the pregnancy had ended the relationship.

"I'll have a Diet Coke, please," she said.

"I've heard that before," he said with a wink. He spent time asking about her work, her parents, her social life and even her two cats. She touched gingerly on the subject of his children, the two daughters and three-year-old son.

"You knew Jeannie and I had split up again?" he said. "This time it's for good. I'm living alone in a condo I bought downtown."

"Maggie told me when she left the *Times* recently that she was dating you," Annie said. "To be honest, she kind of rubbed it in my face."

"I've gone out with her some, but believe me, it's not serious," Jake said.

"She seems to think it is."

"She was just trying to get to you. I sense she's a little jealous. She'd like to be Annie Price when she grows up."

She knew she should disapprove of his cavalier attitude toward Maggie, but instead, her heart beat faster. She hoped her face wasn't flushed and her hands weren't noticeably trembling. She folded them behind her, willing them to be still. He'd always stirred up reactions that embarrassed her.

"You shouldn't lead Maggie on if you're not serious," Annie said, failing to sound stern.

"She's been around the block more than a few times," Jake said. "She flirts with anybody who has power and she's definitely playing the field. Besides, what do you care? You broke my heart and stomped on it with your cowboy boots."

"Let's not fight about who got hurt the most," she said. "You know why I left."

"The point is that I'm making a fresh start, and you should, too," he said.

"What am I supposed to do, Jake? I haven't even seen you for three years." Her voice rose and she could feel herself beginning to get emotional. She saw that Jake knew it and wanted to defuse a difficult conversation.

"Let me find you that Diet Coke," he said, exiting the conference room. "Sorry, I guess I'm moving too fast. I'll be right back."

Annie got up restlessly, smoothed her jacket and tried to calm herself. She scanned the pictures on his desk and managed to study the silver-framed photograph of the little boy without crying. It was obviously Jake's son, a serious-looking child with blue eyes and dark curly hair. If they'd had a son, would he have looked like this? There were several other framed pictures of all three children, but none of his wife.

She slipped back into the conference room before he returned with a large plastic bottle of Diet Coke. He got two glasses and poured the beverage. She smiled and he toasted her with his half-filled glass.

"To you, Annie. Whatever finally brought you here is a good thing."

"Tell me about your colleague, Sam Wurzbach," she said.

"He's a great guy who's made a pile of money with his German bakeries," Jake said. "They're all over the Hill Country. The pastries are unbelievable."

"What do you think of his German-Texas plan?"

"I think he's a little hyped about the subject, but I've been waiting to see where he takes it," Jake said. "So far, I think it's a pretty decent proposal."

"Do you really think so?" Annie said. "I thought you'd decided after the secessionist debacle that any kind of separatist movement was bad."

"I'm not sure that giving streets German names and teaching more German in the schools is a bad thing in the Hill Country," he said. "Calling a bunch of underdeveloped counties German Texas might be a creative way to promote growth and tourism."

"Do you really think that's all he wants?" Annie said. "I'm not sure I believe that."

"I don't know, Annie," he said. "I haven't had time to check it out thoroughly, but Sam's a key legislative ally and a great friend."

"Are you part of this crazy scheme?" Annie asked. "Be straight with me."

"I'm leaning toward it," Jake said. "What's gotten into you? Why are you so suspicious and angry?"

She told him about Kyle Krause, his support of the German-Texas movement and the death of Nate Hardin at his club. Jake of course had read stories about Nate's murder.

"I've only met Kyle Krause once or twice. I would agree that there's something strange about him," Jake said. "But do you really think he killed your reporter?"

"I don't know what I think," Annie said. "He certainly didn't like the attention the *Times* was giving him."

"I get regular reports on the secessionist movement from the Texas Rangers," Jake said. "The last one said Dan Riggins might be border-hopping in Texas, near the ranch of your old boyfriend Tom Marr."

"I don't think Tom's in touch with him," Annie said. "He told me he was finished with the secessionists."

"The plot thickens," Jake said, looking at her flushed face. "Are you seeing Marfa's lonesomest cowboy again?"

"We've talked on the phone a few times," said Annie. "That's all."

He frowned, looked at his watch and back at her. She could see he was wondering about Marr and miffed that they were in contact.

"I've promised to go to Sam's German-Texas fundraiser near San Antonio tonight," he said. "Come with me. It will give you a chance to see what this group is all about. And we need more time to talk."

"Sure," she said. "I'd love to meet some German Texans."

CHAPTER 31

There was something about being in Jake's old black BMW that brought back the sharpest memories. The car smelled like Jake, a hint of lemony aftershave and something she couldn't define. Every person exuded his or her faint aroma if you got close. His took her back to their passionate nights together. The interior of his car as usual looked clean and mostly uncluttered, though the booster seat in the back and a few toys beside it were new. After he'd deposited her in the passenger seat and carefully closed the door, making sure her jacket wasn't caught in it, he got in and put in a Coldplay CD she hadn't heard since the last time they were together.

He drove as fast as the late-afternoon traffic would allow, heading from Austin to Grey Forest, a small town northwest of San Antonio known for its single but substantial landmark, the Grey Moss Inn. Annie hadn't been there before, but she'd always heard about the restaurant and knew that it had the reputation of being impossibly romantic. That wouldn't be the case tonight. The German-Texas Society had rented the whole place for a large party.

"I heard there'll be a good band, with dancing," Jake smiled.

"You know I'm not much of a dancer," Annie said.

"Annie, you're crazy. Those long, sexy legs were made to dance."

She laughed out loud, feeling lighthearted and a little reckless. The sadness she'd felt earlier had evaporated and what remained was the charged-up awareness of his body. She remembered the ten-hour trip they'd made from Marfa to Houston long ago, when he'd renounced the secessionist movement and barged in to take her away from Tom Marr's ranch. That tempered her giddiness somewhat as she wondered if Marr was in touch with Riggins, the state's most sought-after fugitive, as Jake had implied. She didn't really think Tom was lying about forsaking the secessionist movement, but a shred of doubt remained. She'd question him about it the next time he called. She couldn't think about that right now.

They got to the town of Grey Fox in less than two hours, slowed down for its notorious 30-mile speed limit that trapped unwary drivers and soon spotted the secluded grounds of the inn.

They got out of the car, enjoying the rural view. Across the parking lot, in an adjoining pasture, she saw some whitetail deer and a group of smaller animals.

"Are those wild turkeys?"

"Yeah. Cute, aren't they?" Jake said.

She'd always been tickled that he enjoyed animals, especially her cats, as much as she did. It was one of the things about him she found most endearing.

A canopy of huge oaks and a stone wall encircled the inn. The wall was only a couple of feet high, but it still gave the place the air of an ancient fortress. Annie could see that the long, low building and its spacious patio in back were lit up with hundreds of twinkling lights. She and Jake walked through the restaurant, enjoying the buzzing ambience of people anticipating a festive evening. Well-dressed couples stood in clumps or sat at crowded tables, sipping wine and champagne. The partygoers ranged from beautiful young people in white jeans, fancy cowboy boots and flashy jewelry to wealthy-looking retirees in their seventies and eighties in full cocktail regalia. Waiters, mostly younger, tuxedo-clad Hispanic men, were passing trays of fancy canapés.

"I think the serious partying is this way," Jake said, steering her through the room to the outdoors area.

On the patio, a country band was playing some beer-hall tune that Annie vaguely recognized as German. A number of couples, mostly younger people dressed in dirndls and lederhosen, were dancing to the sprightly music. The traditional Bavarian outfits looked cute on the young women, Annie thought, but the leather shorts and knee socks on the guys reminded her of movie scenes depicting Hitler Youth. She halfway expected them either to break out in German drinking songs or hoist guns or knives at a given command. She chided herself when she looked closer and realized that most of them were young, probably high school or college students.

"What do you think?" Jake said. "Very colorful, huh?"

"Seems kind of over the top," she said. "Maybe I'm just not used to the whole German-Texas vibe. Ever been to that big German festival in New Braunfels in the fall?"

"Wurstfest? I'm a Hill Country boy. Would I pass up the festival of sausage?" Jake said. "This is a much more refined bunch of folks. People aren't quite as drunk, either."

Annie studied the crowd and to her surprise, spied Travis with Senator Sam Wurzbach. She waved them over and introduced Travis to Jake. Jake was his usual amiable and talkative self, but Travis seemed stiff and a little angry.

"I left several messages on your cell," he said. "I didn't know whether you wanted to meet for dinner or what. When I didn't hear anything, I accepted Sam's invitation to this party."

"Sorry, Travis," Annie said. "I just lost track of time. I'm glad we're both here."

The six-piece, German-sounding band began playing "Cotton-Eyed Joe," a legendary country tune Annie often heard in Texas-themed bars. Always, when it was played, the native Texans would rush to the dance floor to perform a line dance. The young people in their dirndls and lederhosen enthusiastically joined the partygoers dancing to the rollicking tune. Annie and her companions watched from around the edges and she tapped her toes to the music. Wurzbach told them he planned to deliver his pitch about German Texas as soon as the band finished the number.

"We sold about seven hundred tickets and ended up with a full house," he said with pride. "It's the first in a series of big parties to introduce the German-Texas movement."

"Where did you find the young dancers?" Annie asked.

"They've been going to a German dancing school in Fredericksburg," Wurzbach smiled. "That's the kind of cultural activity we'd like to encourage."

Annie enjoyed chatting with him, Jake and Travis until Wurzbach excused himself, saying he needed to touch base with supporters before his speech.

The band finished its number and people began drifting away from the stone dance floor section of the patio. Some headed to the bar for another drink and others sat down. One of the musicians grabbed the microphone.

"We're playing one last song, so don't leave yet, folks. It's 'Waltz across Texas', so everyone needs to get their sweetheart to the dance floor for a slow one," he said.

"Annie, would you dance with me?" Jake said with a little bow. "You don't mind if we take advantage of the waltz, do you, Travis?"

"Break a leg," Travis said, sounding sour.

Jake led her out on the floor. He put his arms around her waist, pulled her close and they swayed together wordlessly as the song began. Feeling his strong body pressed against hers after they'd been apart for so long made her almost too dizzy to dance, so she focused on the music. She'd never really listened to the lyrics of the classic song and the band's version was soulful.

"When we dance together, my world's in disguise. It's a fairyland tale that's come true. And when you look at me with those stars in your eyes, I could waltz across Texas with you."

The band lingered over the chorus: "Waltz across Texas with you in my arms, waltz across Texas with you. Like a storybook ending, I'm lost in your charms. And I could waltz across Texas with you."

Jake softly sang the words into her ear, kissed her neck and they moved together as if they were making love – again. Annie wished the song would never end.

But end it did with a bang, a strange popping noise. She heard the screams of fear and panic. She looked at Jake and saw her shock mirrored in his eyes. They pulled apart abruptly and stared in horror. The sound had been a gunshot, perhaps coming through the tall trees beyond the brightly lit outdoors area. Sam Wurzbach had fallen on the patio with a spreading red blur on the lower left side of his white shirt.

CHAPTER 32

Annie and Jake rushed to where Sam was stretched out on the patio. His eyes were closed and his body appeared motionless. But a barely discernible groan reassured them that for the moment, he was breathing. In one quick motion, Jake jerked a white tablecloth off a nearby table set for dinner, sending glasses and tableware crashing. He pressed the wad of starched linen tightly against the wound, which resembled a red ink blot spreading across Sam's chest.

"Hang on, Sam," Jake said in a steady, crooning voice. "Keep breathing, man."

Partygoers stampeded across the patio, heading through the restaurant where patrons inside were already clogging the front entrance. It hadn't taken long for panic to set in. Some people on the patio had dived under a group of tables, bracing themselves against further violence. But Annie heard no more gunshots, just the jumbled noise of humans reacting to fear. A large woman in a sparkly white evening gown tried to run, but slammed into a tray of champagne glasses, scattering them across the floor. She teetered against the wobbling tray, trying to regain her balance. An elderly man grabbed her hand before she fell and they hurried through the restaurant with others in the departing crowd.

Annie watched as a small knot of helpers gathered around Jake and Sam. She was relieved to see an older man with wire-rimmed glasses open what looked like a doctor's bag. A gray-haired woman, possibly his wife, was on the phone in what sounded like a 911 call. It had all happened so fast that Annie had trouble thinking straight. She'd been in crisis situations twice before, a knife attack and a horrendous shootout on a freeway, and they'd left their psychological mark – nightmares, flashbacks and a stupefied slowness to act. She realized that she was frozen and wondered if she was having a post-traumatic stress reaction. She mentally shook herself, trying to summon the will to press forward. She grabbed her mobile and located the number of the *Times'* night desk. She looked around for Travis and spotted him crawling out from under a table, notebook in hand. She was relieved to see that he was all right.

Hugh Heller, the paper's best rewrite man, answered her call to the newsroom. Luckily for her, he was on Saturday night duty, covering the police shift. In his usual unflappable, low-key way, he asked questions and she could hear him tapping out notes on his office computer. She described to him, as succinctly as she could, the shooting of Wurzbach and the events leading up to it.

"It felt like a sniper shooting from the woods behind the restaurant, but I haven't gotten that confirmed," she said.

"Is he dead?" Hugh asked.

"No, but it looks like a serious chest wound."

He asked her some background questions about Wurzbach and the German-Texas movement, which she was able to respond to quickly. She was so glad he had the presence of mind she lacked. But she knew she was recovering – her voice sounded stronger and her instincts were beginning to kick in.

"Travis and I are both here for at least a while, so we'll be calling you back with details as we get them," she said.

"You know our formal deadline's passed, but I can get a bulletin in and file online right now," Hugh said. "Let me go, but call back in fifteen minutes."

She hung up, hearing the sound of an ambulance siren coming closer, rounding a bend in the road beside the restaurant. The vehicle screamed to a stop in the parking lot and doors slammed. Four emergency technicians hurried through the restaurant carrying equipment and brushed aside the knot of helpers around Wurzbach. They gently lifted him onto a stretcher as Jake conferred with them in a low voice. A sobbing woman had joined Jake from inside the restaurant and his arm wrapped around her shoulder. Annie hadn't met her during the earlier part of the evening, but assumed that the dark-haired, fortyish woman was Wurzbach's wife. She almost tripped on the hem of her evening dress, but Jake helped to steady her. It looked like she was preparing to accompany her husband's stretcher in the emergency vehicle.

"Marie, I'll meet you at the San Antonio medical center," he assured her as she left the restaurant. He glanced in Annie's direction and stopped to hug her.

"I'll be back as soon as I can," he said. "You and Travis need to stick around and talk to Mark Ingram. He's on his way and he'll need your help."

"Of course," she said. "I'm glad he's the Ranger taking the call."

In her opinion, shared by many local law enforcement officials, Texas Ranger Mark Ingram was the state's top criminal investigator. She knew him well, having worked with him while both were investigating the secessionists four years ago. They'd been together in an East Houston apartment when Alicia Perez had stabbed him and tried to kill her. Surviving that violent encounter had cemented their relationship.

The Texas Rangers, now a part of the Texas Department of Public Safety, had formed the famous squad in frontier days before Texas became a state. Among their accomplishments, they'd captured and killed the outlaws Bonnie and Clyde, stopping the couple's murderous rampage across Texas. The modern-day Rangers generally handled the state's most serious criminal cases.

Annie stationed herself with Travis inside the restaurant with staff and party stragglers, waiting for Ingram's arrival. Local and state police were swarming the scene and had roped off the patio to safeguard evidence. She could hear them out there, talking to each other on walkie-talkies and searching for clues.

Travis took charge of calling in news updates to Hugh, for which Annie was grateful. She still felt a bit numb. But she was doing her share, talking to people about what they'd seen and heard, and giving her notes to Travis, who organized the story.

Finally Mark Ingram arrived, dressed in Saturday night casual clothes, his short red hair neatly brushed. He was a stocky man with tortoise-shell glasses and his freckles stood out in his suntanned face. He smiled when he spotted her.

"Annie, I'm surprised to see you, but I shouldn't be. You have a habit of showing up whenever things are happening," he said. He shook hands with Travis, who also knew him.

"I'm just glad you were on duty tonight," she said. "Travis and I were doing interviews in Austin and got invited to Sam's party."

She filled him in on what they'd seen before he broke away to interview other partygoers trying to leave.

"I'll talk to you two later after I corral some of these people. Just hang on for a while."

Annie drank coffee and she and Travis continued their reporting. Ingram brought one person at a time to interview at a table in a corner of the restaurant. Police had also talked with people separately, trying to collect as many impressions as they could while witnesses were still at the scene.

The front door opened again. Jake had come back. Annie could tell from his somber face that the news was bad. He still had blood spatters on his white shirt and his eyes were bloodshot.

"Sam's gone," he told them quietly. "Died a few minutes after we got to the hospital. Marie was holding his hand, but I'm not sure he was aware of it. He'd lost a lot of blood."

"Oh, Jake," Annie said. "I'm so sorry. I know he was a great friend. Wish I'd gotten a chance to know him better. He seemed like a good person."

"He was the best. I just feel sorry for Marie and their three kids."

"What'll happen to his bakeries?" Annie said.

"He's got a brother and an uncle in the business," he said. "I feel sure that they'll step up to keep it going."

Ingram joined them, shaking hands and commiserating with Jake. He'd apparently finished his first round of interviews, so the four of them sat down at one of the quieter tables.

"Questions? Comments?" Mark looked each of them.

"What do you and your guys know at this early stage?" Annie asked.

"We think Wurzbach was killed by one good shot from a high-powered rifle. We've found a place on the hill in back of the restaurant where the killer must have waited, taking time to get the right vantage point."

"Any clues at the scene?" Annie asked.

"A tube of lip balm was found, apparently a brand made in Mexico. It must have fallen out of the killer's pocket," he said. "Obviously, it could have belonged to either a man or a woman. A couple of damaged shells were also picked up and sent to the lab."

Annie looked at Ingram to see if he had the same thought that immediately occurred to her.

"Alicia Perez?" she said.

"I'm not ruling her out," he said. "It's certainly possible that she and Riggins were so concerned about Wurzbach's German Texas campaign that she might have slipped across the border to try to kill him."

"Have you heard anything lately about her and Riggins?"

"Yeah, I can't go into specifics, but we have reason to believe they're being protected in their movements around Mexico by a drug cartel," Ingram said. "They've traveled around there and have crossed into West Texas periodically."

"Our sources have told us that Riggins has been seen near the border and he still directs the Nation of Texas group's activities," Annie said. "We haven't been able to confirm that, though."

Ingram nodded and continued with his analysis.

"The secessionist movement is still pretty active online, though the groups don't surface in public the way they used to before Riggins and Perez fled," he said. "The Nation of Texas hasn't put up any billboards or solicited members in a while."

"I meant to tell you earlier. We ran into Rob Ryland yesterday at a restaurant outside Austin," Annie said. "It seems like a thousand years ago."

"Yeah, we've asked Ryland to come to headquarters in the morning and give a statement," Ingram said. "But we've kept an eye on your former colleague and it looks like he's behaving himself."

"He said he's working at the *Austin Comet*," Annie said. "He denied having anything to do with the Nation of Texas, but I wondered. He still seems awfully emotional about the subject."

"He's definitely working as a journalist at the *Comet*," Ingram said. "Got stories all over that liberal rag. As long as he's not causing trouble, we don't have any justification to follow him around. Don't have the manpower either."

"What happens next?" Annie asked.

"We do the normal kind of death investigation, looking at Wurzbach's life, his friends and enemies. We also try harder to extradite Riggins and Alicia Perez."

Ingram stood up and said goodbye, telling Annie he'd be in touch. She was glad he wanted to continue sharing information, which had helped them both in the previous case. She looked at her watch, surprised that it was nearly 5 a.m.

"Annie, let me take you to breakfast," Jake said, putting a hand on her arm and pointedly leaving out Travis.

"I'm not hungry, I'm exhausted. I'd like to get a few hours of sleep before Travis and I have to head back to Houston," she said.

"I'll take you back to your motel," Jake said. "That okay with you, Travis?"

"Sure," Travis said with a notable lack of enthusiasm. "What time should we leave, Annie?"

"How about 11 a.m.? I'll set my clock. We'll get a few hours of sleep and still get away before the traffic gets bad," Annie said. "Since Brandon's taking the lead on the Wurzbach story for tomorrow, we can get back later."

Jake opened the door to his passenger seat and drove quickly to the budget motel, neither of them talking. He took her hand and walked her to the door of her room. He pulled her into his arms, kissed her hungrily and reached for her keys to open the door.

"Could I join you for a while?" He moved to come inside, but she paused.

"Think I'd like to just curl up by myself," she said, trying to let him down gently. "It's been a horrible night. I need to be alone and you probably do, too."

He looked hurt.

"Okay, Annie. It sure would be nice to cuddle up for a little while."

"We both know what would happen," Annie said. "I'm not sure I want to go there yet."

"I can tell you still love me," Jake said. "Saw it in your eyes on the dance floor. I'm finally a free man. Don't you want to see me?"

"You're right, Jake. I care about you," she said, measuring her words. "But we've got a lot to figure out before we jump into bed. When things quiet down, we need to talk."

He shrugged. "Have it your way, babe. Why don't you call me tomorrow?"

"I'll call you soon," she said. "We should get back to our lives first and think about what we want from each other."

"I still love you, Annie. I want to give things another shot." He looked at her for a long moment, kissed her cheek, and retreated to his car.

She shut the door and collapsed on the bed. She knew that if she'd let him stay, by now he'd be stripping off her skirt and panties and pushing her up against the wall. He'd make love to her quickly, the way he'd always done when they'd been apart. Then they'd probably make love again, more slowly in the creaky double bed. She'd be swept up in a frenzy of lust. But did she really want to go there again?

She thought about Rhett Butler in *Gone with the Wind*, one of her favorite old movies. Her girlfriends joked that she used the movie as a guide for life. She thought about the fictional Rhett, carrying the torch for the stubborn Scarlett O'Hara, hoping that she'd finally get over her crush on Ashley Wilkes. In the movie's climactic scene, Scarlett finally realizes that she loves Rhett. But he tells her that it's too late, that even the most passionate love can wither and die. Today she felt kind of like Rhett. In the three years since she and Jake had split up, she'd pined over him, refusing to look at the relationship in a realistic light. But being with Jake for the tumultuous day and night had revived her doubts. She saw a handsome, basically decent man, but one who'd gotten spoiled by the limelight and constant attention from women. Would she have to compete with other women and get her heart broken again? She wasn't ready to admit she was done with him. She only knew she was relieved to be by herself in the quiet room, stretched out alone in the bed while life whirled by outside on the freeway. She pulled up the thin white sheets and closed her eyes for a few delicious hours of sleep.

CHAPTER 33

STATE SENATOR FROM FREDERICKSBURG KILLED; CHAMPION OF THE GERMAN TEXAS MOVEMENT

By Brandon McGill and Travis Dunbar
Houston Times Reporters

AUSTIN – Samuel Barker Wurzbach, owner of a prominent Hill Country bakery and a state senator from Fredericksburg who championed the nascent German-Texas movement, died early Wednesday after a sniper attack outside the Grey Moss Inn near San Antonio.

Wurzbach, 41, a Democrat, twice elected to the Texas Legislature, had served for four years and was vice-chairman of the key appropriations committee. He was fatally shot while hosting a party to raise money for a controversial campaign to get a ten-county Hill Country area designated as German Texas.

Authorities, still combing the scene of the shooting, said on Sunday they have no suspects. They vowed an intensive statewide investigation.

"Sam Wurzbach put his energy into making Texas a better place and honoring the contributions of tens of thousands of Texans who came here from Germany," State Senator Jake Satterfield, a Democrat from Kerrville and a close legislative ally, said today. "He will be missed terribly."

"There was no better citizen of Texas than Sam," Fredericksburg Mayor Joe Schuler said. "He was the author and chief advocate of a far-sighted plan that would greatly increase jobs and visitors to Fredericksburg and the entire Hill Country."

Wurzbach had located his German Bakery stores throughout the Hill

Country and had expanded the chain considerably in recent years. The business currently employs about 900 across the state. He started the enterprise in Fredericksburg ten years ago using his German-born ancestors' recipes for strudel and other traditional desserts.

"With his considerable energy and drive, he created a strong new business in an area that needed it badly," Schuler said. "With family members continuing at the helm of the business, his legacy will survive."

Wurzbach's proposal for German Texas would earmark millions of dollars for a cultural and tourist center to recognize the contributions of hundreds of thousands of Texans who emigrated from Germany in the 1800s. He envisioned German language teaching in the schools, German signage on streets and highways, and a program to attract German industries to job-starved areas of the Hill Country.

Texas Ranger Mark Ingram said Wurzbach's attacker apparently hid in the hills behind the restaurant and waited to strike in the darkness as the state senator was preparing to speak to the gathering. Ingram said authorities believe that whoever hit Wurzbach once in the chest with a high-powered rifle was a skilled marksman.

"There will be a significant reward offered through the German-Texas community for details leading to an arrest," Ingram noted.

More than 700 partygoers had filled the Grey Moss Inn to raise money for the German-Texas cause. Much of the activity, including a band and dancing, took place on the patio area behind the legendary restaurant. Police said Wurzbach's assailant must have gotten details of the event in advance because he or she was able to escape undetected.

Emergency workers rushed to the scene, but attempts by paramedics to revive Wurzbach were unsuccessful. He died soon after arriving at the San Antonio Medical Center, authorities said.

The killing of Wurzbach could be a crippling blow for the German-Texas movement, Satterfield said. The Fredericksburg politician had raised awareness for his initiatives, but hadn't consolidated enough legislative support and was raising money for a long-term campaign.

Wurzbach was a graduate of the University of Texas, who majored in business before returning to Fredericksburg and starting the bakery business.

He leaves a wife, Marie, and three daughters at home. Two brothers, two sisters and three uncles in Fredericksburg also survive him. He'll be buried Tuesday in the town's German cemetery after a 2 p.m. service at the German Lutheran Church in Austin.

•

CHAPTER 34

Travis dropped off Annie at her house late afternoon Sunday. They hadn't talked much on the way back from Austin to Houston. She reckoned that Travis still felt shell-shocked. She was worried about the complexity of reporting that awaited them on Monday.

Annie really wanted to talk to Matt Sharpe. Spending time with Jake before and after the shooting had been emotionally exhausting. She was eager to visit Matt at his peaceful apartment, get the detective's take on the shooting and perhaps go out for a relaxing dinner. She'd texted him about her return and suggested getting together. He'd said he wasn't working and would love to see her. She thought she'd surprise him, so she drove quickly to his Montrose apartment, ran up the stairs and used a key he'd given her recently to unlock the door.

She opened it and immediately realized she'd made a mistake. The view from the door of his studio apartment left no doubt that he was entertaining a female visitor and they'd probably just had sex. She almost slammed the door and left, but curiosity took over. Matt was sitting up shirtless in his bed, his arm encircling an attractive woman with dark curly hair and distinctive eyebrows. She leaned casually on his shoulder in what looked like a contented post-coital languor. Both appeared to be naked, though they were partly covered with a sheet. Annie thought with a pang that they seemed very comfortable together. Matt looked surprised, but not terribly bothered, by Annie's appearance. She couldn't immediately place the woman, though she looked familiar. Something about her shocked expression at Annie's appearance also held an element of triumph.

"Annie, come in and we'll talk. Why didn't you call?" Matt said. "You probably remember Monica Gardiner, the officer I introduced you to that night at the Texas Girls Club."

"Hi, Annie," Monica said. "I know this is extremely awkward. Sorry. I'll be out of here as soon as I get dressed." She grabbed clothes from the floor and padded to the bathroom, carrying them in a bundle in front to cover her nudity.

Annie realized she felt regretful, but wasn't really surprised, to see the two police officers in bed together. She'd sensed a connection at the strip club, watching them talk across the room. With a reporter's instincts, she could usually detect when a man and a woman were lovers just by observing their behavior. She blamed herself for refusing to acknowledge the electricity between Matt and Monica when she met the policewoman. Since she'd gotten to know Matt, she'd let her guard down. He got out of bed, looking resigned to a confrontation.

"Let's go talk on the balcony, Annie," he said, pulling on his pants and a shirt. "Want me to get you a beer?"

She shook her head and walked out the balcony's sliding door, settling herself in a plastic chair facing the backyard trees. It was better than looking toward the apartment where she knew Monica would be scrambling to dress and make herself presentable before leaving. Matt came out carrying a cold beer and took his time to settle into the chair beside her. He wore an appropriately serious expression, but she didn't detect any remorse. If she interpreted his reaction correctly, it was one of irritation with her for barging in unannounced. His next words confirmed that impression.

"I'm sorry that you didn't at least let me know that you were on your way," he said. "I would have gotten Monica out of here."

"I'm just surprised that she's here, since you knew I was coming this afternoon," Annie said, trying for an even tone. "What's your relationship with her?"

"We've seen each other on and off since I separated from Sue," Matt said. "Well, to be perfectly honest, I was seeing her during the last year of my marriage. Sue found out about it and threw me out."

"Is she single?"

"She's married to another cop. He's a nice guy in the robbery division," he said with no trace of irony. "They have a couple of kids."

"What're your intentions?" Annie thought without humor that she probably sounded like the gun-toting father of a pregnant teenager.

"She's not going to leave her husband or family to be with me, if that's what you mean."

"Her behavior seems incredibly stupid," Annie said. "Why would she endanger her marriage to be with you?"

"It's just a sex thing," Matt said quickly. "And we look out for each other on the job. She's a good police buddy."

"You mean a good fuck-buddy?" Annie didn't like that crude term, but in this case, it seemed to fit.

"Call it whatever you want. Monica's not a bad person."

Annie knew she'd made her share of mistakes but wondered about the policewoman. Why would someone lucky enough to find a good husband and father for her children jeopardize something that precious? How many single women wasted their fertile years searching for a decent man?

"Is she the only woman you're sleeping with besides me?" Annie asked.

"Well, to be honest, no," Matt said. "I've been seeing another woman who's a little older than me."

"Is she married too?"

"Yeah, her husband travels a lot," he said. "She's a librarian and she gets lonely when he's away. She says I'm good for her because she's more interested in sex than her husband."

"At the risk of sounding judgmental, that's sad and wrong," Annie said.

"There's a lot of that going around these days," Matt said. "Women want what they want."

"That may be," Annie said. "But what about you? Don't you want something better for yourself? Why would you want to waste your limited time with married women who're just using you for sex?"

"Is that so bad?" he said. "What's wrong with playing the field?"

"Where does that leave us?" She knew she probably wouldn't like the answer.

She could see him hesitate, perhaps trying to spare her feelings.

"I've enjoyed getting to know you, Annie," he said. "You're a wonderful girl, but I'm not ready for a relationship now, or maybe ever again. I stayed married way too long."

"I'm not saying that I'm looking for marriage, or even a long-term relationship with you," Annie said. "But I don't want to be part of someone's harem."

"That's a little harsh. Three women is hardly a harem," Matt said. "I never asked you to be exclusive."

"I know. Wish I hadn't seen you and Monica together," she said. "It just spoils it for me. I'm guessing you're not going to give her up."

"I'm not leaning in that direction," he said. "But why give me up?"

"It's obvious we don't see this in the same way," she said. "Let's just say goodbye, Matt."

She stood up, sorry she couldn't stay. The view at dusk on Matt's balcony was one of the best she'd found in Houston. She'd enjoy sitting there for another hour, drinking more of the Scotch that burned her throat, and making love as the lights flicked on across the city. Monica had slipped out while she and Matt were talking. It was time for her to leave, too. Better to do it fast, like pulling off a scab. She walked back through the apartment, glancing at the crumpled sheets on the bed and leaving her key on the kitchen counter. She opened the door and shut it gently behind her.

CHAPTER 35

Zogu steered the borrowed van into the parking lot at the Texas Girls Club off the Gulf Freeway. He hadn't been there since the *Houston Times* reporter was found dead behind the club two weeks ago. The police had called it murder and he'd wondered about what really happened, knowing that his boss, Kyle Krause, hated the news media almost as much as he feared the local cops. Would Krause really have the nerve to kill a reporter? Zogu didn't think so, though he could easily visualize Juliana Souza bashing in someone's head without a second thought.

It was Juliana the girls had to win over today, and Zogu was jittery about what might happen. Beside him in his brother-in-law's beat-up van was Genta, calm and lovely as usual, with their nine Albanian girls: Leka, Ardita, Edona, Afrodita, Elvana, Rita, Mimoza, Vera and Bora. A couple of weeks ago, they'd been nothing more than a crew of unruly girls to him. Now despite his resolve to stay aloof, he knew them all by their names, their looks, their favorite foods and their capacity for making trouble. Elvana and Afrodita, for instance, were the risk takers he'd really had to watch. They'd sneaked out to a bar one night last week, met two truckers and spent the night with them in a nearby motel before straggling back shamefaced the next day. Since then, he'd put them in different rooms and monitored their movements more stringently. Vera and Bora were the youngest, just eighteen, and they seemed the most homesick for their families back in Albania. Mimoza was the prettiest, slender with Barbie-doll proportions and big blue eyes. Rita had a fiery temper, knew more swear words in Albanian than most sailors and quarreled frequently with her more attractive cousin, Ardita. Leka was still his favorite. She was the smartest with the most assertive personality. She was the leader they all wanted to follow.

He'd visited their motel rooms every day with groceries and other supplies and marveled at the incredible progress Genta was making in rehabilitating them. Under her exacting tutelage, they'd metamorphosed from loud and messy to polite and orderly – well, most of the time. His wife worked miracles through the sheer force of her will. The girls were afraid of disappointing her and igniting her sudden, lightning-blast temper. Zogu could relate; he felt the same way. Right now she was looking at him inquiringly.

"Let me speak to the girls for a moment before we go inside the club," she said in a low voice.

Zogu parked in front of the club and turned off the van's ignition. It was nearly 2 p.m., two hours before the club officially opened for customers. Krause and Juliana had scheduled this time to see each girl dance before deciding where to place them. It was essentially an audition. He couldn't begin to guess what might happen if any of the girls failed to measure up. What would become of them? Would Krause keep his bargain to find a place for all of them? Above all, would he pay Zogu what he'd promised? Since it was the first time he'd brought over girls from Albania, he wasn't sure what was supposed to happen next. He knew that in the past, Krause had gotten dancers through the Russian Mafia. But he felt that if he asked too many questions about those shadowy deals, he'd risk Krause's anger.

Genta had finished her coffee and he could see her preparing to speak. She half-turned and blew the little whistle she wore around her slender neck while she was training them. The girls filled three rows of seats behind her. They'd been talking and laughing among themselves, but they immediately became quiet. She spoke English mixed with Albanian, since she'd discovered that most of the girls remembered bits of English from elementary and high school days. Leka, the star student, had worked for two years as a maid at a tourist hotel in Tirana. She was nearly fluent in English.

"Girls, we have worked hard for two weeks in anticipation of this day. This is the time for you to look your best – and to dance your best," she said. "Your hair and makeup are perfect, your clothes are nice and we have practiced our dance steps enough that you should know them well."

She paused, fixing her magnetic gaze on each of them in turn. As usual, Zogu could see that they were spellbound – and so was he. What a woman she was!

"Please remember that you are dancers, an honorable trade. You can perform with grace and show your beautiful bodies without losing your dignity," she said. "You must always act mysterious and a bit out of reach.

Men will value you more and give you bigger tips if you hold yourselves apart from them."

The girls nodded sagely, taking in Genta's message of empowerment. Zogu was proud of his wife and her wisdom, but also baffled. Would her advice work in a strip club where things could get down and dirty awfully fast? Could the girls refuse the salacious imperatives of the VIP room? It was all too confusing. He found himself hoping that Genta's words would help keep the girls hopeful and unsullied. He didn't like the thought of them being pawed by drunken refinery workers and pot-bellied old men. But he'd worked in the strip clubs too long to ignore their reality. What were they here for, anyway?

The girls cheered and spilled out of the van, carrying their makeup cases containing an abundance of mysterious female paraphernalia. Zogu rang the doorbell and nodded to Bobo Simmons, the club's sleazy bouncer. He hated the tattooed, ill-tempered giant with a passion he reserved for the worst of Texas rednecks. He glared at Bobo for leering at Genta and the girls before he directed them to dressing rooms behind the stage. Zogu's dirty look didn't seem to faze the bouncer. He just led Zogu to the table where Krause and Juliana waited.

In contrast with the curt behavior Zogu recalled from their previous meeting, Krause rose and shook his hand. Juliana threw a half-smile in his direction before motioning for him to sit down at their table.

"Time to see if this little investment pays off," Krause said. "Hope the girls are up to the challenge."

"My wife Genta has worked very hard with the girls," Zogu said. "They are all blondes now and looking good. They know dance steps and many English words."

"Bring them out as a group and let's look at them all together first," Juliana said. Though she was a shade friendlier, Zogu resented that she directed everything at him as an order and never said please.

"Of course," Zogu said. He tipped his head and walked backstage.

Genta had picked out all of the music, so he would tell the deejay what to play for each girl's performance. Zogu watched with pride as they paraded onstage in a group, smiling and waving. Genta and her two friends had helped the girls select cheap but attractive clothes to show to advantage their physical attributes. Mostly, they were decked out in short black skirts, flattering tops that revealed some décolletage, and sexy black heels. Each girl took a turn strolling down the runway, pausing, smiling and turning around, displaying a rear view before disappearing offstage. Zogu could see Genta directing things on the sidelines.

It reminded Zogu of the carefully scripted beauty contests his wife enjoyed on TV, like the Miss America pageant. What would these girls have to do next? Twirl fire batons, model bathing suits or convince a host that they really wanted to save the world? The girls were trying so hard, he realized with a pang of admiration mixed with guilt. But at least it appeared to be paying off. Krause and Juliana looked impressed.

"Your wife should work as a beauty pageant consultant," Juliana said. "These girls look so much better than when I first saw them."

Now it was time for each girl to strut and dance on the runway, as she'd do at whatever place she'd be assigned to work. Genta had decided that Zogu's favorite, Leka, would go first because her natural confidence would give the other girls courage.

The deejay shouted her name into the microphone, his reedy voice resounding through the room. Leka thrust herself into the spotlight and Zogu was thrilled at her transformation. Gone was the girl he'd despaired over with the muddy complexion, unibrow and wobbly thighs. Her honey-blond hair fell in soft curls below her neck, her artfully embellished brown eyes looked enormous and her legs were long and toned. Genta had been especially impressed with Leka's self-discipline. She'd dieted conscientiously and excelled at tedious boot-camp exercises like planks and squats. She looked like she'd lost ten pounds and gained muscle in all the right places.

She danced un-self-consciously and smoothly, stripping down to a black girdle-like garment and shedding her black bra at the end. Her performance came across as provocative, but somehow escaped looking sleazy. The other girls, taking it in anxiously from the wings, applauded with gusto. Leka dipped her head modestly before bounding offstage with her winsome smile.

One after another, the other girls danced and stripped with varying degrees of proficiency and style. Throughout their abbreviated appearances, Zogu tried to decipher the reactions of Juliana and Krause. Juliana scribbled a continuous stream of notes and Krause conferred with her in whispers. By the end, they both looked slightly glazed, but had given a decent amount of attention to each girl's performance.

Finally, to Zogu's relief, the music ended and the stage was empty. Krause asked Zogu to bring the girls out again for a last look. Genta appeared with the group and he proudly introduced her. The girls arranged themselves around the stage and smiled hopefully. He could see Bobo loitering at the side of the room to leer at their legs.

"So this is the woman who runs the Albanian charm school," Juliana said to Genta in the snarky tone Zogu hated.

"All of these girls have given their best to please you," Genta said. She waited for Juliana to speak.

"Here's what we've decided," Juliana said. She pointed to Leka, Mimoza and Afrodita. "These girls will dance at this club six days a week. They can stay in a room of the apartment we own near here."

She motioned to Elvana, Ardita, Rita, Edona, Bora and Vera.

"These six will go to our ranch in the Hill Country and work for a year or so," she said. "Then they'll be free to try out again for our clubs or do whatever they want."

The room suddenly went silent. Zogu looked at Genta for guidance, but couldn't glean anything from her expression. In their negotiations, Krause and Juliana had never mentioned the ranch. Genta pursed her lips and nodded, a signal for Zogu to speak. He saw the girls glance at each other with unspoken but urgent questions.

"Shouldn't the girls all stay together?" Zogu said. "They need each other to get used to a different country and a new life."

"There's no place for all of these girls at our clubs yet," Juliana said. "Their dancing and their looks are not top of the line, but they will get their chance later."

"What would they do at your ranch?" Genta asked. "They're city girls, not used to farm work."

"We will find something for them to do," Juliana said. "They can help with household work, tend the animals or help us in other ways. They must earn their keep."

Zogu didn't like this at all and he could see uncertainty in some of the girls' faces and anger in others. One of the girls, the younger one named Vera looked like she was about to cry. They'd come from Albania hoping for glamour and, if not riches, at least solvency. They'd all worked hard to learn to dance, not tend cattle.

"All of these girls must work to repay the money we pledged to bring them from Albania," Krause said. "The dancers won't be given a salary yet, but can earn money in tips. We will provide them with IDs and help with costumes."

"When we get the girls to the ranch, we'll give them more instruction about our needs there," Juliana told Zogu and Genta. "Take it or leave it."

Zogu nodded and Genta helped the girls gather their belongings.

"I'll pick up the girls tomorrow morning at 9 o'clock and drive them to the ranch," Juliana said. "They will enjoy their life in the beautiful Hill Country."

On the way back to the motel, Leka sat with a comforting arm around her cousin Vera. Zogu knew that the two were close. Vera was petite, with chin-length, platinum-colored hair and a perpetually frightened look. She'd been so tense during the audition that she hadn't done well.

"Zogu, you must think of a plan to change this," Leka told him in her usual decisive tone. "If they must go to the ranch tomorrow, we need to think about how to get them back soon. Vera and Bora are only eighteen."

"It's not that simple," he said. "It is true that the money must be paid back."

Zogu tried not to panic as he wove through the proliferating afternoon traffic. He was worried about the girls, but also concerned that Genta would blame him if Krause and Juliana didn't come through with their final payment.

He knew in his heart that whatever went on at the ranch was unsavory. He'd heard rumors about how girls were used there, but didn't know if the stories were true. He'd delivered girls there, but had left them just inside the guard gate as instructed. He knew it was forbidden to linger, or to ask questions.

CHAPTER 36

The next morning, Vera was the last of six reluctant girls to board the van headed to the ranch. Leka could see that behind the wheel, Juliana was tapping her foot and scowling, but she didn't try to rush them.

Leka, at least a head taller than Vera, practically smothered her cousin in a parting hug. How could she let Vera go, after she'd promised her mother and her aunt that she'd look after the younger girl? She smiled and tried to concentrate on keeping the inner turmoil off her face. Otherwise, she'd just add to Vera's angst.

"Bye, little one," she told her. "You will be in my heart and we will talk every day."

She'd given Vera her cheap cell phone, which she'd convinced Zogu to buy for her at a bread-and-beer store near the motel. She hated to give it up because it was the girls' emergency link, but she'd get another as soon as she danced her way into some tips. She'd hide some of her money for emergency purchases, including a phone.

Leka could tell Vera was trying to act brave, but she looked heartbreakingly tiny waving from the van. Dressed in jeans and a T-shirt, she'd fitted her pitifully small bundle of belongings into a compact duffle bag. She sat in the far back seat. All six of the departing girls waved to Leka, putting on the jaunty front she'd advised last night.

"Don't let the cold-hearted Juliana see that you are afraid," she'd told them. "Stay together and pretend you are happy to be going to her place. She will treat you better."

She'd instructed Vera to call her at the motel when they arrived at the ranch, which Leka had heard was located about three hours from Houston. After the van disappeared, she fretted as she washed her clothes in the laundry room and tried to get Mimoza and Afrodita to help her clean. She could tell they were also despondent, though they didn't talk about the other girls. The three of them would be leaving the motel today, moving to a room in the house that Mr. Krause owned near the club.

Nearly four hours after the van left, the motel phone finally rang. Leka was pleased that Vera sounded less frightened and even a little excited. They'd arrived at the ranch, which she described as beautiful, with nice-looking buildings and lots of trees. Vera and the five other girls were headed to the dining room.

"How was your trip, little one?" Leka said.

"Good. We went through a gate with guards," she said. "They were very friendly to Ms. Juliana, treating her like the big boss. We could see a fence all around the property. The guards let everyone in and out."

"Has Ms. Juliana treated you properly?"

"She's trying to act nice, but she watches everything we do. I think she's afraid that we'll escape," Vera said.

"Has she told you what you'll be doing at the ranch?"

"She says she will explain our duties after our lunch. I have a room…" She trailed off and Leka heard some noise in the background that sounded like a struggle.

"Please give my phone back," Leka heard her cousin say in a pleading tone. Then someone disconnected the call. Vera was gone.

CHAPTER 37

Betsy Marr peered from behind the stage as a woman the deejay had introduced as Leka finished her dance routine at the start of the happy-hour shift. She hadn't met her yet, but Betsy was struck by Leka's poise and graceful moves. The blonde dancer was tall with pretty legs and a nice smile. She might be close to Betsy's age, unlike some of the other dancers who looked decades older and kind of hard. Something about Leka's turned-up eyes looked appealingly foreign, like the glamorous Russian models Betsy had seen in fashion magazines and on TV shows. She was sure she wouldn't ever meet anybody like Leka on the poky streets of Marfa. Coming from West Texas, where everyone was either Anglo or Mexican, Betsy was intrigued by the international flavor of Houston. Patrick had taken her to Chinatown recently, south of the fancy downtown area, for a lunch of spicy chicken skewers with peanut sauce. She had been surprised that so many Chinese and Vietnamese people lived in Houston. Patrick told her that the hot, humid climate reminded them of their Asian homelands. Houston was the biggest and most exotic city she'd ever seen, so much more exciting than San Antonio. She'd gone to the Alamo City a few times with her dad. The Alamo was sweet, the river walk was fun, but Houston seemed more like a place where important things happened every day in those amazing skyscrapers.

The Texas Girls Club wasn't exactly empty, but Betsy counted only about twenty people in the big room – all men, naturally – drinking at scattered tables near the stage. A small audience suited her just fine. This was her first shift at the Texas Girls Club and a big, rowdy crowd was the last thing she wanted. Her legs felt rubbery, and despite the wheezy air-conditioning, her forehead was clammy with sweat around her hairline. A half-hour ago, Patrick had dropped her off in his black pickup, turning away her pleas to stay for a while during her first shift.

"Baby, you've got a job to do, so put on your big-girl pants," he grinned, giving her a big smacking kiss on the mouth and leaning across her to open the passenger door at the club's front door.

"I'd feel better if you were with me." She waited until the last possible moment to get out.

"They don't want boyfriends hanging around," he assured her. "You'll just be distracted. You need to focus on the big tippers in the audience. You know we need the money."

"What're you going to do while I'm gone?" she asked.

"The band will probably practice for a while at Donnie's," he said. "Maybe go out for a few beers afterwards. Call my cell and I'll pick you up whenever you're done."

She wasn't happy to hear that. Donnie was the least attractive of Patrick's friends, kind of a no-manners cowboy who began every sentence with the words fuck or shit. Betsy was no prude, but she didn't care for his constant stream of profanities. Donnie lived in an unbelievable pigsty of a garage apartment and always had slutty-looking girls hanging around. She'd been over there a couple of times and the girls would flirt shamelessly with Patrick, right in front of her. Of course, her handsome boyfriend was the best-looking member of the band, no doubt about it. But she didn't want to get into a fight with him about Donnie.

"Okay," she said. "Wish me luck."

"Honey, you'll be great," he said. "The customers will go crazy over those boobs." He waved as he speeded up and drove away, looking sexy with his newly trimmed black beard.

Now she was walking out onstage and she'd better not think about Patrick or anything except swaying seductively to the thumping rock music she'd chosen. She'd heard the deejay announce her made-up name, Sugar, and that was her cue to get out there and prove herself. Her jittery lips made it hard, but she somehow managed a half-smile. She'd dressed in a black lace mini-dress she thought was kind of sexy and she could tell right away that most of the men liked the way she looked. She saw a couple of them nudge each other and nod.

She just danced the way she'd learned with her friends, mostly by going to the boring school dances in junior high. She shimmied and shook a lot, avoiding fancy footwork. It wasn't anything special, but she could tell the men were watching every move she made. A lot of them were focused on her breasts.

The tempo of the music speeded up and she unzipped the dress, pulling it over her head while trying to keep a slow wiggle going in her hips. She couldn't do it as gracefully as the girls she'd watched earlier, but she guessed that came with practice. She was wearing red satin tap pants, which were kind of like low-slung boxer shorts, with a matching lacy tank. A few of the younger men whistled and cheered, which gave her more confidence for the second number. It was slower, and she took her time, shrugging off her red tank top and bra to reveal the blue pasties that sort of covered her nipples.

It gave her a funny feeling deep in her stomach to show her breasts, but it wasn't as bad as she'd feared. Several men whooped and hollered and a few came up and shoved bills in her tap pants or laid them on the stage. She smiled, feeling shy but pleased they'd liked her. She picked up the bills, her garments and bounced offstage. She didn't really know what to do next, so she ambled into the dressing room and found her pink terrycloth robe.

There were about ten women in there, and she caught the eye of Leka and her posse, two girls with the same foreign look around their eyes. She smiled at them encouragingly and was rewarded with friendly looks. Leka conferred with them briefly and they all came over to introduce themselves.

"You are Sugar, no?" Leka said in foreign-accented English. She shook hands with Betsy and introduced the other girls, Afrodita and Mimoza. They smiled and said hello, but not much else. Leka explained that they didn't speak much English yet, but added, "They will be your friends, like me."

"My real name is Betsy," she told Leka. "This is my first day. I was really scared out there."

"I know how you are feeling. We all were scared when we started working two days ago," Leka said. "Are you a Texan?"

"Yeah, from West Texas," said Betsy. "Came to Houston with my boyfriend. Where are you from?"

"Tirana, in the country of Albania," Leka said with pride.

Betsy didn't even know where Albania was, but Leka explained so that she kind of understood, though her grasp of geography was hazy. She listened eagerly to Leka's story about their journey to Houston hiding as stowaways. She'd never heard anything so exciting from girls her age. She sat with them at a rickety table in the corner of the dressing room, feeling that she'd finally found some friends. They seemed so much nicer than the nasty girls she'd met at Donnie's house. What a crazy trip the Albanian girls had been through hiding on a ship to Houston. She promised she wouldn't tell anyone about it. She felt sorry for them when Leka told her about her cousin and the others who'd been sent to a ranch in the Hill Country. She'd lived on her dad's ranch all her life and knew that it was hard work and not at all glamorous.

She reveled in the girls' companionship until a large woman butted in by clapping her hands and shouting orders in Spanish. She scolded that they needed to get in line because they'd all be dancing again soon. The girls on shift duty would take turns performing on stage, giving Betsy and the others more opportunities to dance as new customers arrived.

"That's Mrs. Jimenez," Leka told her. "Be careful around her and do what she says. She is very mean."

"And stay away from Bobo, the man who guards the door and looks at you with evil in his eyes. He will try to touch you." Leka grimaced and her friends wrinkled their noses with distaste.

Every time she left the stage, Betsy gravitated toward Leka and her friends. They giggled about some of the older men in the audience and exchanged more stories about their lives. Leka translated to the girls so they could all participate in the conversation. It was nice to have someone her own age to explain how things worked. She wasn't sure she totally understood the club's operation. There seemed to be unwritten rules in this strange world. She'd looked, every time she was onstage, for Mr. Krause, the owner who'd been so nice to her. But he wasn't in the audience.

Midnight approached and Betsy ached all over from dancing, smiling and standing for so many hours. Mrs. Jiminez told her to punch her time card and leave. She put on jeans, packed her duffle bag and called Patrick to pick her up.

He pulled into a parking space and opened the passenger door. She sank into the passenger seat, so glad to sit down. She could smell the acrid marijuana and sour beer on his breath across the seat, which she resented after working all night. But she decided not to say anything. She didn't have the energy for a fight.

"Well, babe, how much did you make?" He said eagerly.

She hadn't added up the pile of crumpled bills she'd stuck in her purse. She rummaged around and counted it.

"It's $276 dollars," she said proudly.

"That's a start, but not great for a whole night," he said. "You've got to do better than that for us to be able to stay in the fancy motel you picked out."

"I thought you'd be so happy," she said in a small voice.

"Houston's music scene is slow right now," he said. "Just worried about money. Might have to do a couple of months on a rig, or go back to Greece for a while. I don't want to have to leave you."

"Well, if you don't blow it on pot or booze, we should be okay."

"Don't nag me, Bets. I won't put up with it."

"Can't you see I'm dead on my feet?" She wasn't going to smooth things over for once. "Just get me out of here."

CHAPTER 38

Lila Jo's luck had been remarkably consistent that night at the poker game. She and Travis had found the fancy host house on a Memorial-area street where about half the 1960s ranch-style houses had been torn down to make way for grander two-stories festooned with columns, stone accents and three-car garages. Travis hated neighborhoods that looked neither one way or another, that were always in process of becoming something else. But he understood the impulse for transformation, even though it didn't always result in improvement.

For the past couple of weeks, both he and Lila Jo had lost money most of the nights they'd ventured out to private games. But tonight she'd bested everyone at the table and was taking home close to $1,000 in cold cash. He'd won a few hundred, after a long losing streak. Normally, Lila Jo would be taking celebratory swigs of bourbon, but she'd left the good stuff on the table and had sipped Diet Dr. Pepper all night. She seemed less animated than usual and didn't make her usual jokes about beginner's luck.

They said their goodbyes to the boisterous group and Travis drove the fifteen or so miles to his apartment on the north side. Was she angry with him? He opened the door and stepped aside for Lila Jo in a faux-ceremonious bow, expecting her to make some kind of wisecrack about his gallantry. But she rewarded him only with an absent-minded smile.

"Wow, you blew everyone away at the table," Travis said, puzzled by her silence. "Thought you'd be on Cloud Nine."

She turned and looked him over slowly, as if she were trying to make up her mind about something. He feared that she was about to call it quits, that she realized she could do better than a short, financially-strapped journalist who wasn't all that good at poker. He dreaded her next words and hoped that if it were a kiss-off, she'd make it mercifully quick. Instead she appeared to want to drag it out.

"Travy, let's sit down for a moment and talk," she said in her usual pleasant drawl. He tensed up, but sat down on one of his two folding chairs.

"Sweetie Pie, I'm pregnant. I know that's the last thing you expected to hear from this old babe, but there it is."

"Well, damn, Lila Jo." He was shocked. "I thought you said you and Beebe couldn't have children."

"I guess Beebe couldn't, but you, on the other hand, apparently are prime daddy material," she smiled. "To tell the truth, I thought I was past all that, since I just turned 45. In fact, I went to the doc thinking he'd tell me I'd gone into menopause."

He didn't know what to say, but he felt a surprised tingle of excitement.

"When did you go to the doctor?"

"Yesterday. He did a test, felt around in there and said I was nearly three months gone."

"How do you feel about it?" He asked, putting a hand on her stomach. It felt warm under her black top and by no means flat. But then it'd always looked slightly poochy, which he'd never minded.

"Baby, I'm thrilled," she said. "I always wanted a child, or two, or six. I just didn't think it would ever happen. My luck's usually like the girl's who fell into a barrel of peckers and came up sucking her own thumb."

He guffawed, sensing that she was trying to deflect tension from her announcement.

"Where'd you get that one?"

"My cousin Ida Mae from Vidor. She always had the dirtiest mouth in the family. Think she ended up peddling her ass at a truck stop."

She settled back on the sofa, looking happier than he'd ever seen her.

"Beebe and I tried for fifteen years, working with the best doctors he could buy at the Medical Center. We knew we had some issues, but no matter whatever crazy procedure we tried, it didn't work. It was one reason why we split up – it brought out the worst in our relationship."

"So you want to have it, or I guess I should say her, or him?"

"Oh, yeah," she said. "But you don't have to be a part of it. I know that this wasn't part of our deal."

"But I think I'd like to be part of it," he said. "It's my kid, too."

"I'm seventeen years older than you, honey," she said. "I don't think you know what you're getting into. What would your mama and daddy think? They don't even know about us."

"I don't care what anyone thinks," he said. "I love you. I know that we started out as poker buddies, but don't you think we've grown into a lot more than that?"

"Sweetie, I love you, too, but you're a highfalutin' journalist," she said. "I'm just a country girl from Tyler. I don't even have a college degree, just a silly real estate license."

"You're as smart as any woman I've ever met," he said, putting an arm around her waist. "Would Beebe give you a divorce?"

"I think so," she said. "There hasn't been much going on between us in the last couple of years. I could probably sell the house in Katy pretty fast and offer to split the profits and go away."

"Would you marry me?"

"Whoa, guy," she smiled. "Lemme get the divorce first."

"We'll have to give up our poker games," Travis said. "I can't keep losing money. In fact, I probably need a better job."

His mind flew ahead six months, thinking about everything he needed to do before he became a father.

"One thing at a time," she said, her smile fading. "I'm like that leopard, can't change my spots overnight. Neither can you. Besides, you know I make money setting up the games."

"Maybe I can get a promotion," Travis said. "I'll talk to Annie about it tomorrow."

"Sweetie, can we go to bed now? We don't need to figure out everything tonight. I'm craving the chance to stretch out on your nice air mattress."

"Sure, Lila Jo." His head was swirling with ideas. He was surprised at how happy he felt. He'd never thought of Lila Jo as a potential wife, but he realized that she just might be everything he wanted.

CHAPTER 39

Annie looked up in surprise at the front of her glassed-in office. It was only 9:30 and reporters usually ambled into the newsroom after 10 a.m. But there was Travis, knocking on her door, looking showered, combed and happier than he reasonably should be at such an early hour. She motioned him in.

"Hey, Trav," she smiled. "What can I do for you?"

"Got a minute? I know it's early, but I wanted to talk to you about my future. I think I got engaged last night."

"You think? Don't you know?"

"Lila Jo is pregnant. And I want to marry her."

Annie stood up, walked around to where he was standing and hugged him. She was surprised, but not exactly shocked, because Travis could be unpredictable, particularly in his personal life. But he looked undeniably jubilant. She'd only met Lila Jo a few times and liked her, but hadn't exactly thought of her as a marriage partner for Travis.

"Congratulations, guy," she said. "Sit down and tell me more. I've got a few minutes before the morning news meeting starts."

"She just told me last night," Travis said. "We want the baby, but Lila Jo has to get divorced before we can get married."

"Yeah, that's the way it usually works," Annie said. "So what are you thinking about your future?"

"Mostly I'm thinking about how poor I am," he grinned. "Wondered if that assistant editor's position is still open in Business?"

"Well, I'm hearing that the Business section has withdrawn the posting. I didn't know you were interested in business reporting. You didn't do it in your previous job, did you?"

"No," Travis said. "To tell the truth, I'm interested in making more money. Moving into editing seems like the quickest way."

"Don't go into editing for the money," she said. "It doesn't pay that much more than reporting and it's got a lot of hassles. I thought you loved the work of a reporter."

"I do," he said. "But I'll have a family to support soon. What's happening with the editing job? Does Business have an internal candidate?"

"No," said Annie. She hated the thought of him moving from Metro, the local news desk, to the newsroom's Business desk. She'd miss him, but it wasn't just that. She hesitated a moment, wondering how much she could say without betraying the managing editor's confidence.

"To be honest, I think they decided not to fill the position because there's going to be a big announcement soon about changes in the newsroom."

"Again? Another round of layoffs?"

"Could be, but it sounds much more extensive than that. Rumors are flying, but the announcement won't be until the end of the week. I'm guessing it might be another change in ownership."

"Whoa," Travis said. "Doesn't sound good."

"Tell you what. What if I let Greg know you might have interest in the assistant business editor's position if it opens back up? Or would you rather talk to him yourself?"

"What day is the announcement?"

"I think the corporate suits will be here Friday morning."

"I can wait a few days," he said. "Thanks for talking to me, Annie. Can you keep what I said about Lila Jo under wraps for now?"

"Of course, Trav. Mum's the word. Literally, perhaps."

He smiled at her feeble attempt at humor and left, headed in the direction of the coffee room. He must feel pretty good to come by before he got his first cup of coffee. She was happy for Travis, especially considering he was still mourning the loss of Nate. She made a mental note to talk to Brandon about the progress of Nate's murder investigation. The police still seemed stumped and she felt more than frustrated about it. Then there was Friday's announcement from the bigwigs. She'd tried to be nonchalant about it with Travis, but her synapses all ticked with worry. What would happen next – to her, to Travis and to all the other staffers in the money-starved newsroom? What was left to cut in what was already a bare-bones operation? She looked in her side drawer for her bottle of antacid.

CHAPTER 40

The *Houston Times* newsroom seemed to stop in its tracks when the delegation of California executives got off the fifth-floor elevator. Barry McKnight, the CEO of the *Times'* parent company, McKnight Newspapers, led the delegation that included two other men Annie thought looked like bankers. McKnight, a blond surfer wunderkind who'd metamorphosed into a balding, self-important executive, wore a sober-looking gray suit and blue tie. Annie had seen him a few times previously in more relaxed outfits with a gold chain or two. She thought today's sartorial formality must be a bad sign.

She didn't like McKnight, and it wasn't just for his knack of combining glib California-speak, faux-good messages undergirded with bad news for the *Times* and the other papers his company owned. She didn't think he really understood or cared much about the news business or the communities the company's papers served. She didn't doubt, as he had often reminded them, that the papers' ad revenues and circulation had plummeted for nearly a decade. But he seemed to embrace every crackpot solution that came along, rather than having a sensible, long-term plan. Who knows what he'd say today?

The computer message flashed on her screen that the stand-up meeting was about to begin. She gathered with other editors, reporters, copy editors, and photographers in the center of the newsroom where big announcements and going-away parties took place. Amanda Weeks chatted with McKnight, trying to conceal the strain on her face. Weeks, an attractive woman with short black hair and tall black boots that accentuated her tiny body, was a strong editor-in-chief with an even stronger personality. Annie admired and believed in her proven leadership while steering clear of her changing moods. But she always studied Amanda's moves closely, thinking her somewhat of a role model. Since more than a hundred staffers had gathered, the editor tapped a microphone for quiet.

"Let's all welcome Barry McKnight, our CEO, from California," Amanda said in her clear voice. "He's got some important things to tell us."

"Hey, guys," McKnight said, stepping up to the microphone, his stomach leading the way. "First, I'd like to introduce you to new partners in our newspaper enterprises, Russ Williamson and Cal Parnell of Agamemnon Partners. I'm sure some of you have heard of Agamemnon, the incredibly successful hedge fund started by Russ and Cal ten years ago.

"As you know, we've had some challenging economic times during the four years since McKnight bought the *Houston Times*. We thought the newspaper industry would stabilize, but profits have continued to fall. No one knows when it will bottom out. Things are especially bad in Houston since the collapse of oil prices. Despite city boosters' claims of a more diversified economy than when the big recession ruined the 1980s, Houston's heart still beats on oil. The *Times'* advertising and circulation have suffered tremendously."

"So in the last six months, we've been talking to experts about what to do with our newspapers, especially the *Times*. As a result, Agamemnon Partners has decided to buy the *Times* and make some radical changes. We hope Houston will become a national model for the industry. Now I'll turn the meeting over to Russ."

Annie stood beside Travis and her boss, Managing Editor Greg Barnett, during McKnight's comments. She looked at them without masking the worry she could see they shared. How could this be happening? The *Times* had changed hands less than five years ago. They'd barely had time to get used to McKnight's ownership and the company was dumping them already? They'd seen and reported on what happened to companies acquired by greedy, bottom-fishing hedge funds. The funds seemed interested only in stripping newspapers of their assets, including the most experienced, best-paid staffers, and eventually offloading them.

"Did you know about this?" she whispered to Greg.

"No, I could tell that something was going on, but they've managed to keep it secret," he said with a warning finger to his lips. "Better be quiet and listen."

Russ Williamson, a lean man with a prominent widow's peak in his graying half-pompadour, took the microphone and tried to lighten the leaden atmosphere by beaming at the assemblage. No one smiled back.

"Well, to put it in a nutshell, we're going to attempt something the industry has talked about for several years," he said. "We're going to shut down the daily paper and put our whole focus on the website."

Annie sucked in her breath and looked at Greg and Travis, who appeared as shell-shocked as the rest of the room. There were scattered murmurs, but mostly people waited.

"This is a bold move and it won't be without some pain," he said. "But we'll offer good severance packages, including a week of pay for each year the person has worked at the *Times*."

"Cheapskates," Annie whispered to Greg. "They know that the industry standard is at least two weeks."

Greg raised his hand a few notches and said, "When will the daily paper be shut down?"

"We'll phase in all these changes in the next three months," Williamson smiled.

Why does he keep smiling, Annie wondered. He's either very nervous or an idiot. Can't he see that people's hearts are breaking?

"How many people will be laid off?" she asked.

"You have 223 in the newsroom," Williamson said. "We expect that about eighty will be offered jobs on the website. As you know, previous layoffs have done away with the copy desk and most of the photography staff. But we believe that we can achieve many more economies. Reporters who stay will also take photos and video to stream with their stories.

"We have studied this carefully and believe that print has no future," he said. "People read the newspaper, if at all, mostly on their mobile devices. We will give them what they want – shorter stories, more celebrity news and a very scan-worthy product that won't take up too much of their valuable time."

He still looked pleased with himself, but at least didn't flash another inappropriate smile, Annie thought.

"Of course, we'll have a lot more details over the next couple of months," he added. "We'll post a slate of all new jobs for the website and everyone will need to reapply to be considered. If you're rehired, you'll be part of a ground-breaking experiment in American journalism."

He stepped back and Amanda moved to the microphone.

"I know this is difficult to digest for those of us who've spent our careers at traditional newspapers," she said. Her eyes looked wet, but her voice was steady. "But let's not rush to judgment yet. We still have our jobs for a few months. And those who stay will be part of a national model."

Most staffers drifted away, some stopping to grab a free can of soda or a few cookies from the refreshment table. Some staffers broke into dejected-looking clumps, talking among themselves in low voices.

Annie noticed that Abigail McEwan, a bright, young business reporter, had waited to interview Williamson and McKnight after the meeting. Abigail was taking notes in longhand, her long brown curls bobbing as she asked questions and listened closely. Annie could see that she was hurrying to file a website story about the paper's sale and changes. She wondered what would happen to Abigail. The youngest, lowest-paid journalists were the ones they'd keep in a slimmed-down operation. The young woman likely would land on her feet, but lots of older reporters would be gone.

Greg beckoned Annie and Travis toward his glass office. She went in with Travis and they sat in straight-backed chairs opposite his desk, looking at each other glumly.

"I just wanted to reassure both of you that I'll do what I can to keep you," Greg said. "You're valued members of our staff. But there's no guarantee that I'll be around either."

"I can't believe Houston will lose its only daily newspaper," Travis said. "First the *Post*, then the *Chronicle* disappeared, and now the *Times*. More than our careers are at stake."

"It's terrible for the city," Annie said. "It's incredibly bad for Houston's politics, government and cultural life. Of course, that's not something hedge fund managers would consider."

She thought about other cities where newspapers had moved from daily publication to several times a week – New Orleans, Cleveland and Ann Arbor, Mich. None had lost the whole print product. She felt a lump in her throat. What would happen to journalists like her and Greg who'd grown up with print? Would Travis, the expectant father, survive in the new environment?

CHAPTER 41

Dan Riggins smoked his last cigarette outside the front entrance of the hospital in Ojinaga, Mexico. He hadn't indulged in months, trying to give up the noxious habit for good. But he'd taken a pass today after three days at the bedside of his dying Alicia. The gut-wrenching vigil was almost over. Alicia probably had only a few hours left before she succumbed to the brain tumor.

The nurse had sent him out while she adjusted the morphine drip that was easing Alicia into oblivion. He'd hated to bring her to the hospital, but couldn't keep her pain-free any longer at the rented house a few miles outside of town. The brain tumor had moved quickly and relentlessly in the last few weeks. She'd become seized by nightmares and he couldn't bear to hear her cries in the dark. He could travel around Mexico freely, thanks to a bodyguard provided by his friends in the Zetas. He wasn't afraid of being detained or arrested if he took her anywhere. He'd just wanted her to have a peaceful death at home. But she was past caring now.

He stubbed out the cigarette in the sand around the desert plantings that decorated the walkway. He walked back into the building. The two-story hospital was clean and decent, but its operators weren't wasting their money trying to make it beautiful. The mud-colored adobe exterior of the building blended into the arid landscape in a kind of comforting plainness.

He climbed the tiled stairs, rather than taking the balky elevator, mostly to stretch his legs after hours in a straight chair beside her bed. He walked into the room, saw that the nurse had finished stoking the drip and was tucking Alicia's sheet and blanket around her thin shoulders. His lover's eyes were closed and her body seemed at ease. Dan motioned to the nurse that he'd take over and she bowed and left.

He thought about his and Alicia's life together, separated for long stretches by work but punctuated by rapturous reunions at the West Texas house. In the quarter-century since they'd met in the mountains of Peru, he'd never tired of her company. She'd had occasional affairs with men and women, but he believed what she told him – that he was the only man she'd ever loved.

He listened to her shallow breathing for an hour or so, losing track of time. He dozed off, waking only when the nurse came back, checked Alicia's vital signs and said she was gone.

"*Muchas gracias,*" he said. After signing a required form to retrieve her body later, he left abruptly before the doctor could return to offer condolences.

He sat in his car for a moment before rummaging in his back pocket for his mobile phone. He'd made up his mind what to do after her death, the only thing left that made sense.

Within an hour, Riggins had changed the course of his life. He'd struck the deal he wanted and now he was headed through Marfa, perhaps for the last time. Again, his fake passport was good enough to get him across the border without questions, a blessing in his current state of mind. He'd decided that when he fled Texas four years ago he'd change vehicles often to avoid detection. Today, he drove a dusty white Honda Accord with a large trunk.

It was a clear day in the little town, just 85 degrees with low humidity. He stopped at a convenience store for bottled water, sipping it as he surveyed the quiet landscape and blue sky, treasuring its peace. On impulse, he parked the car on a side street and walked through the downtown area, savoring its understated charm one more time. He strolled into the courtyard of the Hotel Paisano, a restored cattleman's hostelry, and went inside. He remembered one cold winter when the outdoor fountain at the entrance had been crowned with icicles. He knew the look of the sweeping lobby by heart, its cowhide chairs, buffalo heads and original green, gold and orange tile, but he needed to see it again. He admired the pictures and memorabilia from the filming of the 1955 movie, *Giant.* He left the hotel and walked to the restored Presidio County Courthouse. He looked at its pink and beige hues shining in the sun before heading back to his car. It was time to get on with the sad business that had brought him here.

He drove a few miles to the yellow stucco house where Alicia had lived for eighteen years. He'd had so many wonderful times there that he regarded it as home, though he'd never actually lived with her.

He spotted Tom Marr's pickup in the back yard, so he drove there, parked and accepted Marr's hug. He'd called his friend before leaving Ojinaga.

"Buddy, I'm so sorry," Marr said. "Didn't think it would happen so fast. Was Alicia in pain?"

"Kept her comfortable," Riggins said. "Got painkillers from the doc in Ojinaga and later at the hospital. He said the tumor had grown so big before we found it that he couldn't do anything. She knew I would have taken her anywhere for treatment, but she wouldn't allow it. She was tired of running."

"Glad you called right away," Marr said. He pointed to the trunk of the Accord. "Is she in there?"

"Yeah. I'll leave it closed until we dig the grave. It doesn't have to be very deep. She would have wanted a green burial, so I didn't bring a casket."

When Alicia had begged him at the end to bury her body at her house on the property Marr had given him, he'd immediately thought of the leaning oak tree in the back yard. Marr had gone to the house when he called and staked out a gravesite under the lone tree. He'd also brought shovels, so they got to work.

They paused when they heard the sound of an approaching vehicle and put down their shovels to greet Rob Ryland. Riggins's nephew parked his pickup in the driveway and got out, dressed in old jeans and carrying a shovel. He embraced Riggins, apologized profusely for being late and offered his sympathy in a faltering voice. Like most young people, he wasn't comfortable with death, though Riggins remembered that he'd been stoic as a teenager at the funerals of his parents.

"I'm so sorry, Uncle Dan," Rob said. "I was shocked when you called. I didn't know Alicia was that close to the end. She was one of the most alive persons I've ever met."

"Thanks, Rob," Riggins said gruffly. "Let's get this done. You and I will talk later."

After the three men dug a little longer, the plot was ready. Riggins opened the trunk and motioned to Marr. Alicia body's was draped in a cotton shroud and a burial sling, but her soft white hair and her closed eyes were visible. He and Marr each took an end of the sling and carried it to the grave, placing it gently in the arid caliche soil.

"Do you want to say anything?" Riggins asked Marr and Rob. "You know I'm not a religious man, but could you each say a few words? Alicia didn't like most people, but she always felt good about the two of you."

"Dear Lord, please hold close the body and spirit of your daughter Alicia," Marr said. "Forgive her many sins and transgressions. Please give comfort to your son Dan and sustain him in his journeys. And bring my Betsy home. Amen."

"Amen," Riggins said. He didn't even mind when Marr mentioned her sins, though he couldn't bring himself to regard her as sinful. As a skilled assassin, she'd always performed repugnant tasks that needed doing.

"Dear God, please bless Alicia for her bravery and commitment to Texas," Rob said. "Let her rest peacefully on the plot of land she held so dear. Give her a place in heaven alongside the heroes of the Alamo."

"Amen," Riggins said again. Rob had become his surrogate son in the absence of his twin boys, now grown and gone. He'd been thinking about them in the last couple of days. Would he ever see their faces again? He'd even miss his two brothers in San Antonio, who'd taken over his parents' grocery chain and lived the dullest of lives.

He and Rob and Marr all fell silent for a few minutes. The bare-bones funeral had been sobering, especially the sight of Alicia's frail body. They soaked in the stillness, broken only by a bird's solitary song and a car honking in the distance.

After they covered the grave, they went inside the house and washed up. Marr brought out the picnic basket that Maria, his housekeeper, had packed for them. It contained steak sandwiches, fruit salad and cookies. She'd also thoughtfully included a bottle of good red wine.

They toasted Alicia solemnly, clinking the hand-blown, blue wine goblets they found in the cupboard. Alicia had collected unique glassware and pottery during the nearly two decades she'd run a crafts business in San Antonio.

"You said something on the phone about changing your life, Dan," Marr said as they ate. "What's that all about?"

"I couldn't imagine staying in Mexico without Alicia," Riggins said. "I hate that place and I hate my life running from the law. I called some of my old contacts in the CIA and worked a deal."

"What kind of deal?"

"They'll clear up my fugitive status and wipe out all of my legal problems. In exchange, I'll go anywhere they want and work undercover – for as long as I'm physically able," Riggins said. "I'll do whatever I can for them."

Marr whistled. "That's quite a deal. But it's kind of a life sentence in some ways. You sure you want to do that? Where are you going?"

"I'll be leaving for Venezuela in a few days," Riggins said. "Not sure how long I'll be there, but as you know, that country's a big mess. Got to get rid of my stuff in Ojinaga first and tie up loose ends," Riggins said.

"What about this house?" Marr said.

"Save it for Betsy. Alicia would want her to have it. She didn't have anyone left she cared about in Peru."

"When my Betsy comes back, the little house will be hers. I know she'll treasure it," Marr said, his face somber.

"One more thing," Riggins said. "I'm leaving a package for you. The note will explain everything. Just tell the authorities you found it on your doorstep. Don't tell anyone you saw me – or that Alicia is buried here. Who knows what people would do to her grave?"

His chin trembled and he covered it with his hands for a moment. He gave Marr a wobbly smile.

"You got it, buddy," Marr said. "What about the Nation of Texas? They'll miss your leadership. Are you really giving up on Texas secession?"

"Of course not," Riggins said. "That's one reason I invited Rob today. We'll leave you now and go somewhere to talk about what needs to happen."

He hugged Marr again. After a moment, so did Rob. His nephew walked a few feet ahead, giving the two older men time to say goodbye, a lifetime of memories between them.

"Goodbye, Tom. Don't forget my Alicia. Come by and visit her when you can."

"I'll take care of her, Dan. You take care of yourself."

Marr looked over at Rob.

"You know I'm not going to get involved in the Nation of Texas again. But good luck, son, and don't get yourself killed."

CHAPTER 42

Annie sat in her living room with her cats. As usual, Marbles attached himself to her right side on the sofa, as close as he could get without climbing into her lap, while Benjy lounged on the Queen Anne chair across from her. The silky red upholstery probably felt soft and cool, she thought. She didn't care how much black hair the cats left on her sofa and chairs – their silent presence comforted her.

She drank her light beer with its three orange slices slowly, because the single glass would be all she'd have tonight. She'd been fairly successful kicking her nightly wine habit in favor of one beer. It tasted refreshing after the heat of the day.

Today was the first full day of work since Barry McKnight and Agamemnon had announced their plan to shut down the newspaper and shore up the website. Across the country, journalism pundits were still obsessing over the terrible decision to do away with the only daily paper in the nation's fourth largest city. Television news was all over it, with TV reporters doing live shots in front of the building and in the newsroom about the latest nail in the industry's coffin. It was all so depressing.

Annie had gone to the first planning meeting today with top editors discussing how to staff the website-only operation, which would be phased in soon. What really upset her was seeing the faces of the reporters who'd have to fight each other for the small number of jobs that soon would be posted. She'd refused to think much about her own dwindling prospects. But she felt heartsick for so many others, including Travis and his excitement just a few days ago about marriage and fatherhood. He was quietly going about his business, not saying much but looking anxious.

She needed to stop thinking about the whole newspaper catastrophe because she was waiting for Tom Marr. He'd called her at work to say he was on his way to Houston and wanted to stop by briefly. She had no idea what he wanted, but she looked forward to seeing him. After the debacles in her love life lately, she wanted to be around someone whose constancy she was beginning to trust.

The doorbell rang before she'd finished her beer. She opened the door and there he stood, in his usual jeans, scuffed cowboy boots and white shirt.

"Hi, Tom," she said and he stepped inside. She looked into his blue eyes and suddenly he was holding her tightly and kissing her, their first real kiss. He'd kissed her on the cheek and the head, like a fond friend, but his kiss on the lips felt warm and sensual. He smelled of sunshine and Ivory soap mixed with a fresh breeze. After the disturbing collapse of her reunion with Jake and the disastrous ending with Matt, being with Tom felt new and fresh. After a minute, she broke away, but held his hand and steered him into the living room.

"You look great," she said. "I'm so glad you're here."

"Can't stay long, because I'm meeting with a detective about Betsy," he said. "But I've been thinking about kissing you ever since I saw you last."

"Well, we better talk about whatever brought you here," she said. "Can I get you a beer?"

"No, but I'll sit down for a few minutes while I explain."

"First of all, what's the news on Betsy?"

He shook his head. "She's somewhere in the Houston area with her boyfriend. Maria persuaded her to talk to me on the phone briefly and she said she's fine, she's happy and she's working. But she says she'd disappear if I pressure her right now."

"Well, that's progress, I guess," Annie said.

"I feel like my hands are tied," Marr said. "But I'm getting together with the detective who's been working behind the scenes for me."

"I understand," Annie said. "You don't want to lose her for good."

"Betsy knows that if she needs emergency help, you're here," he said. "She has your address, phone numbers and knows where you work, of course."

"Tom, you know I've always loved Betsy. I'd be glad to help any way I can."

He leaned toward her and kissed her again, lightly this time, but she felt its incipient promise. He reached into his pocket.

"I've got a copy of a letter here from Dan Riggins. He attached this note to a package he left on my doorstep. I'll let you read it first."

He handed her a copy of a handwritten note. She went through it quickly.

"Attention Texas Ranger Mark Ingram: I offer this package as possible evidence in an ongoing investigation. It's a rifle I found in Alicia Perez's car. When authorities fingerprint and test it, I expect they will conclude it's the weapon that killed State Senator Sam Wurzbach. Ms. Perez is dead of a brain tumor. She assassinated Wurzbach to protect the interests of the now-defunct Nation of Texas. No one was involved in his death besides the two of us. I have left Texas for good and won't return to the United States. If you check, you'll find that the charges pending against me in Texas have been dropped at the behest of the federal government. I'm returning to the work that I did before I retired. I leave this weapon with you in the hope that the senator's family can find closure. Goodbye, Dan Riggins."

"How strange," Annie said. She was quiet for a moment, thinking about Wurzbach, Riggins and Alicia Perez. Marr put his arms around her, but she wanted to talk. There was so much she needed to understand.

"Can you explain this?" Annie said. "Has Riggins been in touch with you?"

"Yes. I can't lie to you," Marr said. "We've talked over the past couple of months and I knew Alicia was sick. She died two days ago in Mexico and I helped bury her in a secret place. I said goodbye to Dan and I know he won't be back. If I get in trouble for seeing him without turning him in, so be it."

"Why did Alicia kill Sam Wurzbach?"

"Here's what Dan told me. Alicia heard him talking about Sam Wurzbach and how Sam's German-Texas campaign could ruin the plans of the Nation of Texas. She got fired up, sneaked away from their home in Ojinaga and crossed the border into West Texas. She drove to Austin, where she stalked Wurzbach and plotted how to kill him. She saw her chance on the evening of the big German-Texas fundraiser. Dan said she was angry and wanted to take action before she died from the brain tumor. I'm sure Dan also wanted to harm Wurzbach, but I think she jumped the gun, so to speak, by killing him at the party."

"How terrible," Annie said. "Do you believe him?"

"In his note, he shares responsibility for Sam's death with Alicia. But he's definitely telling the story he wants the Texas Rangers to believe," Marr said. "I don't believe the Nation of Texas is dead. He's probably saying that to protect people active in the organization."

"Where's Riggins?"

"It's impossible to know for sure. But I have a pretty good idea. He spent his whole career with the CIA, as you know. After Alicia died, he called high-level folks there and offered to go anywhere if they'd make his legal problems disappear. They agreed and I'm betting he's on his way to South America."

"I can't believe the government would just forget about the killings he ordered here in Texas," Annie said. "How can the CIA wipe the slate clean?"

"You know it happens all the time," Marr said. "Dan's an unparalleled CIA field agent and they're happy to get him back. With Alicia gone, he has nothing to lose by making a deal. His ex-wife and sons cut off contact with him a long time ago."

"What'll he do?" Annie asked.

"Whatever the CIA wants him to do," Marr said. "I expect he'll be stirring the pot in South America or Central America. That was his area of expertise."

"Do you think we can get any kind of confirmation from the CIA?"

Marr laughed. "C'mon, Annie. You know better than that."

"What about the Nation of Texas? Do you think he'll lead it from afar?"

"I seriously doubt it," Marr said. "The CIA will probably keep him on a tight leash. But I suspect that he'll stay involved with whatever that organization becomes."

"Did you come all the way to Houston to tell me about this?"

"No, I have to see the detective," he said. "But I also needed to see you."

"I'm glad you did," she said. "But I've got to ask you. Are you entirely free of the Nation of Texas? Can you put it all behind you?"

"I know I've got a lot to prove to you," he said. "But yes, now that Dan's gone, I won't have further contact with any secessionist."

She lowered her eyes and thought for a moment. "I'd like to believe you, Tom, but it's hard, given everything that you just told me."

"I know you're disappointed that I was in contact with Dan again, but I've come clean. Can we move on?"

"Let me think about it, Tom," she said. "You know what's happening at the paper right now. I'm slammed."

She stood up and he followed her to the door, put his arms around her and kissed her lightly.

"I hope that within a couple of weeks, Betsy will be back and you can come to the ranch to visit us," he said. "I want to court you properly."

"No promises, but I like the sound of that."

CHAPTER 43

STATE SENATOR'S SLAYING AT RESTAURANT MAY BE
SOLVED, TEXAS RANGER SAYS

By Travis Dunbar
Houston Times Reporter

Texas Ranger Mark Ingram said Tuesday the state's law-enforcement unit
has recovered the weapon used to kill State Senator Sam Wurzbach, who
died earlier this month after a sniper attack at a restaurant near San Antonio.

Ingram said the department received a package containing a rifle "almost
certainly" used to kill the state senator as he prepared to speak at a party held
at the Grey Moss Inn in Grey Forest. Wurzbach, 41, was a native of
Fredericksburg and represented his district in the legislature.

Authorities are still examining the rifle, but Ingram said Wurzbach's
likely killer was Alicia Perez, a fugitive in a four-year-old federal case federal
case involving two murders and a drug conspiracy. He said Perez died
recently at a Mexican hospital from a brain tumor. She was 54.

Wurzbach, the leader of a fledgling movement to create a German-Texas
enclave in the Hill Country, had received several threats from the
underground Nation of Texas, according to Ingram. The state senator had
spoken against the secessionists' plans for winning Texas and converting it
into a republic. Wurzbach wanted to carve out a place where German Texans
could celebrate their culture.

Ingram declined to discuss the whereabouts of Dan Riggins, the de facto
leader of the Nation of Texas organization and Perez's partner. Riggins, a
former CIA field agent, has also been a fugitive, but Ingram said federal

charges against him have been dropped.

He said he couldn't answer questions about why there is no longer an indictment against Riggins and Perez.

"It's a matter of national security," he said. "I'm prohibited from saying anything more."

CHAPTER 44

Betsy sat with her head in her hands at a table in the dressing room at the Texas Girls Club. She was scheduled to dance during the afternoon shift, but she was so tired she'd rest until the hateful old lady, Mrs. Jimenez, started lining them up.

She was almost asleep when she felt a gentle hand on her shoulder. She sat up, startled until she realized Leka and her two Albanian friends were hovering over her with concern.

"Betsy, are you okay?"

She was so glad to hear Leka's sweet voice that her lips trembled and she started crying. She sobbed for a few minutes while the three young women sat down beside her and Leka held her hand. It was only Betsy's fifth shift at the club, but she and Leka had become fast friends, talking as much as they could between their times on stage. She'd learned a lot about the three Albanians, including their increasing worry about the six girls who'd been sent to the ranch in the Hill Country. Leka couldn't get in touch with her cousin because her cell phone had been taken. She thought they might be prisoners, though that seemed kind of crazy to Betsy.

"Are you sick?"

"No," Betsy said, reaching into her duffle bag to find a tissue. "Patrick and I had a bad fight last night. I didn't sleep much."

"Poor girl," Leka said soothingly. She translated to the other girls and they nodded vigorously in empathy. They'd learned a lot about men behaving badly during their short lives. It didn't matter where you lived or what language you spoke. Men made life difficult for women all over the world.

"Why did you fight with Patrick?"

"He had lipstick on his face and neck when he picked me up," Betsy sniffed. "I think he's been screwing one of the skanky girls at Donnie's."

"What is screwing and skanky?" Leka asked with a puzzled look.

"Bad sexy," Betsy said. She mimed the sex act, complete with thrusting and faux moans. The Albanians understood immediately. They giggled helplessly, then recovered and shook their heads at the perfidy of men.

"You must stop giving him money," Leka said. "He is a bad boyfriend and cannot be trusted. He might give you a disease."

Betsy started crying again and the girls surrounded her with hugs and pats. But she saw that Mrs. Jimenez had arrived and was giving them the evil eye. The large woman shook her finger menacingly and ordered them in her odd mixture of English and Spanish to quit wasting time and line up.

For the remainder of her shift, Betsy danced and stripped lethargically. Her meager tips showed that her heart wasn't in it. She'd just come off the stage when Bobo the bouncer stopped her at the entrance to the dressing room.

"Hey, Sugar," he said leering at her pasties-tipped breasts. "A customer in the VIP room wants a lap dance from you."

"I don't do lap dances," Betsy said without the usual aplomb that kept him at bay. "You know that, so stop asking me."

She hated Bobo with his shaved head, disgusting beard and persistently nasty manner. She stayed out of his path and knew never to be alone with him because he'd grab a feel – or worse. He was so creepy.

"Well, Miss High and Mighty," he said. "I say you do, or you're out of here."

She glared at him, wondering what she'd do next. Would he physically escort her to the VIP room upstairs? So far, he'd abided by Krause's directive that she didn't have to do lap dances. She'd seen other girls do them upstairs, waggling their breasts and butts close to customers' faces. Who knew what went on after that? Her refusal was a bone of contention between her and Patrick, who was always pestering her to bring home more money.

To her relief, she could see Leka and the girls headed their way. Bobo stepped back a few inches.

"Bobo, Betsy needs to go with us," Leka said diplomatically. "Mrs. Jimenez is looking for her in the dressing room."

"Okay, girls. Behave," he said lightly, walking away. Betsy knew he was afraid to bully the Albanians because of their friend, Zogu, who worked for Krause. The Albanian man stopped by often to make sure they were treated properly. Bobo seemed cowed by Zogu, though Bobo was at least six inches taller and one hundred pounds heavier.

"Thank you, girls," Betsy said. "He's such a horrible man."

"If you talk with him like a friend, he loses some of his meanness," Leka said. "But he looks at you with evil in his eyes, so we will watch out for you.

"Zogu is coming to take us home in a few minutes," she added in a whisper. "Would you like him to take you to your motel?"

"Sure," Betsy said. "I won't have to wait for Patrick. I'll surprise him when I get home and maybe we can make up."

They dressed quickly and waited under the striped awning for Zogu's car. He showed up promptly at 7 p.m. He smiled and nodded when Leka asked him to drop Betsy off at her motel room.

Betsy didn't see Patrick's pickup in the parking lot, but she had her key. Leka told Zogu to wait until she got inside safely.

She opened the door, looked around and gasped. Her belongings were strewn throughout the room, as usual. But Patrick and all of his things were gone.

CHAPTER 45

Annie sat at her kitchen counter eating a simple supper of yogurt, raspberries and bananas and reading the paper, something she hadn't had a chance to do earlier. She'd gotten up at 6 a.m. for another planning meeting about changes in the newsroom.

She was startled to hear a knock on the back door. It was turning dark and visitors usually didn't go to the back. She got up and looked out. Four young women and a short, scruffy-looking man waved and smiled at her. She opened the door, leaving the screen door latched.

"Annie, you probably don't recognize me, but I'm Betsy Marr," the tallest woman with long, honey-blonde hair said in a West Texas twang. Annie looked closer and she could see Tom Marr's luminous eyes shining in the woman's face.

"Betsy, is it really you?" she said.

"Yes, and these are my friends. Could you let us in? We'll explain everything."

She opened the door and Betsy enveloped her in a hug. The young woman looked healthy, but from her swollen face, Annie could see she'd been crying.

"Oh, Annie. I'm so glad you're here. These are my friends: Zogu, Leka, Mimoza and Afrodita. Zogu works for Kyle Krause at his Texas Girls clubs and the girls and I dance at the Gulf Freeway club."

"I'm glad you're here," Betsy," Annie said. "Please, everyone come in."

Annie shook hands with the man and three other women and motioned them into her living room, bringing in a few straight chairs. She was shocked that Betsy was dancing at a topless club, but didn't want to say anything that sounded judgmental. The young woman and her companions seemed nervous and probably needed her help.

"What brings you all here, honey?" Annie smiled. "Your dad was in town just a few days ago. He misses you so much."

That was probably the wrong way to start the conversation, she realized. Betsy's face crumpled and she started wailing.

"Patrick, my boyfriend, left me," she said between sobs. "We had a fight last night and he moved out while I was at work."

Leka, sitting beside Betsy on the sofa, moved closer to hug her.

"If it weren't for my friends, I wouldn't have been able to get to your house," Betsy continued. "I don't even have a car. I want to go home."

"Sweetie, of course you do," Annie said. "We'll call your dad after we talk to your friends."

Betsy wiped her eyes and grasped the hand of the woman introduced as Leka.

"I told my friends that you were a reporter and that you could help them with their problem," she said. "Would you listen to their story?"

"Of course," Annie said. "Can I get you all some snacks?"

"Yes, please," Betsy said. "We've been dancing all afternoon and we don't get a break. They brought me here instead of stopping to eat dinner."

Annie rummaged through her refrigerator and pantry and brought out crackers, cheese, hummus, peanuts and a carton of lemonade with plastic glasses. Zogu and the women fell upon the food hungrily, thanking her with many smiles, and suddenly the visitors seemed more at ease. Whatever their story was, Annie wanted to take her time and listen properly. They were obviously foreign-born and probably wary of trusting anyone. It had taken courage for them to support Betsy and bring her here. It appeared that two of the women spoke little English, while Leka and Zogu sounded fairly fluent.

"I will tell you my story," Zogu said. "But I beg of you not to go to the police. We need to get the girls back first."

He told Annie about coming from to Houston from Albania seven years ago, meeting his wife Genta and finding his job with Kyle Krause. He'd learned that Krause had paid the Russian Mafia from time to time to bring girls in from Eastern Europe. So he offered, with his brother's help, to smuggle ten girls from Albania after Krause had said he needed more dancers.

"But I did not know enough," he said. "I did not know that Ms. Juliana was so cold-hearted and that she ran another business. I didn't know that bad things would happen."

"Was the body found floating in the ship channel last month one of your girls?" Annie asked. She looked at Leka, Mimoza and Afrodita with dawning recognition.

He nodded solemnly and the girls leaned forward to hear his explanation. All this time they hadn't gotten answers about the tenth girl's fate.

"Arlinda got too friendly with one of the sailors," he said. "She was kind of the wild one, always looking for adventure. She drank vodka with him at nights on deck, though she wasn't supposed to leave the rooms below. One night she drank too much and slipped overboard. He tried to rescue her, but she couldn't swim."

Leka picked up the thread, wanting to support Zogu and his story.

"Our families in Tirana are very poor and we had few chances to make a living," she said. "Coming to Texas was a chance we knew would be hard, but we all wanted a better life.

"Zogu picked us up and took us to a motel for a few weeks," she said. "He treated us well, brought us food and his wife Genta helped us. She and her friends cut our hair, took us to stores to buy clothes and makeup and taught us how to dance," she said.

Zogu looked grateful and resumed the story.

"All went well until we brought our nine girls to show off their dancing at the Gulf Freeway club," Zogu said. "Ms. Juliana decided to keep Leka, Mimoza and Afrodita to dance there. But she said the six other girls would have to go to the ranch."

"Is this the ranch that Kyle Krause and Juliana Souza own in the Hill Country?" Annie asked.

Zogu nodded. "She drove our girls there, took away their cell phones and we haven't been able to talk to them."

"What do they do at the ranch?" Annie said.

"Ms. Juliana wouldn't tell us why she was sending the girls there," Zogu said. "It is supposed to be a big secret, but I have heard whispers from other people who work for Mr. Krause."

He paused for maximum effect. "They say the girls are forced to make babies for rich people to buy."

"That's terrible." Annie was horrified, but everything Zogu said sounded truthful so far. "Have you tried to check this out?"

"No, Miss. The ranch is guarded with fences and maybe electricity."

He hung his head. "I know that I've done wrong, but please don't let Mr. Krause and Miss Juliana know that I've told you. They will kill me."

"I understand," she said. "We will send a reporter there right away. Give us a few days to check it out. Perhaps you and the girls should go about your business as usual and not let on that anything is different. Can you tell the manager that Betsy just decided to resign?"

Zogu nodded, and Leka spoke to the girls briefly in Albanian. They all got up to go, looking relieved. Zogu brought in Betsy's suitcase and the girls hugged her goodbye. Betsy and Leka cried and promised to call each other.

After they all left but Betsy, Annie picked up the phone, where she had Marr's number on speed-dial.

"Are you ready to talk to your dad?" Betsy nodded.

"I'll leave you alone," she said, walking to the spare bedroom to make up a bed for her visitor. She didn't know how long Betsy would be with her, but it would be good to reconnect with the girl she'd loved. She couldn't quite believe that Betsy had lived with a man and danced at a topless club. Annie could only hope she wasn't too traumatized to bounce back from her experiences.

She heard Betsy crying again this time with relief.

"Daddy, I've missed you so much … Yes, I love you too, very, very much."

CHAPTER 46

Annie and Travis had spent two days in the Hill Country trying to unravel the mysteries of Kyle Krause's ranch before making a frontal assault. They'd done the obligatory courthouse search on the first day, confirming that Krause and his girlfriend Juliana had owned the property for a few years and had added even more acreage since their initial purchase. Construction permits showed plans for additional buildings and Annie and Travis were able to study them. The expansive ranch property included two motel-style structures plus one-story administrative offices and a cafeteria building. The operation had a bed-and-breakfast license, but appeared to accommodate only those travelers who made arrangements privately in advance. Since Fredericksburg was the largest city near its rural location, they'd tried to find people in town who'd worked there. But they hadn't come up with any.

Next, they studied its security arrangements by driving roads in the ranch's vicinity. The property was heavily wooded and its buildings were set back and hidden by large oak trees and tall rail and wire fences. They couldn't tell for sure, but worried that the fences might be electrified. A manned guard gate off a two-lane rural road and a locked back entrance off a dirt road appeared to be the only entrance and exit. Numerous signs around the property warned: Keep out. Exotic animals. Dangerous!

Lots of Hill Country ranches were getting exotic animals, mostly varieties of deer and antelope to adorn the property around palatial second homes. There'd been news stories about a few ranches that stocked rhinoceros, zebras, lions and other safari-type animals that amateur hunters could pay big money to shoot and kill. Annie thought that was a horrid practice, but she knew it was just another way that Texas catered to rich and feckless hunters. There wasn't much anyone could do to stop it. She wondered, though, whether the signs at the Krause ranch were phony. She and Travis had driven around the area a lot and never saw any wildlife near the edges. It could be just a ruse to keep the curious at bay.

Annie had shared with Travis everything she'd gleaned from Zogu about the possibility that the ranch forced captive women to produce babies for sale. She and Travis had gone quickly to Fredericksburg with the goal of getting inside the compound. As they worked at night in separate, cheap motel rooms, Annie researched adoption on the Internet and found a long, sad history of legal and illegal practices in Texas. Much was perfectly legal. For instance, she learned that one of the most famous Texas agencies, the Gladney Center for Adoption in Fort Worth, had placed 30,000 babies in its 125-year history, attracting couples from all over the United States. The agency started as a last stop for the infamous orphan trains that traveled west with unwanted children.

In more recent years, infertile couples still flocked to Texas in droves, oddly because of its conservative social and political climate. Large number of teenagers who got pregnant in Texas had been brought up to oppose abortion. They'd opt instead to carry an unplanned baby to term and relinquish it for adoption. Plenty of wiggle room in state laws also abetted semi-legal private adoptions, where clandestine amounts of money changed hands between lawyers, couples and expectant mothers. Mothers-to-be could get many expenses legally paid during pregnancy and could postpone school or working for a while. If this tipped over into baby-selling territory, usually all the parties kept quiet.

Travis regaled Lila Jo with bits of research during his calls to Houston. She naturally had a keen interest. She was excited that her pregnancy at last was becoming visible. She felt good, too, after a few weeks of mild morning sickness. Lila Jo had told her estranged husband, Beebe Lemmons, about the baby and he'd been surprisingly gracious. Travis suspected that his goodwill stemmed mostly from the fact that Lila Jo would be willing to divorce him quickly without lobbying for a financial share of his construction business. She just wanted half the proceeds from the sale of the couple's big house in Katy. Lila Jo reported brisk traffic on the property from her marketing efforts, but no offers yet.

Both Travis and Annie were glad to be away from the newsroom because of its suffocating angst. Every day a new crop of rumors emerged, usually bogus, but the inescapable fact remained that after the new owners finished chopping jobs, only about one-quarter of the journalists would remain. This might be their last big story for the *Times*, so they were determined to go out with a bang.

On the third day, they saw their chance. They'd noticed that each morning, a truck from the local grocery store arrived at the ranch at 10 a.m. The driver looked barely out of his teens. They went to the store early and hung around until Travis saw the guy, clean-cut in jeans and T-shirt, and struck up a conversation. His name was Jared Wells and it turned out that he and Travis shared a love of fishing, skateboarding and some of the local bands that played in Austin. Travis helped him load the bags and boxes of groceries into the van and it emerged that he was headed to the Krause ranch. Travis told his new friend that he had a girlfriend at the ranch that he and his sister desperately wanted to see. He offered Jared $50 to allow Annie and him to accompany the delivery. Travis assured Jared that he'd help unload numerous bags of groceries at the ranch's big kitchen.

"What does your girlfriend do there?" Jared asked.

"I think she cleans rooms," Travis said. "What's the place like?"

Annie stayed quiet in the back seat, letting her so-called brother do all the talking.

"Hard to put your finger on it, but there's something strange about it," Jared said. "Lots of pregnant women walking around, like it could be a maternity home or something."

"Interesting. How many people are usually around?" Travis kept his voice casual, but his skin suddenly prickled. Annie was right. This was going to be a monster of a story if they lived to tell it. Jared was driving like a maniac on the curving country road, but Travis didn't dare say anything.

"Maybe about thirty, including a few maids and kitchen workers," Jared said. "Sometimes visitors come and stay in one of the bunkhouses. I've seen cars parked with out of state tags."

"Who's in charge?"

"All of the bills go to a woman named Juliana Souza. Sometimes she's there and sometimes she's not. I've seen her and she's a real looker, but I hear she's kind of a bitch."

Travis and Annie listened in fully absorbed silence, wishing they could jot it all down in their reporter notebooks. Annie surreptitiously took a few notes in the back seat. They tried to look casual when Jared stopped at the guard gate. The guard was playing some kind of game on his iPad and impatiently waved them through. Inside the ranch, they drove on a ring road and then turned into what appeared to be a pleasant compound of ranch-style buildings. Travis didn't see any exotic animals, but thought the majestic oaks and scrub vegetation likely sheltered plenty of deer. They parked near a central building that appeared to be the cafeteria. He and Jared jumped out and began unpacking boxes and bags of groceries. Annie wandered off toward the barracks-style buildings. Her mission was to find Leka's cousin, Vera.

"Looks like lunch has started," the ever-helpful Jared told Travis. "You might be able to find your girlfriend if you go through the dining room."

"Good idea," Travis said. "How about if I carry these two bags through to the kitchen and scope it out?"

"Whatever, dude," Jared said. "Meet you in the back."

Travis grabbed the bags and walked slowly through the dining room. It was nicely appointed with soft green walls and pine tables and chairs, giving it the feel of a summer camp for grownups. Some women trickled in for lunch, several in visible stages of pregnancy, sitting at tables of four to six. He'd been shown pictures of two women Annie's informant had given her. He didn't see anyone who looked like them. Maybe they'd be in as the lunch hour approached. He carried in more bags and helped Jared put things away in a giant storeroom.

Travis lurked at the edges of the dining room until he felt a sharp tap on his shoulder. He whirled around and saw a heavyset woman wearing a uniform, an old-fashioned hairnet and a stern look on her face. He guessed she was the cafeteria manager.

"Who are you? What are you doing in my dining room?"

"Sorry, ma'am. I'm just helping Jared with groceries. I'm a writer visiting the area to do a story on Texas ranches. Jared said this one was one of the most beautiful places he'd ever seen."

"You need to leave. I won't have you disturbing my girls during lunch."

"Yes, ma'am," he said. "I'll just get my sister. She's nearby, looking for wildflowers."

"Five minutes and you all better be gone."

"Of course," he said. She walked away toward the kitchen.

"Travis, let's blow this joint." Jared had come up behind them at the end of the conversation. "Get your sister before the old biddy comes back."

"Sure thing, dude."

CHAPTER 47

Annie wandered through the trees to an unadorned building that looked several degrees less fancy than the other one set slightly further back in the greenery. She suspected that the girls were housed in the modest building and the other one was reserved for the well-heeled couples who came to adopt babies. That one looked deserted. She walked inside the first building and wandered down the hall. Doors were closed, but one young woman was walking toward her. Annie put on her friendly, helpful reporter's face. The woman was short, with dark hair, and a chunky figure. Annie couldn't tell if she was pregnant, but she looked about the right age.

"Hello, I'm Annie. I'm looking for a young woman named Vera," she said. "Is she on this hall?"

"Yeah, last door on the left," the woman said. "You a friend? She doesn't speak a whole lot of English."

"I'm a friend of a friend," Annie smiled. "Thank you so much."

Annie knocked on the door and a young woman opened it. She was petite, with drooping blonde hair and a frightened look in her big brown eyes.

"Are you Vera?" Annie said. "I'm a friend of Leka, your cousin." She held out the multi-colored silk scarf Leka had given her to signal that Annie could be trusted. She'd told Annie that Vera had always admired that scarf.

"Leka," the woman said, grabbing the scarf and holding it to her face to sniff the faint aroma of her cousin's perfume. She quickly pulled Annie inside her small room with its single bed, chair and dresser. She shut the door, clutched at Annie's arm and began speaking in a mixture of English, Albanian and impromptu sign language. Tears rolled down her face.

Annie sat with her on the bed and listened carefully, asking questions when she could break into Vera's torrent of talk. Eventually she patched together the story. Vera had been at the ranch for a few weeks with five other

Albanian women who also lived in the building. She and the others had been injected weekly by a nurse with what they believed was sperm. The girls knew they were expected to become pregnant and stay at the ranch until they bore a baby. Vera was waiting to find out if she was pregnant. Most of the girls staying there were in some stage of pregnancy already. They were fed well and examined regularly. Babies were usually delivered on the premises and separated from the mothers. When infants were just a few days old, couples arriving in fancy cars would take them away. Ms. Juliana, who ran the place, threatened to turn the girls over to immigration authorities if they tried to leave before they delivered. She told the girls that they'd go to prison for long stretches because none had immigration papers. She also promised the women expertly forged immigration papers, money for a new start and a job if they delivered a healthy baby, stayed quiet about it and signed the necessary papers. They'd be taken back to Houston or Brownsville to begin a new life.

Annie was mesmerized, listening in silence or asking questions until her cell phone rang. She saw it was Travis and picked up.

"Got to get out of here fast," Travis's voice was jittery. "The cafeteria manager discovered us. Get to the van as fast as you can. It's still parked in back of the kitchen."

Annie hung up and patted Vera on the shoulder. "I have to leave quickly, but we'll be back in a few hours to get all of you out of here. We'll take you back to Houston. Please be patient just a little longer."

Vera nodded, but looked panicky. "Please don't forget about us."

Annie hurried out of the building. She looked around carefully, but saw little activity in the wooded areas between buildings. She walked purposefully across the campus, keeping a deliberate pace but not moving so fast that she'd arouse attention.

She passed the fancy building where baby-seeking couples stayed and walked past what she thought must be the administration building. The campus was quiet and seemed mostly empty, though she noticed two pregnant girls walking toward the cafeteria. It wasn't far, she thought, trying to breathe normally and stay calm. She was almost there – another five minutes and she'd be safe.

Suddenly she heard a pop and felt a burning pain in her side. She looked around, but didn't see anyone. To her surprise, blood was dripping down the side of her blouse. She tried to zigzag, the way she'd been taught to protect herself in an ambush. It was too late. She heard another pop, felt a searing pain in her arm and fell to the ground.

CHAPTER 48

Juliana Souza sat in her office at the Krause Ranch administrative building. She looked through the spreadsheet on her computer with satisfaction. It had been a good month, with two placements finalized. The Benson family from New Jersey had paid $70,000 for the Ruiz girl, and the Robinettes from Boston had given her a check for $75,000 for the Munoz boy. She'd solved the hardest problem, obtaining birth certificates, by finding a worker in the state's records department and paying him under the table to produce authentic-looking documents. Her infertile couples, sorted through and handpicked for their discretion by her Houston lawyer, would pay almost any price for a healthy white infant. Even though many of the mothers had light brown skin, the babies looked sufficiently Anglo to suit the prospective parents. She'd picked male sperm donors who were tall, blond and fair-skinned, part of the German-Texas community. It was a huge selling point. The regular supply of donated sperm from young men in the Hill Country was part of a deal Kyle had reached when he began giving money to the German-Texas cause.

That was the only benefit so far from his extravagant support of the German-Texas movement, Juliana reflected bitterly. She'd become increasingly angry that he was wasting hard-earned money because of a silly high school friendship with Sam Wurzbach. The state senator had persuaded Kyle to donate a half-million dollars to the German Texas cause. Luckily, he'd gotten himself killed, so perhaps Kyle would get back to making money instead of spending it. She knew about the Nazi origins of his late grandfather and suspected that the old man was the reason behind her fiancé's ridiculous outlay. At least the Nazi connection had served the purpose of bringing him to Brazil, where she'd met him, fallen in love and gotten her ticket to America. If he'd only marry her, everything would work out. She'd make sure of that.

An insistent knocking on her door interrupted her thoughts.

"Who is it?" she asked in an unwelcoming tone. Juliana didn't like to be bothered when she was looking at private ledgers.

"It's Helga. I have your lunch"

Helga Schmidt opened the door, depositing a tray with her usual Caesar salad, iced tea and fruit salad on the table. Juliana prided herself on her slender but voluptuous figure and she worked hard to maintain it. She had her own exercise room at the ranch, and usually ran every morning she was forced to be on the property. If only Helga and the pregnant women would follow her example, she thought, maybe they wouldn't get so enormously fat and ugly. Maybe the food bills would come down.

Helga stood in front of her, idiotically waiting for permission to speak. Really, she was a tiresome woman, afraid of her own shadow. Juliana realized that because the ranch was out in the country, she couldn't hire the cream of the crop, or employees who'd question much that went on. By and large, her help was abysmal.

"Do you want something, Helga?" Juliana said, trying to disguise her impatience.

"Just wanted you to know that a writer and his sister came with the food deliveryman today," Helga said in her peculiar lilting German Texas accent. "He said they wanted to see this ranch because they'd heard it was one of the most beautiful in the Hill Country. I told him to leave."

"When was this?" Juliana said, her voice rising.

"About ten minutes ago," Helga said. "I didn't want to disturb you before your lunch time."

"Why didn't you bring them to me?"

"The writer seemed very nice and said his sister was hunting for wildflowers. He apologized and said he'd find her and leave."

"Helga, that was foolish. I've told you before that we have to operate secretly because of the competition. You should know visitors aren't allowed." Juliana tried to speak calmly, but her head was spinning.

"I'm sorry, Ms. Juliana."

"Just leave and come back later for my tray."

Helga closed the door softly and she sprang into action. That stupid woman had ruined everything. Juliana knew it with a certainty born of superior survival instincts. If someone unknown was on the premises, it was disastrous. A writer and his sister, huh? She looked out the window and saw a tall woman walking across the grass, looking around nervously. Juliana never forgot faces and she thought she recognized the woman who accompanied the cop to the club's porn star show. She obviously was a spy of some sort, intent on unmasking the business. Juliana had to work fast before the stranger left with all the ranch's secrets.

She opened her right-hand desk drawer where she kept her loaded pistol. The open window in her office offered a perfect, easy shot before the woman got away. She fired twice and saw she'd hit her target. The woman fell, likely dead, but perhaps only wounded. At least Juliana had stopped her for a crucial few minutes so that she could escape.

She'd rehearsed this scenario dozens of times in her head. There was no time to waste. She took out her key to a small wall safe, opened it, grabbed the stacks of cash money and threw them into her industrial-size briefcase. She'd squirreled away close to a half-million in cash in the safe. She'd planned for contingencies, knowing she might need to leave fast. She'd taken a risk to provide this adoption service, but had hedged her bet by keeping the women there until they gave birth and bribing them with fake immigration papers and money. She'd be damned if she'd take the blame. Kyle would just have to deal with the fallout.

She ran down the hall to where her car was parked in her special space around back. She'd slip out the secret exit road and be on the highway before anyone realized she'd fled.

She'd take the money, use her fake ID and escape to the beach house she'd secretly purchased on a secluded part of the Brazilian coast. Maybe Kyle could join her there later, maybe not. She'd get to the San Antonio Airport within the hour and be on a plane by late afternoon to Brazil.

213

CHAPTER 49

STRIP CLUB MOGUL ARRESTED IN BABY-SELLING PLOT,
REPORTER SHOT AT RANCH

By Brandon McGill and Travis Dunbar
Houston Times Reporters

FREDERICKSBURG – Federal agents and Texas Rangers conducted a joint raid Friday on a 300-acre ranch owned by Houston strip club mogul Kyle Krause and his girlfriend, seizing records and rescuing twenty-three immigrant women allegedly held captive and coerced into bearing babies for sale.

Authorities descended on the ranch after getting a report that a *Houston Times* reporter had been seriously wounded. The journalist, Annie Price, 40, was investigating a tip that an illegal adoption ring was centered there when an unidentified assailant shot her twice.

Price was wounded in the right side and arm, but is in satisfactory condition in Central Hospital and expected to make a full recovery.

Krause, 39, arrested Friday night at his Texas Girls club off the Gulf Freeway, was jailed and held without bond before a preliminary hearing scheduled for Monday in Houston federal court. His lawyer said he wasn't at the ranch, didn't participate in the adoption scheme and had nothing to do with Price's shooting.

A warrant has been issued for Juliana Souza, 36, Krause's girlfriend who allegedly ran the ranch's illegal operations. Officials say she may have fled from Texas to South America. She is a Brazilian national who has lived with Krause in Houston for at least five years.

The immigrant women, ranging in ages from eighteen to thirty-six, were from Mexico, Guatemala, Ukraine, Russia and Albania, according to Mark

Ingram, the Austin-based Texas Ranger in charge of the investigation.

"This was a cold-hearted, profit-making scheme to coerce these women to become pregnant and deliver babies under a false promise of providing immigration documents to allow them to stay in this country," Ingram said. "The women were barred from leaving the ranch until they'd given birth."

Krause and Souza allegedly conspired to bring the women into Texas and transport them to the ranch. The women all were injected with donor sperm and many taken into custody say they are pregnant.

Ingram said authorities believe that the Albanian women were smuggled aboard a ship that landed in Houston nearly two months ago. One woman held on the ship apparently drowned in an incident involving alcohol and an itinerant seaman. Her body was found floating in the ship channel near the Valero refinery on July 22.

The Russian and Ukrainian women also allegedly were smuggled in on cargo ships, Ingram said. Krause and Souza allegedly contracted with Mexican and Central American smugglers to supply them with young Hispanic women.

The Krause Ranch operation allegedly sold the infants through a private lawyer to rich out-of-state couples for prices ranging from $70,000 to $75,000 per baby. Based on records seized in the raid, he estimated that at least 50 infants had changed hands in the illegal scheme, which apparently operated for about three years.

Baby selling is against the law in Texas, and most other states. In Texas, couples are permitted to pay certain of a gestational mother's expenses, but those expenses must pass muster by a judge at the time of adoption. No judges were involved in the transfer of the ranch's babies, Ingram said.

The immigrant women were taken into custody by authorities and placed in a shelter in San Antonio. They will be interviewed and immigration judges will review their cases individually. Many are likely to be deported, Ingram said.

Krause will be arraigned on multiple federal and state charges of violating immigration and adoption laws, according to authorities. South American authorities are cooperating in an international search to locate Souza, Ingram said.

CHAPTER 50

Annie kept running and dodging and trying to hide, but she couldn't escape the people who were hunting her down. They had the faces of strangers and of people she feared – Dan Riggins, Alicia Perez, Kyle Krause, even Rob Ryland. They had knives, bows and arrows and guns. They were chasing her all over a large island with mountainous terrain. She heard a voice telling her to run just a little longer, that he'd be there to rescue her. She thought at first that it was the voice of Matt Sharpe, but he was stalking her, too. She realized that the man calling for her was Tom Marr.

She ran up the mountain to the top of a precipice, overlooking a waterfall with a lagoon bubbling fifty feet below. Tom Marr was standing in the lagoon, holding out his arms.

"Jump, Annie, jump. I'll catch you," he said. But she was too frightened to make the leap and her pursuers were close behind.

She heard another, different voice and opened her eyes. Travis Dunbar was standing over her bed in what looked like a hospital room. He took her hand and squeezed it.

"Are you finally awake?" Travis said. "How are you feeling? I should get the nurse."

"Travis, I'm glad you're here. Where am I? What happened to me?"

"Do you remember that we were trying to get away from Kyle Krause's ranch?"

"Yeah, I think so," Annie said, trying to prop herself up. Travis put a pillow behind her head to make her more comfortable. Her head pounded and she felt weak and tired.

"You were shot, apparently from a window at the ranch's administration building. You were trying to get back to Jared's van so we could escape. We found you on the ground and called 911, but it took them a while to get there, through the guard gate and all. We think that Juliana Souza escaped in her car through a secret back entrance. You're at the Fredericksburg hospital."

"Do you know who shot me?"

"Probably Juliana," Travis said. "We may never find out for sure. Now she's on the lam."

"Will I be all right?"

"Yeah, you have a couple of flesh wounds in your side and arm, but nothing that won't heal fairly easily."

"Did you file a story?" Annie whispered.

"Sure thing, boss." Travis broke into a grin. "You must feel better to be cracking the whip. Brandon's been helping from Houston. All hell has broken loose. Kyle Krause is in custody. The girls from the ranch are talking to police and immigration."

"Will they be okay? Is Vera with them?"

"Yeah. It's a mess, but some good immigration lawyers have stepped up to help those girls. Maybe they'll be allowed to stay in Texas, given what they've been through."

"When can I go home to Houston?"

"Your parents are on the way. I expect you'll be able to leave with them as soon as tomorrow. Tom Marr is on his way here, too."

"Oh, that's nice. Thanks, Trav. Sounds like you did good work."

"Hey, you're the injured heroine here," Travis patted her shoulder. "All I had to do was write a couple of stories."

CHAPTER 51

A week later, Annie came back to the office for a few hours, the first time since she'd been shot. Her arm was still in a sling and her side was bandaged from the bullet that had passed through it, but she was much stronger. Her parents had left today after fussing over her and her cats entirely too much. A bonus was that they'd gotten to meet and spend some time with Tom and Betsy Marr. The Marrs had followed her parents to Houston to make sure she'd be all right. It had gone pretty well. Her mother thought that Tom was handsome and mannerly and Betsy was beautiful and sweet. Her opinion of Tom had jumped a few notches when she discovered that he owned one of the largest ranches in Texas with a profitable cattle operation. Her father was more reserved. He was suspicious of Tom's secessionist past, but his devotion to Annie was winning her dad over.

Greg stopped by her desk with a broad smile on his face. He liked nothing better than a big story and this one was driving lucrative traffic to the *Times* website. He'd been directing and editing new installments every day in Annie's absence. Their success had been a gift to newsroom morale, since the closing of the print newspaper was looming and hard decisions were being announced every day about staffing.

"Good news," he said. "It hasn't been announced yet, but you and Travis will both get jobs with the new website operation. You'll be an investigative producer, working with Travis and a few others."

"Thanks, Greg," she said. "I'm sure that you had a big hand in that development. I still get my month off, right?"

"Of course," he said. "It'll be a combination of worker's compensation, since you were injured on the job, and your remaining vacation time. If that's not enough, you can take more."

"Can I let you know in a week about the new job?"

"Sure, Annie," he said with a puzzled look. "I thought you'd be pleased and relieved."

"Appreciate your vote of confidence, but I'm not sure what I want to do yet. I guess being shot got me thinking more about the rest of my life. I'm not sure I want to spend it in the crazy news business."

"Understand. You've been through a lot," Greg said. "Take a week to think about the job, but don't think too long. We'll be finalizing the new operation soon."

"Thanks, guy," she said. "After a few more doctor's appointments, I'm heading out to West Texas to enjoy the big skies and empty spaces. I'll get my head on straight, I promise."

"I'm not surprised that West Texas and Tom and Betsy Marr figure into your vacation schedule," he smiled. "Call me sometime in the next week."

He walked away as Travis headed toward her desk, looking excited. At this rate, she didn't know if she'd get to her mail and messages today.

"What's the latest on the case, Trav?" she asked.

"The dominoes are falling," he said. "Behar Zogu is singing like a lark and he's implicated Bobo Simmons and two others in Nate Hardin's murder."

"That's great news," Annie said. "Glad something's finally breaking loose about Nate. The Hardins deserve an answer. Tell me about it."

"The indictment says Bobo killed Nate, at the behest of Juliana Souza. Juliana apparently tipped him off that Nate was headed to the club to cause big problems that could destroy the business. Bobo was so much under Juliana's influence that she knew he'd do anything to please her. She allegedly told him to attack Nate and make it look like a late-night robbery. There's a third unindicted co-conspirator who allegedly tipped off Juliana that Nate was coming to the club. Police won't identify that person, but I bet I'll be able to get it from my sources."

"How did Zogu find out about Bobo's role?"

"He's told police he overheard Juliana talking on the phone with someone and later to Bobo," Travis said. "Zogu searched Bobo's locker and found the tire iron apparently used to kill Nate. Police have identified Bobo's fingerprints on it."

"Interesting," Annie said. "Keep digging. What's in it for Zogu?"

"He's so crucial to the whole case that he'll get a light sentence for his part in the smuggling piece of it. Also, police have agreed not to prosecute his wife Genta."

As Travis hurried away to work on the latest installment, her desk phone rang. She saw that it was Matt Sharpe and picked it up with reluctance. She'd avoided talking to him ever since she'd caught him in bed with Monica, the married cop, and found out about his other amorous adventures. If he wanted to go out again, she'd turn him down.

"Hi, Annie," he said. "Wanted to see how you're doing. Sorry I haven't called earlier. I've been following the story in the paper and worrying about you."

"Thanks, Matt. It's been a tough time, but I'm recovering. What have you been up to?"

"Wanted to tell you something before you hear it from anyone else," he said. "I'm going to work for Kyle Krause, managing his Texas Girls clubs while he works out his legal problems."

"Are you serious? Why would you do a thing like that? You're a cop."

"Just for a few more days," he said easily. "My retirement from the force starts Monday. Remember I told you I'd be leaving once I got my thirty years in?"

"Yeah, I remember. But why would you go to work for a felon?"

"He's not a felon," Matt said. "He's accused of some serious things, but he and his lawyer think he has a good chance of proving his innocence. Juliana masterminded the whole thing and he knew very little about what she was doing."

"Matt, give me a break," Annie said. "Surely, you're too smart to believe that."

"Who says I don't believe it? The Texas Girls clubs are very profitable and I think I can make them even more so," he said. "Over the years, I've learned the pitfalls of the strip club business and how to avoid them."

"You're selling your soul for a few dirty dollars? I can't believe you're doing that." Annie raised her voice a few notches and didn't care who heard.

Matt chuckled. "Quite a few dirty dollars, I must say. I told you I'm tired of being a poor, disrespected cop. I can do this for a few years, pay off all my debts and enjoy a retirement on a nice lake."

"Have you really thought this through? You did so many good things on the force."

"I've been bored for a while," he said. "Same old crimes, same old red tape, same old problems that never get solved. Idiots and crooks have always run this place and they always will."

"You're trying to justify a terrible decision. I don't think you really believe that."

She'd apparently touched a nerve, because his voice turned harsh. "Why are you acting so high and mighty, Annie? Your newspaper's going to be a second-rate website. You have no job security and unless you leave, not much of a future."

"You may be right, Matt," she said. "But at least I'm not exploiting women and pandering to the worst in men. I can look myself in the mirror."

"That's not going to get you much in Houston, Annie," he said. "See you around."

CHAPTER 52

Travis had invited Lila Jo Lemmons to stop by without giving a hint of what he wanted. So she showed up in a good mood and accepted his offer of a diet drink. She looked good, he thought dispassionately. Her pregnancy was barely visible and her beautiful skin and eyes glowed with good health.

"Lila Jo, I learned something this afternoon I wish I'd never found out," he said. "It's about what happened that night we met Nate at Ninfa's. It was the same night he got killed in the parking lot of the Texas Girls Club."

He knew instantly that his guess had been right. Her eyes narrowed, she bit her lip and took a big gulp of soda.

"You called Juliana and warned her Nate was headed to the club. You probably told her he intended to cause big trouble for Kyle Krause," Travis said. "Juliana told Bobo, and he killed Nate to stay in her good graces. Why would you do that? He was a great guy who'd never hurt anyone."

"Trav, honey, you have to believe I had no idea it would turn out that way," she said. "Nate said he was investigating illegal gambling, and I knew he must be talking about the poker games. I've run them for Kyle for years and we make a bunch of money. I bring in new players, set up the games and we split the profits. It's my bread and butter."

"Was I just another mark for you?" he said.

"Of course not. You know how much I love you."

"How can you say that? You killed my best friend."

"I don't think Juliana meant for Bobo to kill Nate. She just wanted the bouncer to scare him a little, maybe rough him up or rob him in the parking lot. We didn't know it would all turn to shit."

"That's the understatement of the year," Travis said. "How did you get to be the unindicted co-conspirator?"

"The police came to talk to me and I told them I was pregnant," she said. "I promised to do anything they wanted to avoid prison for me and the baby.

I'm helping them shut down poker and maybe even find Juliana. Everything will be all right."

"Everything will never be all right again," he said. "We're over. I'm done with you."

"Trav, you don't mean that," she said. "Think about it long and hard. You need me – and I'll sue you for child support."

"Go ahead, Lila Jo. Is the baby even mine?"

"Yes, you bastard. Don't mess with me or you'll be very sorry." She slammed the door on her way out.

CHAPTER 53

Rob Ryland ducked into a coffee shop for a quick latte. The cozy place near the *Austin Comet* offices was where he always headed for his afternoon caffeine fix. He was surprised to see Annie Price standing in line directly in front of him.

"Annie?" he said. "Is that you? Are you following me again?"

He said it lightly, because he didn't want to create the kind of scene that had festered since their last meeting a few weeks ago. That had been stupid and unnecessary. She turned around and smiled at him. She looked good and seemed happy, despite her bandaged arm.

"I've worried about you, getting shot on that crazy ranch," he said. "How are you doing?"

"Better, Rob," she said. "Thanks for asking. I had to stop in today at the Texas Rangers to give a statement about the ranch conspiracy, as they call it. Now I'm craving a coffee before I hit the road."

"Heading westward, to Marfa? He smiled. "Going to see Tom Marr?"

"Now you know that's confidential information. No comment."

"No problem," he said, matching her playfulness. "I have unimpeachable sources."

She turned serious. "I wanted to congratulate you on the *Comet's* cover story about the ranch's operations and the attack on me. It was beautifully written and researched and I appreciate the nice things you said about my investigative reporting. The paper's lucky to have you."

"Thanks, Annie," he said, genuinely pleased. "Can't you sit down with me and enjoy your latte? I promise I won't keep you for more than fifteen minutes."

"Better not," she said. "Got to get going before rush hour. But I'm glad to get the chance to apologize. I've felt guilty ever since that day Travis and I followed you to the Comet office. I must confess I doubted that you were actually a reporter."

"Don't worry about it," he said. "You see I haven't let your good mentoring go to waste. Since I can't persuade you to sit down, I'd better head back to the office. Got to file a story this afternoon."

"Bye, Rob," she said. "Take care and happy writing."

"Do you still have a job? I can't believe that the stupid hedge fund that bought the *Times* doesn't recognize the importance of continuing a great daily paper."

"I have an offer, but I haven't decided what to do yet."

"You mean you might leave the *Times?*"

"I'm trying not to think about it for at least a week," she said. "I need a vacation first."

"I can't believe you'd leave journalism. You're so good at it."

"Well, I honestly doubt that I'll leave, to tell the truth. I still need to make a living – and most other jobs are so boring."

"Isn't that the truth? As someone once told me, reporting's the most fun you can have with your clothes on."

"That wasn't me, I hope?" she smiled.

"No, but I'm sure I heard it at the *Times*. Good luck, Annie." He shook her soft hand.

"You too," she said. She left quickly, sashaying out with the suggestion of a sway in her hips that still moved him. He'd always remember the night he'd stayed over at her place and had his way with that sweet, long-legged body. She'd been so wrong when she threw him out the next day. She'd likened his lovemaking to rape, but that wasn't true at all. It wasn't rape to take a woman you really wanted. Real Texans had always taken what they'd wanted and they always would.

He liked Annie, her fire and her intelligence. He just hoped he wouldn't have to kill her. But he suspected he'd have to do it sooner or later, because she kept getting in the way of his secession goals. She seemed to have a sixth sense about secrets the Nation of Texas needed to hide. She'd always be a nosy reporter who wouldn't give up. He'd kill her, but only after he'd enjoyed that body one more time.

He walked back to the newspaper office, pleased with the way the unexpected encounter had gone. Right now, Annie believed in him. She'd made it clear that she thought he was a bona fide journalist for life. It wasn't true of course – he couldn't imagine himself ever again being such a chump.

Pretty soon, he'd give up his cover job at the *Comet* and devote full time to rebuilding the Nation of Texas. This afternoon he'd cut out early to lead a training exercise with his militia in the hills outside Austin. He and his key lieutenants were picking up new recruits for their army every day. The money Uncle Dan was sending from Venezuela was having a tremendous impact.

Dan Riggins would always have a role in the Nation of Texas, but his uncle finally had anointed Rob as supreme leader. Uncle Dan had proved his ultimate devotion to the cause by placing the blame on Alicia for Sam Wurzbach's shooting. It had been so easy for him to wipe the rifle clean of Rob's fingerprints, let the dying Alicia handle it and turn it over to the Texas Rangers with a note that exonerated Rob. He'd known his uncle would shield him from the murder to promote the greater good of the Nation of Texas.

Rob had ridden a wave of exhilaration when he'd staked out the state senator at his silly German-Texas party and fired a perfect shot from the hills behind the restaurant. All his rifle practice had paid off. He'd never killed anyone before, but was surprised at how easy it had been to execute a man bent on destroying the secessionist cause. He'd felt no guilt when Wurzbach fell on the patio, bleeding and dying. He hadn't been able to stick around to enjoy the results of his handiwork, but the chaos following the assassination was thrilling.

Now he'd crippled, perhaps even dealt a lethal blow, to the German-Texas scourge. He'd keep an eye on those Nazi bastards. Texas would be a country of its own, just like he and his compatriots had spent years planning. It would be a pure, strong and true nation, a place that would become the envy of the world. Winning Texas was squarely in his sights. He'd do anything to make it happen. Winning Texas was everything.

ACKNOWLEDGEMENTS

With great respect and deep appreciation:

For the support of my mentors and early readers:
Stefan Kiesbye, Tony D'Souza, Kevin Moffett, Pam Kelley, Karen Garloch, Dannye Powell, Leslie Gerber, Judy Tell, Don Mason, Diane Hall, Julia Edmunds, Naomi Zeskind, Kenneth Ashworth and Ian Graham Leask.

For the support of my family, especially my mother, Phyllis Pruden; son, Jeffrey Stancill Norman and siblings, Diane Hall, Melinda Poe, Steve Stancill and Jane Stancill.

For the support of my fellow students and wonderful teachers in the University of Tampa master's program in creative writing.

For elements of the cover design created by Christine Long.

ABOUT THE AUTHOR

Nancy Stancill is a writer and award-winning investigative reporter and editor who formerly worked for the Houston Chronicle and the Charlotte (N.C.) Observer. She has a B.A. degree in journalism from the University of North Carolina and an M.F.A. degree in creative writing from the University of Tampa. Her first book, *Saving Texas*, featuring newspaper reporter-sleuth Annie Price, was published by Black Rose Writing in 2013. She lives in Charlotte, NC.

Purchase other Black Rose Writing titles at
www.blackrosewriting.com/books
and use promo code PRINT to receive a 20% discount.

CPSIA information can be obtained
at www.ICGtesting.com
Printed in the USA
FFOW04n1158030516
23710FF